Chasing Jenna

by Micki Fredricks

Chasing Jenna

ISBN-13:978-1503260146

ISBN-10:1503260143

Editing by Kathy Anderson, Klassy Editing and Writing Services

Cover Design by Robin Harper, Wicked by Design

Dedication

You can always tell when two people are best friends because they are having more fun than it makes sense for them to be having. ~Author Unknown

This book is dedicated to my best friend, Lori Rattay.

Thank you for walking beside me through every tear, laugh and emotional breakdown that happened along this journey. You are the reason I had the courage to finish this book. I love you, Friend!

Prologue

I couldn't look at him; so afraid of the pain it would cause me to see him in a different way. He was all I had left, my second chance, my escape.

The paper I held in my hand told a different truth, one I was unable to accept. Over and over I read the name that would change everything I perceived to be good and safe.

I struggled to contain the fear buried deep inside of me since childhood, while it poured out into this small, dungeon like room … drowning me. Drawing in even a shallow breath became nearly impossible.

I swallowed, attempting to wet my dry throat but my words were only a raspy whisper, "What is this?"

"Don't be afraid," he whispered. Heat radiated off his body as he leaned into me slowly – like a lover wanting to gain access.

I closed my eyes and melted into him, welcoming his closeness, while terrified of it at the same time. My mind understood, but my heart refused to believe my protector was now my biggest threat.

"What is this?" I asked once more. His two word answer shattered my already broken world.

"The list."

>CHAPTER ONE<

Three months earlier

"Breathe," I whispered to myself. My knuckles burned as I gripped the steering wheel like a prized possession. From inside the safety of my car, I took in my massive surroundings. The campus looked picture perfect and scary as Hell. This was college.

Anxiety attacked my body, shaking me from the inside out. I dropped my hands and wiped the sweat from my palms onto my jeans.

Taking classes at the community college in my home town for the last two years, had given me a warped sense of what college was. Nothing had changed when I started classes there, except the building I drove to. I continued to waitress at the restaurant my Mom and I lived above. She worked the day shift, I worked the night. My life consisted of school, work and homework. While other people my age went to football games, parties and lived the college lifestyle, I worked to pay the electric bill.

I wasn't a mama's girl by any means. That's a hard thing to be when you feel like the adult most of the time. But right now the two hundred miles between me and my mother made me feel little again. I wanted my mom, or at least the comfort zone she represented.

She'd been ready to ship me off the day I was awarded my scholarship. We argued about it actually; I thought college could wait a year but she'd insisted I go as soon as possible.

"Jenna, listen to me," she said. "You can be anything you want to be. This is your opportunity, your chance." She really meant this would be my only chance to avoid ending up like her.

It's pretty terrifying to know you have just one chance to carve out a different path for yourself. It wasn't that my life was horrible, it just wasn't good. I wanted good.

Gathering up my courage, I tried another deep breath, relieved that the threat of hyperventilation seemed to have passed. My new life tempted me, waiting ... just outside of the car. I was ready – but for what I wasn't sure.

The fresh air rushed in as I cracked open the car door, teasing my senses with an invitation to the outside world. The old car door moaned in opposition as I pushed it fully open and stepped out into the sunshine.

The atmosphere seemed different, almost alive. A typical fall day – the air felt refreshing and crisp. Multiple conversations went on around me and blurred into a musical hum of excitement. The grass was greener and the trees taller than anything I'd seen before.

I turned in a circle, staring in admiration, at the tall buildings surrounding me. A huge clock tower stood in the middle of campus like a sentinel of pride. The brick buildings had an authenticity to them that gave the account of generations of students. I could feel the traditions and practically hear the stories these buildings whispered.

I gazed around, like a tourist on vacation. All that was missing – a Camera and a fanny pack. Seriously, I have to pull it together before I change my mind, jump back into my car and drive home.

My heartbeat jumped into overdrive when I stopped gawking at the inanimate distractions and noticed the people around me. I dropped my gaze to the ground, avoiding any possibility of eye contact with way. A side effect of growing up poor, in a small town. Pity in someone's eyes is recognizable, even to a child. I'd gotten enough of those looks to last a lifetime. In response, I mastered invisibility. I could blend into a crowd before anyone was aware of me.

I found, if I didn't look at them, they wouldn't notice me. Juvenile, I know, but usually effective.

Even at the restaurant, in the middle of a room full of chaos and noise, I could fade into the background. I wasn't socially awkward; at least I didn't think I was. Talking to people actually came easy. It was something that had to be done if I wanted decent tips.

But today I was intrigued. This was my new life, right? Maybe I could be a new Jenna, a better Jenna. Maybe I would look at everyone. And maybe today, I would let everyone see me.

Lifting my eyes, I scanned the crowd. People milled around, some walking arm and arm, yelling hellos and waiving to their friends. They smiled and laughed, comfortable in their own skin. No apprehension about starting school shown on their faces, no anxiety – induced sheen of sweat on their foreheads. Nothing. It looked like they were filming a commercial for the college and soon someone would yell, "CUT! Get that strange, new, girl out of here."

To make matters worse, people here were beautiful ... Magazine beautiful.

My throat began to constrict as I blinked through tears. I felt worthless wondering if the beautiful people could tell the differences between me and them. Was it obvious I came from a small town and had never been away from home before? Could they see how terrified I was and hear my heart pounding against my chest? I became painfully aware that my clothes were all wrong and my hair was different from everyone's. I wasn't invisible like I preferred. I dropped my eyes back toward the ground to regroup my thoughts and try to control the panic that surged.

Unfortunately, when I looked down at my Goodwill jeans and Wal-Mart shoes, I realized I'd never be able to compete with these girls. Compared to them I was average, at best. I pulled at the bottom of my t-shirt hoping to release some of the wrinkles pressed in the material from the long drive. I half laughed, half groaned when a good portion of my blonde hair fell out of my messy bun onto my face. Nervously, I tucked it back in, begging it to stay put. If I had known I might be inspected by the entire student body, I would have taken more time to get ready.

I had tried so hard to make sure I wouldn't stand out in the crowd; in case I needed to fade away. But, here in this new life, being the small town girl with nothing special to offer *was* 'standing out'. I was in serious trouble.

I opened my trunk and grabbed a small bag out, hoping it looked like I knew what I was doing. I leaned onto the bumper, staring at my campus map. Directions had never been my strong suit. As my nerves raged out of control, I wasn't even sure what way to hold the damn map. A sarcastic giggle slipped out as I realized this map might be my total undoing.

The final straw that sent me screaming back to my old life.

The sound of someone else's voice interrupted my personal joke. "Can I help you find your dorm Miss?"

Everyone reacts differently when surprised. Some scream, some run. I jump at whatever surprises me. It's a ridiculously poor coping method and completely involuntary... and, what I do almost every time.

"Easy," he said while holding his hands up in front of him in case I made another unexpected move. "I was only wondering if you needed help finding your way around campus. I don't mean you any harm."

"Oh my gosh, I'm so sorry!" I scrambled to retrieve the bag I had thrown in his direction when I launched myself at him. I frantically collected my scattered items, muttering under my breath about how awkward I was.

"Are you okay?" he asked. I think he was questioning my mental stability. He kept his hands outstretched in front of him. I glanced at his hands, realizing how insane I must look to him. He was huge – at least a couple inches over the six foot mark, if I compared him correctly to my petite five foot three. Yet, he felt a need to protect himself from me.

"Yes, I'm fine. A little stressed out I guess. You scared me. I'm really sorry."

He dropped his hands and smiled but still appeared nervous. "It's okay. I know how stressful the first day can be. Let me help you." He was already bending down and picking up eye shadow and lip gloss. Of course it was my make-up bag I used as a weapon ... I quickly kicked a loose tampon under my car.

"Is it that obvious?" I already knew the answer. I went after a Velcro roller that had escaped across the sidewalk.

When I turned to say thank you, I caught my first real look at him. He looked official wearing leather loafers and freshly pressed khakis. My eyes leisurely moved to the navy polo stretched perfectly across his broad shoulders. His skin was tan and looked like he had just returned from somewhere tropical. It was a noticeable contrast to my naturally pale skin. I wasn't sure if it was the softness of his green eyes or the ease of his wide smile, but something made me trust him. Normally, I don't trust people ... ever.

"Well, you're staring at a map." He pointed to the now wrinkled and torn paper still in my hand.

I snapped back to the here and now. "I guess that would give me away," I said under my breath. "Thank you. That's kind of you." I took the make-up from his perfectly manicured hands.

"My name is Cale Davis and I'm a member of The Brotherhood House. We volunteer every year to help new students move into their dorm rooms."

When I realized I had once again gotten lost in those eyes and he was waiting for a response, I blurted out the first thing that came to my mind.

"Well, I definitely need help." I clinched my lips together, praying for a sudden case of laryngitis.

He shook his head and chuckled. Probably thinking I needed more help than finding my dorm room. Possibly a trip to the medical center for meds to cure stupidity. I couldn't argue with that.

His sandy blonde hair, clipped close, highlighted the strong features of his face. I couldn't help but be embarrassed by how attracted I was to him. His smile made me want to know more about him.

"Okay, where are we headed?" he asked politely. I fumbled around trying to straighten the map so I could read the dorm room assignment again.

"Tower two, room 407."

"Easy enough, the Towers are just down the street." He grabbed two boxes from the trunk. Following his lead, I grabbed my bags and locked the car.

"Conversation might go a little easier if you told me your name," he teased.

I smirked at him, enjoying the fact he wanted to joke with me even after I had made an attempt on his life with my mascara.

"People might be more willing to introduce themselves if you didn't use scare tactics to get attention."

He raised a questioning eyebrow at me, a sexy grin lifting the corners of his mouth as he nodded his approval of my comeback. My stomach flip-flopped...he was so out of my league.

"I'm Jenna, Jenna Clausen."

"It's nice to meet you, Jenna."

>Chapter Two<

We walked in the warm fall breeze. I wanted to look ultra-relaxed and unimpressed; however, I couldn't help but let my eyes roam over the campus. There was beauty everywhere. Tall trees lined the busy street that led to the dorms, and made for a stunning display of autumn colors. Even as a little girl, I loved the changing seasons. There was comfort in knowing the end of one thing, allowed the beginning of something new.

As we walked, he pointed out buildings that would be important to me. "The library where all the studying happens." And, "The student center, where everything else happens."

I felt more at ease the closer we got to The Towers. People on this part of campus looked like they had no idea what they were doing. This is where I belonged, in an endless sea of the unknowing...floating along with the current, waiting for someone to give me direction.

After only a few blocks, we stood in front of a tall industrial looking building. I guessed this was one of the towers since there was an identical building farther down the street.

"Welcome to your new home, Miss Clausen." He motioned to the building.

"Why thank you, Mr. Davis." I gave him a quick curtsy and headed up the steps onto the sprawling cement patio.

The front of the building was glass from top to bottom. It showcased the stairway filled with people filing down from the upper floors, instead of waiting for the elevator. They moved in waves, stopping and starting together as they flowed down toward the ground floor. The simultaneous movements made the building look alive.

Someone had propped garbage cans in front of the doors, making moving day easier.

"Ready?" He asked, his smile warm and reassuring. I nodded my head. It wasn't a lie, I was ready. However, I had also never been so terrified of something.

Maybe it was the look he gave me, but something told me he understood.

I followed him into the packed entryway. It should've been easy to blend in, especially since as soon as we entered the building, all eyes were on him.

"Jenna, don't lose me," he yelled over the people who had unintentionally gotten between us. Like I could lose him, he was a beacon. So much for blending in. I pushed up next to him and he shifted to give me more room.

"Is that where I get my mail?" I asked nodding toward the desk behind us. A few seconds of awkward silence passed between us. Enough time to fully process the stupidity of my question. Of course that's where I get my mail … hence the mailboxes on the wall behind the desk. I rolled my eyes and turned away from him. I kept looking more intelligent as our conversations progressed. I should be quiet, better yet, mute. I bit my bottom lip, hoping it would be a reminder to keep my mouth shut. He let the opportunity to make me feel foolish pass and I was grateful.

"Sign in and they'll give you a key to check your mailbox. I'd wait until later or even tomorrow." He pointed to the lines, most being five or more people deep. No one would send me anything anyway.

We maneuvered into line for the elevator. My shoulder stung where the bag straps had started to cut in. I dropped them all to the ground. They landed with a thud, gaining me unwanted attention from the people around me.

"So, The Brotherhood, is that a fraternity?" I asked even though I didn't remember seeing it listed in the brochure. He reached over and picked up the heaviest bag from the floor and added it to his load.

"No, it's a privately owned house that a select group of guys stay in while they go to school."

"A bunch of guys, huh? I bet things get a little wild around that house." I pictured an entire house full of perfectly pressed khaki's and navy polo's. I frowned at my vision, not exactly a picture of wild frat boys.

He laughed and shook his head. "No, not in the house. Don't get me wrong, we like to have fun, but our house is governed by a strict set of rules that have been passed down from generation to generation. And unfortunately, the older generations like to check up on us often."

"I've never heard of a privately owned house, that a bunch of guys live in, that wasn't classified as a fraternity."

He just smiled, shrugged his shoulders and looked back toward the elevator. Clearly this conversation was over. I'd been on campus for approximately ten minutes, who was I to question it?

The elevator doors jumped open and a group of people shuffled out. *"Going out for another load"*, I thought as I watched them. I wondered how many trips it would've taken me if my "*knight in a navy polo*" hadn't shown up.

We followed the crowd and loaded into the overly full elevator. The nervous tension was thick and gave me an uneasy feeling. Maybe it was the moving, or all the people crammed into this small area, but I felt I could scream, laugh uncontrollably, or cry and any of it would be acceptable. Some might even join in. Following proper elevator etiquette, I kept my eyes locked on the floor numbers as they clicked away.

I flinched when the doors opened. He placed a hand on the small of my back and gently guided me out. We walked to the second door on the right side of the hall.

"Here it is, 407."

I looked to him for direction, he quietly said, "You can go in."

"Oh, right." I reached for the handle but before I could grab it, the door swung open.

"Jenna!" She rushed at me, a blur of excitement, wrapping her arms around me.

"I hope you're Katie." The words came out as a forced whisper because she held me so tightly. We had talked on the phone a couple times since finding out we were roommates, so I wasn't completely shocked that this was her introduction. She was funny and loud, liked to talk and loved to shop. She was also sure that we would be lifelong best friends.

I dropped my bags when she released me and tried to fill my lungs with needed oxygen. Cale stood in the doorway but had placed my bags next to one of the wardrobes.

"Katie, this is Cale Davis."

He extended his hand and politely shook hers. "Nice to meet you, Katie."

"Nice, to meet you too," she replied, looking back and forth between Cale and me.

"Jenna, if you're comfortable with the idea, I could take your keys and get the last of your bags out of your car while you two get aquatinted." I reached into my pocket and handed him the keys.

"I'll be right back," he said as he ducked into the hallway.

I turned back to face my new roommate, but she stood staring at the spot where Cale had been.

"Is that your boyfriend?" she asked, pointing to the empty doorway.

"Are you kidding me? I should be so lucky! I just met him. He's from some house on campus that does volunteer work. They help people move in. I think he called it, The Brotherhood ..." She gasped and lunged at me, gripping both of my shoulders.

"You mean there are more of them?" She started a wild dance in the middle of our room and sang a song, something about "I love college". In that second I knew she was right, we were going to be best friends.

"Come over here!" She half skipped across the room and then pointed outside. There was only one window in the room but it was huge. It looked out onto a courtyard that separated the girls' tower from the boys'. I looked down onto a flurry of activity as people ran around setting up stands and stringing lights. "What's going on down there?"

"The Information Fair is tomorrow night," Katie said, she did a jump and clapped. I grabbed her hands and held them tightly in front of her. Her big, silly grin made it impossible to be serious.

"You were a cheerleader, weren't you?" She nodded her head enthusiastically.

"Great," I mumbled. "Mornings should be fun around here."

Katie winked at me.

"Okay, what is the Information Fair?" I asked, releasing her hands and looking back out the window.

"It's when all the sororities, fraternities and clubs have their booths out to recruit for the new school year. There's food and music and my friend said it's a great place to meet guys. Hot guys! Want to go?"

"Sure, sounds fun." I stood side by side with my new friend. We looked out our window, discussing what groups we wanted to talk to. It was easy and comfortable. I exhaled a relaxing breath. Something inside of me settled.

Katie pointed to the fire escape directly outside our window. "The RA stopped by earlier and said that we're a designated fire room. That's why our room is a little bigger, so if the dorm starts burning down, everyone will come to our room to get out. I think it'll be great for sneaking out after dorm curfew." She wiggled her eyebrows up and down at me.

I choked on a nervous laugh, looked down to the ground and then back at her. She was serious, well, as serious as I guessed she could be.

"Since I'm terrified of heights, I'll leave the sneaking out to you." We leaned against the window sill, surveying the room. Our beds were built on stilts and only a couple feet from the ceiling, Katie's was to the left, mine to the right. A couch and a small fridge she brought with her sat under her bed and two dressers and a stand for the TV stood under mine. At the end of each bed was a small desk and wardrobe. Home sweet home.

We began the daunting task of unpacking and discussed how we wanted the room set up. The idea of having a close friend seemed so foreign to me. I didn't really know how to act. I'd spent all my time taking care of my mom and working. It hadn't left a lot of free time to hang out.

"Hey Jenna, here's the rest of your things." A familiar face walked into the room with arms full of my things. I took the bags hanging off his arms, dropping them by the end of my bed.

"Thank you so much. You've been a huge help." Turning back toward Cale, I realized he wasn't alone. Someone stood behind him. This guy was olive skinned with dark hair which made his vivid blue eyes stand out.

'I'm sorry," Cale said quickly, noticing me smiling in the other boy's direction. "This is Marcus, a first year brother in the house. Marcus, this is Jenna and Katie."

I glanced at Katie, hoping she wasn't doing her 'I love college' dance again. She was quiet … and still. Strange.

"Hello," he said in Katie's direction. I wasn't sure he knew I was in the room, and suddenly, Katie was shy.

"Hi." I moved to my friend's side giving her some moral support. Marcus, unable to avoid my presence in the room then, looked at me and smiled.

"It is nice to meet you both." His stare immediately returned to Katie. Her eyes bounced between the floor and Marcus.

Cale put my bags with the rest of my belongings and took my small TV from Marcus.

His large biceps peeked out from under his sleeve when he sat it on the stand. I looked away, not wanting this guy to think I was a creeper when he'd been so nice to me.

Katie and Marcus weren't talking, but had also not taken their eyes off of each other. I shoved my hands into my pockets, rocked back and forth a little, trying to look anywhere but the two of them. I felt uneasy, like I was watching something that was intimate, and I shouldn't be involved in.

I caught myself biting my bottom lip, a stupid habit when I was nervous. My mom always told me it made my emotions too readable.

"I hope you don't mind that Marcus helped with the rest of your things."

"No, not at all."

I was relieved Cale had broken the silence and snapped the tension in the room a bit. I smiled when I looked his way, praying he would forget all my awkwardness. His eyes locked onto mine and the side of his mouth rose into a smirk. I nearly died.

"Do you ladies need any more help?" he asked.

"No, but thanks again. It was really nice of you."

He held my car keys out to me. I reached for them and was surprised when he grabbed my hand with both of his.

"You're welcome Jenna. It was nice to meet you and I hope to see you around campus." He turned to leave but before walking out the door, he glanced back at me over his shoulder, "Try not to attack anyone tonight, okay?"

I shifted my weight to one side and crossed my arms in front of my chest. "Very funny."

He laughed, tapped Marcus on the shoulder and walked out the door. Marcus looked embarrassed as he turned to follow.

We stood in silence, staring at our closed door for several seconds until we both started giggling. We grabbed each other's hands and danced the *'I love college'* dance together.

>CHAPTER THREE<

I yawned and fell onto the couch with a loud sigh, pulling my aching feet up underneath me. Exhaustion from the drive here and crazy amount of unpacking Katie and I accomplished in the last few hours hit hard. "I can't do anymore," I said dramatically and threw my arm over my face.

Katie flopped down next to me, laying her head onto the back of the couch. She took a deep breath in, exhaling slowly. The moment of silence granted me the window I had been waiting for. I needed to get the short version of my life out before she asked about it. Ripping off a band-aid quickly was always the better option as opposed to inch by painful inch.

"It's just me and my mom," I said. Hesitant to look at her, I adjusted so I could stare straight ahead. She'd spent the last hour talking about her big family.

Her life sounded like a fairytale with Katie the star of every story. She was an only child, like me, but that is where the similarities ended. She was loved, cared for and protected. She had childhood memories ... happy ones. Her favorites being the holiday celebrations thrown in her parent's backyard. Cousins, grandparents and neighbors all came to spend time together.

Holidays meant better tips for me. No special memories, no pretty family pictures.

I kept my eyes forward, no turning back now. "My mom was an only child, her parents died before I was born. No cousins, no aunts or uncles. Only us." I felt the heaviness of her stare, but didn't turn her way. Seeing the same pity in her eyes that I'd been getting for years would be too difficult right now.

"I'm sorry ..." she whispered.

I held up my hand, interrupting her. I didn't need the old 'feel sorry for the poor girl with no family' routine. I sat a little straighter as I spoke this time. My tone a bit more terse than I wanted it to be, but I couldn't help it.

"Don't feel sorry for me." I felt my face warming as emotions I tried so hard to keep buried fought to be revealed. "My father left my mom when he found out she was pregnant. Judging from the string of losers she's brought around since, it was probably a blessing in disguise. It's always been just me and her. It's been fine."

She put her hand softly on my leg. My eyes darted down to where she touched me, and back to her face.

Her dark eyes blinked against tears that threatened to spill over. "Oh Jenna, I didn't mean that I feel sorry for you, I meant I'm sorry that I'm such a bitch. I blabbed on about my life without letting you get a word in." I nodded slightly, acknowledging her apology. "She is all you know, it must have been so hard to leave her."

A small tear surprised me and escaped down my cheek. I brushed it away, trying to turn away from her but she wouldn't allow it. She gathered me into her arms and hugged me ridiculously tight.

"I'll be your sister." And just like that, she claimed me as her own. No one had ever made an effort to be part of my life. My body involuntarily stiffened and I clumsily patted her back. I didn't know how to care about someone in this way ... with a level of concern about their well-being. It certainly didn't come naturally to me, but I couldn't deny I liked the way it sounded in theory. Still, the thought of sharing my messed up world with her was inconceivable.

When it became clear she wasn't letting go, I relaxed into her arms slightly and into my first real hug.

She whispered, "You can tell me everything or nothing. It doesn't matter to me. But I promise to never leave you."

Hope sprung inside of me; maybe good people really did exist. I knew I couldn't believe her completely, although part of me wanted to. I clenched my lips together, trying to keep the sobs at bay while tears slid down my cheeks.

Although her words had given me hope, they had cemented something else in my mind as well. She would never be privy to the darkness I endured … I would make sure of it. Her fairytale would stay intact.

~~~

Katie popped her head up over the side of my bed at eight o'clock. "Good morning, Sunshine. Time to get up!"

"Are you kidding me?" I growled, pushing her head back down. "This might be the first Saturday in my entire life I don't have anything to do and you want me to get up early?"

"That's right. We have things to get done today. Get that tiny ass out of bed so we can go exploring!"

I rubbed my eyes, propping myself up on my elbows. "We need rules about sleep time. The rule is, I need more sleep than you." I fell back onto the mattress, using the pillow to drown out the sunlight and the sound of my roommate's chipper voice. When that didn't work, I rolled onto my stomach and pulled the pillow tighter over my head.

"We can't look like newbies, Jenna. Don't you want to know where things are?"

"I thought you said you cased the whole campus while you were waiting for me." I stuck one hand out and twirled it in a dramatic circle around my head while I talked. "And isn't that what maps are for?" I yelled into my mattress and tucked my arm back under my pillow, securing my decision to stay in bed.

A sharp sting bit into my right butt cheek. I jolted to a sitting position. Katie ran out of the room laughing but stopped in the doorway, grimacing and shaking the hand she had slapped me with.

Good, it hurt her too.

"Did you seriously just …"

She interrupted in a singing voice, "See you in the shower, beautiful!"

She danced her way out of our room but left the door wide open. I fell back onto my mattress, stared at the ceiling and said, out loud, to no one, "Oh my God, I live with sing-along, cheerleading Barbie."

~~~

Katie wiggled her way toward the front of the mail desk line. I stayed at the back of the line, where we had waited entirely too long for her liking. She gave a little wave to one of the male workers and held up two fingers. He reached over the people who were lined up in front of her and handed her two maps. She gave him a sweet smile, turning back to me.

"Impressive," I teased. "Do you even know that guy?"

"Yes, that's Carter. He lives in the boys' tower, he's a sophomore. He likes Mocha lattes."

"How do you know that?"

"I hung out at The College Cafe yesterday. He works there." She laced her arm with mine, turning us toward the doors.

"I don't know where that is," I admitted.

"It's the coffee shop in the Student Union." She smiled at me thinking she'd proven her point.

"See, this is exactly why we need to be exploring today." I guess she had.

The Student Union was as big as the rest of the buildings, but looked more modern. Black lampposts lined the walk leading to the front doors. A sign with solid black lettering read, 'The Student Union', and was lit by spotlights. Even in the day, this building appeared to be a big deal. Judging from the amount of people outside in the sitting area, it was the place to be.

Katie and I wound our way through the crowd to the doors. This is what I pictured college life to be. The excitement began to bubble up inside of me. I had no idea what to expect when I walked into the Student

Union. If it was anything like what I had already experienced from college, it would be awesome – and I hadn't even started classes yet.

According to my daydreams, this would be the place where the extremely hot guys hung out. One of them waited inside to sweep me off my feet with a heated glance or an undeniable attraction. The S.U. was where the good stuff went down – I was sure of it!

Katie gave me a quick wink over her shoulder as she pulled open the door. I followed her, expecting the true college experience to start as soon as we got inside.

A sarcastic sound escaped my lips and echoed around the cavernous space. The few people, who sat at the round tables scattered all over, looked in our direction. I giggled into my hand. This place was a glorified mall food court. The only thing missing was an escalator. I bit my bottom lip as I looked around the empty area. I wouldn't be having any mind-blowing, romantic encounters here today.

The walls were lined with several types of shops, making it look even more 'mall-ish': The College Book Store, The College Café and The College Outlet store, even a few fast food restaurants. The second floor held study rooms, a computer lab, and faculty offices. Boring … and more boring.

A help wanted sign hanging in the window of The College Café caught my eye.

"I'm going to run in and get an application."

Katie smiled and motioned toward one of the many open tables. "I'll be over there."

"Meet you there in a bit," I said as I walked into the Café. This might be the only place people came to study. Most of the high-top tables were full.

"I'll have a Vanilla Latte please, and an application."

The guy taking orders gave me a second look, reached under the counter and handed me the two-sided piece of paper. "The manager is usually here in the mornings during the week, if you bring it back then, he will interview you on the spot."

"Thanks," I glanced at his name tag, "Bryan."

While I waited for my latte, I watched people come and go from Katie's table. Some, introducing themselves for the first time, others seemed to know her and stopped to chat.

Katie was the perfect roommate for me — at least the part of me that didn't want to be invisible. She sucked for the other part. People radiated to her. She said it was because she was tall, people could see her in a crowd, but I knew her personality drew them in. Her laugh was infectious and the way she tossed her long dark hair from shoulder to shoulder made her endearing. She was the girl every girl wanted to be friends with and every boy wanted to date. And her roommate wanted to be the invisible girl most of the time … how ironic was that.

Katie spotted me staring and motioned for me to join her.

"This is my roommate Jenna," she said, pulling me out of her shadow, thrusting me into the spotlight, as I walked up to the table.

"Isn't she gorgeous?" *Oh my God, did she just say that?*

I slid into a chair next to her.

"This is Chelsea, Marie and Dana. They are from Alpha Delta Sigma, one of the sororities I talked with when I registered for my classes."

The three girls smiled their hellos at me, I gave a small wave. Their attention returned to Katie quickly. Dana flipped her brown hair over one shoulder and handed Katie a piece of paper. It was obvious they were over me. Dana looked like one of the beautiful people from yesterday. Chelsea and Marie were the perfect blonde book ends to compliment her.

"Call me. We would like to meet with you. I think you would be a perfect fit for the Delts."

"Thanks, Dana. Jenna and I will look for your table at the Information Fair tonight."

Katie flashed her award-winning smile. Dana glanced at me; I sat motionless with a mouthful of latte, afraid of what she might do if I moved. She was beautiful but damn if she didn't have a seriously scary edge to her also. I'm sure she wouldn't think twice about lashing out at me with her perfectly manicured nails.

"We look forward to it." She smiled at Katie then turned on a dime with Ding and Dong right on her heels. I swallowed my latte, stood and looked at Katie, my eyes bulging out of my head.

"*That* is who you want to live with?" I asked, pointing toward the trio as they walked away.

"God no," she laughed.

"Whoa, I was worried. That Dana girl seems like a real piece of work."

"Really? I think she seems sweet." I glared at my roommate – she threw her arm over my shoulder. Taking the latte out of my hand, she helped herself to a drink and said, "I don't want to live with anyone but you, girly."

>CHAPTER FOUR<

Our room turned into the *pre*-Information Fair place to be. People mingled in and out, laughing and dancing in the hallway to the loud music that came from somewhere down the hall.

I stood in front of the mirror, amazed at what Katie could do with a straightener.

"You need more color," she announced, coming at me with a make-up brush.

When Katie looked in the mirror she saw flawless, tanned skin, so I'm sure my ivory complexion did look transparent to her. I let her work her magic, admittedly, liking what I saw when she finished.

Holli and Kaylee lived next door and Jennifer a few doors down. We had decided earlier it would be more fun to go to the fair together. Apparently, that also gave us permission to raid each other's closets, convinced we would find the perfect outfit in someone else's wardrobe. Katie dug around until she found my tightest pair of jeans and insisted I put them on. She threw a peach colored shirt at me. It was big and flowing and cut in at the waist with a puckering of elastic to make it stay in place. I held it up, noticing the sheerness of the fabric.

"No way Katie! Are you kidding me? You can see right through this thing!"

"Jenna, wear it, you'll look amazing!"

I laughed while grabbing a white and black striped, v-neck shirt from my closet and pulled on my black boots.

She turned from fixing Kaylee's eyeliner and gasped, "Wow, don't listen to me, you look hot in that!" She surveyed our little group, "Are we ready?"

We walked toward the elevator with an air of excitement, knowing the Information Fair was already packed with people. To be honest with myself, I needed a crowd to melt into. The attention I got walking around with Katie today had pushed me to my limit. Once we were in the court yard ... I hoped for the chance of an escape.

We followed each other into the elevator. A silence fell over the group once the doors closed. Holli held her hands in front of her, rubbing them back and forth. I wasn't the only one having anxiety about what to expect. Katie, however, stood with a smile on her face, full of confidence. She was positive this would be a great night. A *Memory Maker,* she'd called it. I picked at my fingernails, secretly wanting this night to be over.

"Stay with me, don't let me get lost, okay?" She whispered. I forced a smile, knowing her comment was more for my benefit than hers.

The elevator doors opened to a wall of people holding boxes … I gasped at the sudden feeling of being trapped. Relief washed over me when they parted to let us through. I couldn't believe how many people were still moving in. I may not know what the hell was going on, but I was a step ahead of these people.

The music from the courtyard floated into the entryway, getting louder as we neared the front doors. The haze of fall did its best to block out the waning daylight. This time of year, even the sun tried to stay out as long as possible, knowing that soon, cold days and nights would take up residency.

The courtyard looked like an outdoor ballroom. White lights hung on trees along the outside perimeters, defining the area beautifully. A constructed canopy of the same type of lights was suspended across a makeshift dance floor where the D.J. was set up.

Elaborately constructed tables were scattered across the open area. The fraternities and sororities were by far the most impressive though, many of them having twinkling lights, small waterfalls and music. One showcased a replica of their house sculpted into ice.

The tables alternated between information tables, food vendors and club tables. Several of them sold university sweatshirts, bags and anything else you could ever want with the school name on it.

"I don't even know what to look at." I whispered to Holli. She shook her head. I guess I was doing better than her, I could speak.

Katie took the lead of our group and didn't appear intimidated in the least bit. She shopped each table and joked with the attendants while asking intelligent questions and challenging the answers she received.

As time passed, the sun gave up its fight and night took over, cooling the breeze. I ran my hands up and down my arms, trying to warm myself.

"This is really stressful," Katie said with little sigh as she handed me some pamphlets.

"Really? You sound like a natural," I said, looking at a t-shirt she bought from one of the stands.

"I don't like talking to these people. It makes me nervous." I continued to compliment her polished style and her ability to talk about trivial things with strangers until I noticed there was no response from her.

"Hey," I said waving a hand in front of her face. "What's the matter with you?" I turned to follow her stare.

Marcus came from around the corner with two other guys. I looked back at Katie – who had turned so her back was to me. I walked around her, catching here terrified eyes, and teased, "Are you going to make a run for it?"

She twisted her hands together in front of her, making a pained expression. "He's so cute. I can't even be around him. It makes me want to pass out."

I peeked over her shoulder and quickly looked back at her.

"Better put your head between your knees then because here he comes." She looked like she could cry.

"Hi Katie, Jenna." Marcus said.

I stepped around her... she didn't move.

"Hey, Marcus." I tapped her arm with my elbow, she whimpered so softly only I heard. I bit lightly on my bottom lip to stop the laughter trying to make its way out. She turned slowly.

"Hi," she said calmly, but I heard the small tremble in her voice. I leaned toward her until our arms touched, reminding her she wasn't alone.

As soon as she spoke, he was lost in her again. I'd never seen two people stare at each other like that. It creeped me out a little bit. I slowly nodded my head, looking back and forth between them, waiting for one of them to speak again. Marcus' friends seemed to notice the lack of conversation also.

"You must be Jenna. I'm Nolan Mcguire. We live with Cale and Marcus. They told us about the two of you. We were hoping to get to meet you." He didn't talk *to* me, he talked *around* me and *over* me. I watched as his eyes jetted off in either direction over my head, looking for someone more important than me. He extended his hand toward me, but I couldn't focus on anything except what he'd said.

Cale told them about us? I couldn't begin to fantasize why he would've mentioned me. It must have been about Marcus and Katie's undeniable attraction for each other. I was the roommate in the story ... *"And her roommate's name was Jenna."*

My mind wandered for a second, wishing something about me had intrigued Cale enough to mention Katie and me to his friends. But I wasn't *that* girl ... I was the *roommate* kind of girl.

I grasped Nolan's hand, realizing I had left him with his hand outstretched for a rude amount of time, and looked into his eyes. They were vacant of emotion. A shiver crawled up my spine. I wanted to stop touching him, but he held my hand tightly, making me wait until he let go.

"Nice to meet you, Nolan." I managed to get out. And like that, he had me in his sights. His eyes bore down on me. A cushion of arrogance surrounded him as his mouth raised in a smirk. No one had ever looked at me that way before. I felt naked and exposed. Afraid he could see my secrets if I continued to allow him to stare – I looked away. My heart beat hard in my chest, pleading with me to distance myself from him.

I glanced toward the other boy but he didn't speak. Finally releasing my hand, Nolan introduced him. "This is Quinn."

Quinn didn't extend his hand, only gave me a quick nod – I was thankful. I returned the same gesture.

"It was nice meeting you, Jenna. I'm sure we'll see each other again." Nolan dismissed me, and moved on to the next group of people, Quinn shadowing behind. I watched him work the crowd like a politician, thankful he had tired of me so quickly.

I scanned the crowd, hoping to find a familiar face. Katie and Marcus had regained the ability to speak and were seated at a table near the dance floor having a quiet conversation. I wondered if they realized they were in the middle of all of these people. I doubted it. It must be life changing to find someone who shuts the rest of the world out with their presence.

Finally, my chance for alone time had come. I stopped at one of the tables long enough to buy a sweatshirt before heading back to my room. I wasn't mad at Katie for ditching me for Marcus. I understood and would've done the same thing. Although, considering I had never been in that type of situation with a guy, I guess I couldn't say for sure.

The entryway of the Tower was mostly cleared out and when the elevator doors opened it was empty. I breathed deeply, letting a long sigh out as the doors closed. My arms went slack and heavy next to me as I slumped back against the cold metal walls. I rolled my shoulders feeling every knot in my back. The excitement of the last day and a half had broken me down. I was happy when I finally walked into my room.

My favorite pajamas, a pair of gray sweatpants and an old high school t-shirt, were a welcome sight. The tension in my back began to loosen from the idea of sleep. I couldn't wait to climb into my bed. I changed quickly and grabbed my bathroom bag. Brushing my teeth was the only thing that stood between me and sleep. I would've been giddy, but I was too tired.

I rushed into the hallway and turned to shut the door behind me. With my hand still on the knob I froze as the lock caught. My warm breath bounced off the pressed wood door, with my nose only inches from it. This area had been overflowing with people when we were getting ready for the fair, but now it was empty. I was alone. I tried to push the rising panic down, begging myself for tranquility. Sometimes the most frightening things are the monsters your mind makes up to fill emptiness.

The buzzing of florescent lights echoed in my ears, attaching themselves to my nerve endings. I shuddered, trying to shake off the uncomfortable feeling that slithered down my spine.

"There's no one there. Nobody wants to hurt you." I whispered, trying to keep my head in the right place. An internal battle raged inside of me. The constant push-pull that comes with anxiety is a Hell I wouldn't wish on anyone.

One side commanded me to do more, be more. The other side screamed – be smart, be safe. My days became a constant back and forth, each time one side winning the immediate battle, but never the entire war.

I squeezed my eyes shut trying to decide if I would go down the hall and brush my teeth or bolt back into my room and lock the world out behind me. A simple decision for most … But to me, my entire existence hung in the balance.

I held my breath, looked toward the bathroom, nothing, and then toward the elevators. It was clear too. I rushed down the hall, the weight of fear pushing on my back, making me move faster with each step.

I slipped into the bathroom silently and pressed my back against the wall. My lungs burned but I released my breath slowly. If anyone else was in here, I didn't want them to hear me. I slid down the wall, pulling my knees up and resting my forehead on them. Sometimes making myself smaller physically, made my emotions easier to control. '*I am safe. No one wants to hurt me.*'

Once I felt the anxiety recede, I forced myself to my feet. "*Forward,*" I whispered, incase my brain had forgotten to tell my legs the direction I intended to move.

My make-up had started to fade from my eyes and I was glad. I reached up and touched my reflection, wondering if anyone could understand what I was really trying to hide. The make-up changed the way I looked, but not who I was. There was no fix for that.

When I finished washing my face and brushing my teeth, I walked back to the room. A burst of cold air hit me when I opened the door. I grabbed a blanket from the couch, threw it across my shoulders and hurried to shut the window.

Heaviness settled in my chest when I looked out the window. The fair was still in full swing. Regret twisted my stomach. A small part of me wished I would've stayed, maybe looked for someone from my floor to hang out with. I tightened the blanket around myself and turned away from the window, knowing there was a bigger part of me glad I was in my room. I took a pillow from my bed and curled up on the couch.

The music from outside was the last thing I remembered.

My eyes fluttered and I stretched my arms above my head. Something had woken me. Several panicky seconds passed before I realized where I was. I wasn't sure how long it took me to fall asleep or how long I'd slept. A soft knock from the other side of the door startled me, but I recovered quickly.

I mumbled into the darkness, rubbing the sleep from my eyes, "Why do I have a feeling that you will be forgetting your keys a lot?" I shuffled my way to the door, unlocked the deadbolt and turned back toward the couch. A familiar voice stopped me in my tracks.

"Jenna, its Cale. Can I come in?"

>CHAPTER FIVE<

My body froze halfway between the door and the couch. This had to be a dream or possibly a hallucination. Maybe I was experiencing a psychotic break. Considering I had been close to one since driving onto campus, it wasn't a farfetched theory. One thing was for sure, there was no way I actually heard that voice.

Now wide awake, my mind spun with a dozen questions. Why was he here? Was it really him? Should I let him in? What do I look like?

I reached for the overhead lamp attached to my desk and turned it on. Obviously intended for studying when other people wanted to sleep, it was more of a small spotlight on the top of my desk. Lights shining in from the Information Fair did little more than throw long shadows on everything.

Placing one hand on the door, the other on the knob, I tried to decide if it had actually been his voice.

"Jenna?" I dropped my hands. Reality quickly set in – it was him. I needed to let him in, or tell him to go home. This was bad. It didn't feel right. But it felt *so* right at the same time.

I ran my hands over my hair, trying to calm any wild strands. My decision had been made; I reached for the knob, opening it a crack. I peered through the small opening, blinking rapidly as my eyes adjusted to the light of the hallway. His face lit up with a kind smile.

"Can I come in?" he whispered. My mind was stuttering stupid responses to his question that I thankfully had enough sense to not blurt out, which in turn, made me mute.

Was this one of those "*situations*" that everyone warns you about before you go to college?

Cale cleared his throat and leaned closer to the door. "Not really supposed to be out here, standing in the girls' dorm, after curfew. If you don't want me to come in I totally understand, but could you say something so I know if I need to leave or not?"

Really? Could I be any more awkward? I opened the door wider and stepped behind it.

Hello "*situation*", *welcome to my room*. He turned sideways to fit into the opening, glanced back down the hallway and slid in. We stood in silence, me in my pajamas, hair a wreck, sleep in my eyes ... and Cale.

I shut the door behind him, the whole time wondering what the hell I was doing.

"Hey," he said. He seemed both surprised and happy that I had let him in. Although I found myself unbelievably attracted to him and excited beyond words that he was here, I wanted to make sure he couldn't read it on my face. I tilted my head and looked at him through suspecting eyes.

"You aren't some weird serial killer that picks out unsuspecting girls and murders them before their first day of classes, are you?"

"No. I wait until after your first day." The beautiful smile returned to his face and I nearly died. His eyes dropped to the floor and he pushed his hands down into the front pockets of his dark jeans. His tight-fitting Henley hoodie was proof that he had spent many hours in the gym. He was perfection and I was ... me.

I lightly hit him in the stomach as I walked past. "Well, that's a relief."

He laughed and turned to follow me to the couch. We both flopped down, him on one side with one of his arms draped across the back and the other resting on the arm. I sat on the opposite side using the arm as a backrest with my legs up on the couch toward him. I grabbed the blanket and pulled it around my shoulders, realizing how silly it was to think that this thin blanket gave me any protection against this guy.

"What time is it?" I asked as I positioned the pillow behind me.

"It's 11:30 you party animal." He nudged my feet in a teasing way.

"I know, I should've stayed longer but Marcus showed up and whisked Katie away. The other girls had gone their separate ways so I decided to come back and relax for a while. I met some of your friends there."

"I heard," he said with a smile. "I saw you talking to my brothers but by the time I got through the crowd you were already gone." He seemed disappointed. "You looked beautiful by the way."

My heart skipped and I shifted on the couch, uncomfortable with his compliment. "Thanks, but these sweatpants are really more me than the make-up and silly clothes."

His face softened, and he tugged on the leg of my sweatpants. "You look as beautiful now as you did earlier, maybe even a little more." His fingertip circled on the bare skin of my ankle. It was the slightest of touch, but my body didn't understand that. Warmth flooded through me and I felt the blush in my cheeks. His eyes held mine for a few seconds too long before I looked away. Could this really be happening? Could this guy be interested in spending time with me?

"Will you tell me about yourself? What makes you Jenna?" He seemed sincere but I couldn't possibly tell him the truth. Why would someone like him want to be around me if he found out that my dad left before I was born? If the man who was supposed to love me no matter what could turn his back and walk away, never looking back ... Why would anyone think I was worth sticking around for?

And what if he knew that my mom and I lived in a one bedroom apartment and we barely made it? Living week to week didn't sound so bad when you were living day to day.

I'm sure he could care less that I wanted so badly to be in sports in high school but was too busy working to help pay the bills.

I never had any close friends. I had girls that I was friendly with but I didn't do the party thing or the boyfriend thing.

I could never tell him my mom didn't marry because she continued to hold on to the "knight in shining armor" dream. I tried over and over to get her to understand that it was never going to happen that way. She'd smile, and tell me to have hope. Hope is a hard thing to have when you're standing in line at the food bank. I tended to choose reality.

I didn't want him to know I'd never had a cell phone or my own computer. The fact I was at this school happened to be a miracle totally funded on scholarships and loans.

The room was quiet. I pulled the blanket over my face realizing everything I "couldn't" tell him had poured out of my mouth. I'd told him everything about where I lived, my parents, and my dream of being a journalist. Embarrassment flooded my body. I lowered the blanket enough to make eye contact, "How long have I been talking?" For a second we stared at each other and then both broke out in laughter.

"I may need time to process that information," he said teasingly.

After our laughter quieted down, he began to talk. He spoke about his wealthy upbringing and the social expectations he had to live up to. It all seemed so foreign to me.

"My father expects me to run The Brotherhood house next year. He says it's a huge jump start into my career." His shoulder slumped; I couldn't imagine the weight he carried. He continued, lost in his own head, talking about growing up in a family like his. I listened carefully, fascinated by his world and the way he described it. There were parts he appeared passionate about, sharing them in great detail, while others he skimmed over. He quieted and a waterfall of emotions ran across his face as he internally worked though something. I fought the urge to touch his cheek to remind him I was still there. Instead, I reached out and I lightly stroked his hand.

"You okay?" I asked. He grabbed my hand, linking our fingers together.

"I'm good, you talk again. I like the sound of your voice." He rubbed circles on the back of my hand with his thumb. I struggled to find something to talk about. I had told him everything about myself. "What type of business are you going into?" I asked.

"It's the family business. It has to do with international customer service. We work with companies across the globe." He must have seen the small-town girl look on my face. He released my fingers but laid my hand on his leg and covered it with his.

"Okay, the best way to explain it is," he started, "Company A is trying to impress Company B, because they're trying to make a deal or need money or a certain type of service. Then Company A hires us as customer service. We then send our highly trained employees out to wherever they are needed. Usually, to keep the higher management of Company B happy and taken care of."

"Wow. That sounds so exotic." My mind swirled with a million questions. There was so much of this world I knew nothing about. "What types of services do you provide," I asked.

"All types from chefs to personal assistants, attorneys and nannies. Anything they want and it's paid for by Company A."

It seemed so common to him. But to me, it was a different world. I paused, realizing how huge his family's business must be.

"Your employees must be very dedicated. Do they have to leave their families?"

"Sometimes, but we pay them very well and there are a lot of perks. Most of the time the employees can bring their families with them, sort of like a paid vacation."

I nodded my head as I tried to grasp everything he'd shared with me.

"I'm going to need some time to process this," I said with a smirk.

He smiled wide and his whole face lit up. My heart raced at the thought of me putting that smile there. Warmth started in my chest and I drew in a deep breath. Cale laid his head against the back of the couch, staring up into the darkness. His mouth opened as if to say something, but closed again. He turned toward me, confusion clouding his eyes. I smiled shyly at him and his eyes dropped to my lips then locked back onto my eyes. With a shaky hand, he reached out and tucked a strand of hair behind my ear. His fingertips lingered at the soft skin behind my earlobe. I held my breath, not because I wanted to, but because I wanted to let out a sigh at his soft touch. I leaned my cheek into his hand and he ran his thumb along my jaw line.

"So perfect ..." he whispered.

I opened my eyes as he leaned closer to me. Reality slammed back into me. I hadn't even known this guy for two full days and already I was putty in his hands. My desire fought against this moment of clarity and my body demanded I lean into him. Instead I cleared my throat, and leaned away.

"Have you ever thought about doing something else?" I asked a little too quickly.

He stilled, "I'm sorry?" he asked as he lips turned up into a smirk.

"Oh no, I don't mean …" as I pointed between the two of us. "I'm not critiquing your …"

I covered my face with both hands and laughed. "That's not what I meant."

He reached up and pulled my hands away, smiling and shaking his head in amusement. He kept hold of my hands, laying them gently in my lap.

"I meant, have you ever thought about doing something other than joining your Dad's business."

He lowered his eyes and shook his head, "That's not an option for me."

I melted again. "Does that make you sad?" The words tumbled from my mouth without much thought.

He stared at our intertwined hands for a few seconds before answering. "I wouldn't say I'm sad about it. If I'm upset about anything, it's the loss of choice. My life's path is already laid out ahead of me but it's based on someone else's decisions, not mine."

I understood that feeling. Finally, something we had in common. My entire life had revolved around the poor decisions my mom made. Even though Cale's father's decisions led him toward a position of great power, where my mom's had taken any power from me, we still lived in the shadows of our parents' past lives.

I rested my head against the back of the couch. "You can make your own path, if you want to."

My eyes were getting heavy but I refused to close them. I didn't want to miss a word that came out of his mouth. My heart ached for him. Even though I hadn't had the money or upbringing he had, at least my mom had given me the freedom to decide what was going to make me happy.

"It's getting late." He motioned toward the window. "Looks like the fair is over."

I stood and walked over to the window. The few people left in the courtyard moved quickly, taking down tables and stacking them onto carts. The music stopped and I watched as the lights began to darken, one grouping at a time, as they were unplugged. Except for the moonlight, the room was dark.

A heavy silence settled on the room. My heartbeat drummed against my chest. I looked at the floor, crossing my arms loosely over myself. The air shifted and I felt his warmth behind me. He stood close enough that the absence of his touch was painful … and he continued to deny me. His strong body curved around mine. Close enough to feel his presence, but not close enough to touch. I wanted to reach back and pull him close, but I couldn't be the one to touch him first, somehow I knew this. I closed my eyes and took a deep breath, wishing and waiting for any touch from him. He leaned into my hair – his warm, rapid breath causing an aching in me. A burning I had never known.

The air rushed from my lungs when his fingertips reached under my shirt, softly touching the bare skin of my lower back. One hand teased around until he found the curve of my hip, and began a light massage. He brushed my hair away with the other hand. Holding my shoulder in place, he lowered his mouth to my collar bone, nudging me until I tilted my head and exposed the soft part of my neck to him. He began with small kisses along my collar bone, making a path up my neck. The tenderness sent a shiver through my body. His mouth smiled against my skin as he realized the power he held over me at this moment.

I arched my back, laid my head on his shoulder. His kisses became more desperate as he spread his fingers out across my bare stomach and pulled me tightly against him. The action was so different than his other touch that it startled me.

His mouth hovered over my ear as he spoke, "I feel so comfortable with you. I don't really understand what's going on. I'm not used to letting my guard down so quickly." The vibration of his voice so close to me sent shock waves through me, causing my knees to nearly buckle. I reached back with both hands and grabbed onto his thighs, needing something to ground me. He pulled me even tighter against him, his hand slipping around to the front of my throat. His grip was tight, but not restricting. I gasped at the excitement of someone having such control of me. Somewhere deep inside me, terror rose up...cautioning me, but was silenced by this new thrill of emotions.

"Jenna," my name was breathy and rushed on his lips as he spun me around. His hands grabbed both sides of my face and his eyes connected with mine, desperate for a reply.

Somehow, I managed a few words but instead of the confidence I had hoped for, my voice trembled as I spoke, "I feel comfortable with you too." The sound of uncertainty in my voice brought me some unwanted clarity. His eyes searched my face. He had heard my doubt too.

I closed my eyes against the flood of embarrassment that surged through me. With those few words I had given away my secret. I wasn't comfortable with him right now; actually I had never been more uncomfortable than I was in this very moment.

Although, something about his touch – the way he changed from tenderness to aggression...had made me want to ignore the uncomfortable parts and go with the thrill of what he would do next. But I couldn't ignore what my mind was screaming at me either.

"Stop," I whispered. I reached up and gently took his hands from my face. As they dropped, he intertwined his fingers with mine, pulling me against him. Inhaling deeply, he pressed his lips hard against my forehead. We both struggled to calm our rapid breaths.

I leaned back, breaking our contact. "Comfortable, maybe. Going to have sex with you tonight ... not a chance."

He held my stare as his eyes searched back and forth between mine. Releasing me, he smiled and laid his forehead on mine, running his hands up and down my arms.

"I think you should go," I whispered.

"You're probably right. I'm sorry." He took another deep breath and stepped away from me. "I hope I didn't scare you, or push you too far."

I shook my head, confused about my feelings and what had happened. He stepped around me and opened the window.

"Wait, what are you doing?"

"You asked me to leave. I can't go out the door so I will have to use the fire escape."

"You can't!"

"Jenna, if I go out the door I'll get caught. My father would be furious if he knew I was in the girls' dorm after curfew. He's going to be in town tomorrow so I won't be available, but can I see you on Monday?"

I nodded my head like a little girl pouting because she didn't get her way. Did I want him to stay? No. I wanted him to go. I wasn't the kind of girl who was going to have sex with him tonight, or any other night for that matter.

The emotional dilemma must have played out on my face. He touched my cheek, and lifted my chin toward him.

"You're beautiful, but you don't know that, do you?" His warm breath teased over my lips as his fingertips traced down my face. His eyes lingered on mine like he was committing them to memory. "Be careful Jenna," he whispered, "You could drive a man to do bad things." His lips curved into a smirk. "It's one of the things I like about you." He released me, giving my forehead a quick kiss and climbed out the window.

>CHAPTER SIX<

"Katie! It's seven-thirty. I can't wait any longer. I don't even know where I'm going." I yelled into the steamy shower room, unsure of which stall she was in.

"Yes you do, we've gone over it a thousand times." She laughed from behind one of the curtains. "Just go. My class isn't until 8:30. See you back at the room around noon. Have a great first day!"

"You too," I yelled pushing my way through the crowded bathroom and into the hallway.

People rushed around me as they hurried back and forth. Anxiety over the first day of classes hung in the air wrapped in a cover of excitement.

There were two streams of people; one heading to the stairs, one to the elevator. I followed the crowd onto the elevator. With my map firmly in my hand, I smiled to myself as my fingers traced over the creased and ripped paper. Katie had laid down a firm *"No maps on the first day"* rule. This map was hidden away for other reasons than needing directions.

Cale drifted into my mind. If I was honest, he never really left. The memories of Saturday night lingered with me. The trail of warmth left as he kissed down my neck, his fingertips exploring parts of me that had never been touched before. The entire memory was frightening but for the first time in my life, the fear had not shut me down. When his skin touched mine, I felt powerful in my fear and it was intoxicating. A new world had been opened to me. I found there was something I liked about being out of control. And, as much as it scared the hell out of me, I actually enjoyed allowing someone to have power over me – not because they took it, but because I gave it. Whatever had happened between us altered who I was, and the new me wanted more.

Warmth ran over my cheeks and I fanned myself with the map. I ran my hand through my hair, wishing I could wipe away the vision of us standing in front of the window. As much as I had wanted it – it gnawed at my heart. How could I have let that happen? I knew better. This was insane. I needed to take myself out of this fantasy world. Cale was not an option for me, and he was definitely not interested in me. Saturday night was nothing more than a nice guy, coming to my room to get to know me better. Things got out of hand – lines were crossed. I let him into my room at 11:30 at night when I knew nothing about him. What kind of message did I send? I knew what kind; come in, lie on my couch, tell me your life story, and touch me inappropriately.

But we did talk, a lot. We told each other about our families and our future plans. Do you do that with someone you are hoping to have a one night stand with? I was clueless about these sorts of things.

My stomach twisted inside of me, making me nauseous. How stupid could I be to let some guy I don't even know, into my room? This was a serious lapse of common sense. I told him my whole life story, without even thinking about how that would look or sound to someone like Cale. He had everything, I barely had anything.

Sunday morning Katie and I dissected every possibility of why he had shown up. She was convinced he was interested in me and probably already wanted to get married. Her fantasy included beautiful babies running around in designer diapers and navy polos, calling her Aunt Katie.

I was positive her *'sunny side up'* attitude about everything was going to make me jump off the fire escape.

My take on things; he was a nice guy and probably could see how unstable I was. He was checking up on me to make sure I was settled. There was no way this guy was interested in me. I had nothing to offer him and I was pretty sure if I didn't stop obsessing about it, I was going to lose my mind.

Katie disliked my take on it as much as I did hers.

The elevator doors jerked opened, startling me back into reality. I tucked all of my Cale daydreams away so I could focus on my day. Like the follower I was, I mindlessly trailed behind the line of students heading toward the front door. *Focus, I needed to focus on school. That's why I was here. Not for all of this other silly stuff.*

An unexpected tap on my shoulder startled me and I spun around. Cale jumped back with his arms crossed in front of his face.

"Cale!" I said with a playful slap in his direction. *Goodbye focus.*

"Didn't you learn your lesson last time?

"Excuse me Miss, but it looks like you're lost," he said pointing at my map.

"You *know* I'm lost." I snapped back, not realizing until it was out of my mouth how stupid it made me sound.

He laughed out loud and it was a wonderful sound. I laughed with him while my heart thumped hard against my chest, reminding me of Saturday and what happened when he was near.

"Would you like an escort to your first class? I don't have to be in class until 8:30."

"Really? That would be wonderful. My first class is beginning journalism. It's in the communications building, room 346." I held out the map and tried to point out the building.

"Jenna," he softly said as he pushed the map down. "I know where that is." He lifted his eyebrows playfully and smiled.

"Okay college boy, let's go then."

I followed him out the doors and into the foggy, fall morning. The heaviness of the air penetrated my clothes and made everything thick and cool. I knew the weather was fickle this time of year and it would be warm by the afternoon, but that didn't help me now. I trembled and wrapped my arms around myself. The sun was making a pathetic attempt to warm things, but seemed to be just for show.

"Would you like my sweatshirt?"

"Well," I said, hesitant to take it. He stopped and stripped it off before I could say anymore.

"Jenna, I can see you shivering." He held it up, making it easier for me to slip into.

I was suddenly surrounded by his warmth and scent. It was heavenly. He watched as I folded up the cuffs.

"You're so tiny." He said under his breath and started down the path again. He cleared his throat like he was about to say something but kept walking.

"Yes?" I asked, trying to encourage him to speak. He stopped and turned toward me, running his hand over his face while a frustrated growl escaped his mouth.

"Awkwardness doesn't suite you." I teased as I pushed on his hard chest just enough to make him sway. "What do you want to say?"

He smiled and looked away, obviously trying to choose his words. When his eyes returned to mine, his expression turned serious.

"I'm really sorry about Saturday night."

Oh shit. I almost choked on my own tongue; or maybe I had unknowingly swallowed a tennis ball because that's what it felt like. Was he really going to talk about this? Right here? Now? I might die if this conversation continued. I looked anywhere but directly at him, hoping to develop a quick escape plan – maybe fake a heart attack.

He continued, even though I internally begged him to be quiet. "I really didn't have any intentions of trying anything … out of line." He sighed nervously, it was adorable. My insides instantly softened. This magnificent man was standing in front of me, offering something I'm sure, he rarely offered to anyone, an apology.

I tilted my head and smiled, recognizing in this moment, a small-town girl that stood a good eight inches shorter than him, might have a little power over Cale Davis, once again.

"Really?" I linked my arm around his and started walking. "You mean you didn't intend to sweep into my life like Prince Charming with the intention of stealing my purity?"

He bumped me with his elbow, leaned in and whispered into my ear, "I said that wasn't my intention, but once I got there and saw you in those sexy sweatpants, well, every guy has his limits."

He was teasing, his voice low and sensual making my whole body tingle. I glanced up at his lips— remembering how soft they were and quickly looked back down. Power shifted back to the rightful owner.

He chuckled at my sudden shyness, untangling his arm from mine and throwing it over my shoulders like he owned me.

Guiding me into the building, we stood just inside the main entry. The sea of people coming and going from class parted and moved around us as we stood our ground.

"Your class is on the third floor," he said as he pointed to the stairs. His eyes were focused on me, concern crossed his face. My heart swelled in my chest, loving the feeling of having someone worry about me.

"Thanks. I've got this." I said while readjusting my bag on my shoulder. "Will I see you later today?"

He was quiet. His eyes slowly scanned my body like this was the first time he had seen me. He closed the distance between us. I placed my hand on his chest, just to touch him, not really understanding why I needed it.

"I'll be fine." I looked up at him, trying to conjure up a look of confidence.

"Maybe I should walk you to your class." He grabbed my hand, pulling me behind him.

"Cale, I'm a big girl and I can find this room on my own." I said politely as I held my ground. I wasn't some young girl on my first day of high school. Even if his concern was sweet, I needed to do this by myself.

"Of course you can ..."

"Hey Cale, what's up?" A low voice from behind me interrupted us.

Cale released my hand, reached past me and shook someone's hand. "Hey little brother," he said, "Do you have class in this building?"

I turned slightly to make room for Cale's friend to step in closer, smiling as I glanced toward him. My breath caught in my throat, I turned quickly back to Cale.

"Yes sir, beginning journalism."

Oh no ... no, no. I held my breath, preparing for what I already knew was coming.

Cale patted him on the back and relief washed over his face. He smiled down at me.

"Jenna, this is Ryan Kitson, he's a first year in our house. Ryan, this is Jenna."

Silently cursing my inability to hide my emotions I braced myself to look at him again. I knew I was biting my lip, but didn't care. I looked over my shoulder to greet him, smiling timidly. Ryan nodded in my direction.

An awkward silence stretched out between the three of us. This Ryan guy was hot ... super-hot. I suddenly wondered if there was a secret lab somewhere here, producing beautiful alpha males. If there was, I wouldn't tell.

Where Cale was perfection, Ryan was rough and hard. Cale was Khakis and polos, this guy was baggy jeans and fitted tees. Even though the normal time to shake someone's hand had passed, I turned and stretched my hand out to greet him. He gave it a quick glance before he gently wrapped his large hand around mine. The second his rough hand touched mine, I was sorry I had offered it. My face was burning and my stomach doing flip flops. I said a quick prayer that Cale could not read my thoughts. They were not something a nice girl would think and I was pretty sure Cale thought I was a nice girl.

"Very nice to meet you Jenna." His deep voice touched somewhere deep inside of me. A well-spring of emotions flowed through me. I fought off a small shiver. "I think I've heard Cale mention you a time or two."

"Oh?" I said with a quick glance toward Cale. I'm not sure what emotion crossed Cale's face. *Oh no, he can read my thoughts.* He would have superpowers like that.

Cale cleared his throat. "My class is across campus. Do you mind if Ryan walks you to class?"

He looked at Ryan, "She has the same class as you, could you make sure she gets there?" Ryan smiled and without hesitation said, "Sure."

Cale turned toward me, "I will talk to you later, okay?"

"Sure. I'll be around."

He leaned in and gave me a quick kiss on the cheek, turned and left without saying anything else. I was stunned. I stood there following him with my eyes.

Ryan let out a low laugh, "You may want to close your mouth."

I snapped my mouth shut and looked in his direction. "Did you see that?" I asked him, pointing in Cale's direction. He laughed again and shook his head. "Come on, let's get to class."

>CHAPTER SEVEN<

The doors to the classrooms started opening as the earlier classes began to get out. The new flood of students made it even tighter in the hallway. I took a step closer to Ryan, hoping to avoid being swept into the passing crowd. He looked down at me with a smirk, "Cale was right, you are little."

I tried to take a step back but there were just too many people coming and going through the entryway to get much distance between us. "Ever think that you two are just built like linebackers?"

"Maybe," he said as he maneuvered behind me, guiding us through the crowd to the stairwell. "But you're still little."

I stepped onto the first step, waiting for the people ahead of me to move. When he leaned in to talk to me from behind, his warm breath rushed over my skin.

"It won't be this crowded in a few weeks. People will drop classes or find different ways to get to where they're going."

I followed the crowd because I didn't have much choice. There was only room for two streams of people – one going up, the other coming down. People weren't shoving but there were too many people in too small of an area. You couldn't help but feel like you were on top of each other. I kept my eyes down on the steps. The noise of the crowd was deafening, the sound from the upper floors spilled down to the bottom. It was total chaos.

I stepped onto the first landing and waited as the crowd paused, not noticing the shift in the mood until it was too late. The yells quickly became more intense. People in front of me started backing up, but the people behind me didn't know that. The entire crowd shifted and I was caught in a wave of people. A firm hand grabbed my arm, helping me regain my balance. Suddenly the realization hit. There was a fight happening right in front of me and I was trapped. Panic took over. I started pushing back; I had to get out of here. I frantically searched the crowd, looking for any break between people to make a run for it. But there were too many people – too many bodies. There was no way out. I could hear fists connecting with flesh. Dull thuds, followed by struggles to get away. The sound of violence was something you never forgot. I covered my ears and closed my eyes tight. I could envision the blood. My mom's blood. My blood.

Grabbing me, Ryan pushed through the crowd and shoved me into the corner of the small landing. He pinned me against the wall holding me with one hand up against his back, while he watched what was going on. I grabbed two handfuls of his shirt and buried my face, tears streaming down. No, not here, not now.

I just needed to be quiet, I needed to be a good girl and this would all go away.

Ryan turned and glanced at me. His eyes squinting at me with concern when he saw the terror on my face. "Hey, I am going to get you out of here, okay? You're safe with me."

I couldn't respond. I just stood there, holding onto his shirt, shaking like a child.

He turned to face me, blocking everything out of my sight. I laid my forehead on his chest. The feel of his arms around me calmed me for a second but panic surged when I realized he had turned his back to the threat. "You can't see, you need to see him!" I yelled.

"Everything is going to be fine, I won't let anything happen to you. Hold on to me and don't let go."

He turned once again toward the fighting crowd and reached behind him with one arm, hooking me around the waist. He inched his way along the wall keeping me shielded with his body.

We moved slowly along the wall until we reached the stairs. He used the arm he had around me to push me to the stairs. I sprinted up them pushing people out of the way until I made it to the hallway.

My vision narrowed to a pin point down the hall. Everything around me blurred into stretches of colors; helping to focus on the goal of getting as far away as possible. Each step seemed to require every ounce of my energy. I knew I was crying from the ache in my throat, but the only sound that registered was the rapid beating in my chest. My entire body burned from the surge of adrenalin. I had no idea where I would end up but I needed to be away from there ... away from the violence. It's what I'd been running from most of my life.

I frantically scanned the hallway looking for any escape. The girls' bathroom sign caught my attention and I ran toward it. I rushed in, past the girls standing at the sinks and into the stall at the end. I was all too familiar with what was happening and I didn't want anyone to see it. I leaned my back up against the wall and tried to slow my breathing as I lowered myself to the floor. I closed my eyes, pushing my palms into them until it hurt.

I sat in the corner watching him. He thought I was playing with my Barbie, but really I was watching him. It was always a good idea to know where he was when his walking got unsteady. He dropped into his chair.

"Rose!" I cringed at the way he screamed her name. "Get me another beer." She didn't respond, where was she? He didn't like it when he had to repeat himself. I panicked and looked toward the kitchen where she should be. Stupid! I knew better. If I didn't move, he forgot I was there. But it was too late, he had seen me.

"What are you looking at brat?" I looked back down at my doll, tears filling my eyes. The chair creaked, oh no, he was trying to get up. I gripped my doll tighter as my body flooded with fear. I focused on the floor in front of me, hoping he was drunk enough to fall over before he got to me. My shoulder burned as he ripped me up from the floor, twisting my arm behind my back. "I'm talking to you, you stupid little bitch." The slapping noise rang out before I felt the burning pain on my face that always followed.

"Put her down!" she screamed, running into the room. He dropped me and my bare knees hit the wooden floor, scraping the skin. I grabbed my Barbie and jumped up.

"Hide," she yelled and went after him with her fists. I scurried into the hall and pulled open the closet door. There was a small area that I fit perfectly into. He never found me here. His evil laugh floated into my hiding place. He enjoyed this. The grunts and screams slowed. I squeezed my eyes together, hugging my Barbie up against my face.

I jumped at a loud banging noise, it sounded like when he pounded his fists on the table, but I knew it was my mom. She moaned and it sounded like she was on the floor.

"You are worthless to me," he yelled. And the screen door slammed. I didn't move, frozen in my spot. I knew not to come out until I heard her. I don't know how long my Barbie and I were in there before she whispered my name. I pushed the door open, crawling out and rushing into the other room. She lay on the floor, next to the table.

"Mommy," I cried. I knelt down to her and with my little fingers I tried to wipe the blood from her face as tears streamed down mine.

"Shhh, Jenna. I'm Okay," Her words were strained and she sucked air in like I was hurting her when I helped her sit up. I climbed onto her lap.

"I'm sorry Mommy, I shouldn't have moved, I should have been invisible." Her trembling hand ran down the back of my hair.

"No baby, it's not your fault. Now you don't worry about this, you are starting first grade tomorrow … you will be safe there all day."

"Jenna!" Ryan yelled.

I heard the gasps of the other girls and the shuffle of their feet as they scurried to get out of there.

I didn't want him to find me, but I didn't want him to leave either. He slowly pushed open the door of my stall. I laid my head back against the tiles, my cheeks wet with tears, eyes shut tight. I heard him take a deep breath and felt his presence in front of me. I waited for the questions. It was always the same thing. What happened? Why did you react like that? What's the matter with you?

I jumped when he used his fingertips to wipe the wetness off my cheek. He was leaning on one knee in front of me. His eyes didn't show pity, only concern. Another tear fell but he caught that one too.

"I'm here," he said softly. "No one's going to hurt you." I nodded my head and wiped the rest of the tears from my face. He reached out with both hands and helped me to my feet. He pulled me to his chest, wrapping me up in his strong arms, "You're safe, I can promise you that."

I inhaled a ragged breath. His grip loosened as I gently pushed away from him.

"Give me a second?"

"Are you going to be okay if I leave?"

I nodded up at him and tried my best smile, which must have been pretty pathetic, because he tilted his head and gave me a questioning look.

"Really, I just need to pull it together." He nodded this time and left me standing there by myself.

I stared at the reflection in the mirror. I was so messed up. My mom was right; this was my only chance at making a life for myself. If I continued to let the demons resurface, I was as good as dead. Maybe not physically, but emotionally dead for the rest of my life. I couldn't allow that to happen.

I grabbed some paper towels from the dispenser and wiped the smeared make-up off of my face. I reached down into my bag, reapplied mascara and called it good.

Ryan was leaning up against the wall, his eyes on the ground. He straightened when he heard me come out. I felt the flush of embarrassment starting but to my surprise it didn't last long. His eyes were soft and there was no judgment. He opened his arms and I walked into his embrace. After a short time he let me go and we started walking. That was it. No questions, no awkwardness.

"Are you ready?" he asked as we walked up to the doorway of our first class.

I forced a weak smile. "As ready as I'll ever be."

"Don't worry. Everything will be fine."

He wouldn't be so confident if he knew how far from "fine" I really was.

The classroom was three times bigger than any at my junior college. It was theater style with stairs sloped down to the front where the instructor was set up. Stunned, I looked around wondering what I had gotten myself into. There had to be, easily, three hundred seats in this room and most of them were filled. Ryan softly placed a hand on my lower back and pointed out two empty seats across the room. I made my way past the other students, letting out a small sigh when I finally reached the seats. My hands still shook, an aftermath of my memories, so I tucked them under my leg. I realized I still had Cale's sweatshirt on. I tucked my chin down, hooking it under the collar of the sweatshirt, trying to sink down into it. It was a perfect place to hide.

"Relax," he whispered.

Ryan appeared to feel the exact opposite of me. He was more than comfortable as he dug around in his bag, pulling out a spiral notebook, pen and his laptop. People filed by our desks on the way to their seats, most stopping to say hi or to shake his hand. Even the teacher gave a nod in his direction.

"Do you know the professor?"

He leaned toward me. "The house sponsors a banquet every year for the faculty. It's a good way for the "first years" of the house, like me, to get our names out." His closeness silenced everyone else in the room for me. His blue eyes were fixed on me and I felt honored to have a few seconds of his attention.

My heart grew suddenly heavy. I needed him to forget about what he witnessed only a few moments ago. This was my new beginning, my new life, and I had stupidly brought the darkness here with one moment of panic. Damage control was needed quickly. I didn't want him seeing the bathroom scene every time he looked at me. So up went the walls, and out came the sarcasm – my two best defenses. I whispered back as the teacher began with his introduction, "Well, aren't you the golden boy of the class already?"

He smiled and shot back, "And aren't you lucky to be my friend?"

>CHAPTER EIGHT<

I leaned back against my chair, slightly winded by the exchange that had just happened. After his quick come-back, something passed between us. His eyes settled on my lips for a bit too long. It was only a second, but long enough for my mind to make up the scenario; him leaning into me, his lips brushing lightly over mine.

Just as quickly, he glanced at Cale's sweatshirt and leaned away. Stretching against the back of his chair, he ran his hand through his hair. Someone else caught his attention and he turned around to greet them.

This day was already exhausting. I'd made a huge mess of the morning with very little hope for improvement as the day moved on. My mind continued to play out the fight in the stairwell making it impossible to focus at all. I needed to find a different way to get to class. The idea of passing through the same landing everyday made my skin prickle. I didn't want a repeat of the bathroom scene day after day.

The empty notebook page staring back at me made my restlessness worse. I chewed on my pen, another nervous habit of mine, as the instructor blabbed on about study guides and scheduled quizzes.

I shifted casually in my seat, acting like I was trying to get comfortable. Honestly, it was to sneak looks at Ryan. His relaxed, bad boy demeanor was so sexy. I loved the way he leaned back into his seat when listening to the professor, one arm draped over the back of his chair, the other resting on his leg. He was so confident in himself. I wondered what it would be like to kiss those full lips, or run my fingertips over those amazing arms.

I sighed quietly and shifted in my seat again, glancing over at him. He looked like the perfect student, until I noticed a small smile forming. He ran his tongue over his bottom lip and nipped at the side of it with his teeth. Without looking at me, he reached into his bag and handed me a piece of paper. It was his schedule.

Keeping his eyes down, he leaned into me and whispered, "Why don't you look to see if we have any other classes together? You're making me self-conscious with all that staring." A small gasp slipped from my lips and it felt like the floor dropped out of the room. I had been caught and he called me out. Somehow this morning just got worse.

When I reached for the paper, he grabbed my hand, our eyes locked onto each other's. "And a favor, please? Stop twirling that pen around in your mouth. Unless your evil plan is to make me fail this class miserably."

My shoulders slumped and I tried to fight back the humiliation that rolled through me. I looked away immediately and hid my face behind his schedule. He chuckled and the sound of it warmed my heart.

I dug through my bag until I found my schedule. I was shocked.

"Is this because we have the same major and are in the same year?" I whispered handing back the identical schedules.

"I don't know," He said shrugging his shoulders. "That's really strange. Well, I guess I found my study partner."

~~~

Ryan and I successfully navigated our way through our first day of morning classes. I grabbed at my stomach trying to quiet the next round of growling. Why didn't I listen to Katie when she told me to always have a granola bar with me for times like this?

"Dang Jenna," Ryan said looking down at me as we walked, "everyone on campus must know you're starving. You need some food, girl." He laughed at my pitiful attempt to shove his arm. "Let's stop at the Union and eat. We have time before our next class."

"Can't," I shook my head. "I promised to meet my roommate back in our room. She wants to hear all about my classes. She would go crazy if I blew her off; probably send the FBI out after me."

"Over protective?"

"Oh my gosh, you have no idea."

We stopped in front of the Student Union. He pushed his hands into the front pockets of his jeans and smiled at me. Just a simple, small smile. My heart jumped and I felt my face warming. I looked over toward the herds of people filing into the Union, or anywhere that wasn't directly at him.

"I'll see you in our next class." He turned and started toward the Union. My already racing heart pounded as I envisioned him eating alone. I started down the sidewalk toward the dorms. There was no way someone like him would be eating alone. He was the male version of Katie. There were probably ten tables of people waiting for him to show up. *Just keep walking Jenna. Just keep walking.*

"Why don't you have lunch with us?" So much for walking away.

He turned and started back toward me. "Are you sure Katie won't mind?"

My mind panicked as I rushed through our conversations this morning. How did he know her name? Had I told him? I couldn't remember talking about her. Shouldn't this be another red flag? I'm obviously bad at this stuff. I thought I was a smart girl but I let Cale in my dorm room when everything about it felt wrong. And what had that gotten me? Confusion and an awkward conversation.

Did this feel wrong like that night? No. I don't think so, but shouldn't it? Why did I want to trust these guys? I felt all the years of protection I had built around myself suddenly slipping through my hands like sand.

Ryan stepped in close to me, cutting off my psycho thoughts – stopping all thoughts really. I let my eyes focus in on him.

"Hey, where did you go just now? A thousand emotions just ran across your face."

I took a step back to distance myself. There was no clear thinking when he stood that close to me.

"Are you hungry or not?" That was better. Avoidance; I'm comfortable here.

"Marcus and yes," he said shifting away from me.

"What?"

"Marcus is how I know who your roommate is and yes, I am hungry."

I nodded my head once, feeling like a complete idiot. Of course Marcus was talking about Katie. Without another word, I started toward the dorms.

The temperature had gotten high enough to make it a comfortable day. I could feel the warmth from the sun on my face and it calmed me. He fell into step with me and we walked in silence, pushing through the sea of people. My mind was racing however; going over the morning's events.

I reached the steps of the towers first: quickly ran up several, and turned, so I could be eye to eye with him. He stopped abruptly, not expecting me to block his path.

"I was hoping that maybe …" I twisted my hands together while I gathered my courage. This was the last thing I wanted to bring up, but I had no choice. "Maybe, you wouldn't tell Cale what happened today? Or anyone really, but especially Cale."

Ryan looked out over the crowd of people around us. He put his hands on his hips, shaking his head slightly. A conflicted look crossed his face. He was acting like the possibility of not telling Cale was a huge deal. I needed to plead my case and do it quickly before he made up his mind.

"I mean, I guess I just don't want him to think I'm some sort of freak. I know I overreacted. I should've been able to deal with a fight, it's just …" I couldn't think of another word to say. My eyes searched the sidewalk, hoping that the words would suddenly be clear in my head.

"What did happen, Jenna?" The softness of his voice wrapped around me, his eyes searched my face for some clue to the answer. The people around us continued to go about their day, not noticing he just asked an impossibly painful question.

"What do you mean?"

"I want to know why the fight freaked you out so badly? Haven't you ever seen a fight before?"

Tears threatened again but I fought to keep control. He had no idea what I had seen before. "Of course I have. It just was so, unexpected."

He was silent for a minute while he processed. I put my hands together in front of me and gave him my best puppy dog eyes. I'd never tried this tactic before but hey, this was important, I was willing to try anything.

A small smirk raised one side of his mouth.

"Please, I will never ask for another favor again," I said batting my eye lashes in an obnoxiously, over the top way.

Rolling his eyes, he groaned and I could tell he was caving. "Okay, it's our little secret."

I smiled at him, "Thank you."

He started up the steps, lightly grabbing my arm as he pushed past me. "Let's go little one, I'm starving!"

We got off the elevator and walked up to my door. I stopped and teasingly said as I opened the door, "Now, my room may not be as nice as yours in the house but it's all I have."

Ryan busted out in laughter as Marcus fell off the couch and Katie scrambled to her feet and straightened her hair nervously. Ryan walked past me and offered Marcus a hand.

"Guess we should've knocked. Right, brother?" He pulled Marcus up from the floor and put his arm around his neck, and then it hit me.

"You two are brothers aren't you? I mean real brothers from the same family." The same wide smile lit up their faces, suddenly the resemblance was undeniable.

"This is my little brother." Ryan said as he messed up Marcus's hair. Marcus gave him a shove and went back over to hug Katie who seemed very confused.

Looking at Ryan she said slowly, "I am sorry, who are you?"

"I'm Ryan, his older brother."

"Biological." I added.

"Why didn't you tell me you had a brother here?" Katie asked in a slightly whiny tone that made me frown at her. I hate it when girls whine. But who was I to judge, hadn't I just used puppy dog eyes on Ryan to get what I wanted?

Marcus hurried over to her and put his hands on her hips. "I told you my brother and I went to supper last night. We've talked so much over the last few days I thought I'd told you about him."

"Well, I guess you did mention Ryan's name. But how was I to know, you guys call everyone brother." She laughed and all was right in their world again. She snaked her arms around his waist and hugged him tight.

"Are you hungry Ryan?" She asked naturally taking her place as hostess and digging through our small fridge to see what she could offer.

"Let's order a pizza." Marcus suggested.

"Well I guess fruit snacks and root beer aren't exactly lunch," she laughed.

We had a great time talking and joking around while enjoying our lunch. The four of us were comfortable together.

"See you back here tonight." Katie said as Ryan and I left. She was going to make a great mom someday.

>CHAPTER NINE<

The next few weeks passed and we fell into a comfortable routine. Every morning, Cale waited in the lobby of my building and walked me to my first class where I met Ryan. Ryan and I spent our days together, had lunch with Marcus and Katie and usually studied for a few hours after classes. Cale always showed up sometime after dinner and hung out until curfew. He'd kept things totally platonic since the first night he'd come to my room. Every time he left, I was a little disappointed about that.

Today, however, there was something different about Cale … and it wasn't a good different. He walked at a fast pace, a few steps ahead of me. His body seemed stiff and when I did talk to him, his responses were short. I stopped and cleared my throat loudly so he would know I was no longer walking with him. He turned and looked back at me.

"Have I done something to upset you?" I asked.

His eyes darted around to the people who were walking past us. But then his gaze dropped to the ground as he walked back to me.

"Jenna, I need to talk to you about something." My stomach knotted up from the tone of his voice. He was nervous, that made me nervous.

"What is it? Is everything okay?"

He nodded his head, "Yes, everything is good, but I have something to ask you."

I raised my eyebrows and smiled, trying to encourage him, but he said nothing. "Cale, you're freaking me out a little."

"When I came to your room the night of the Information Fair, I mentioned a little bit about the traditions that go on in my house, do you remember?"

I mostly remembered the kisses on my neck but vaguely my mind recalled him talking about how the traditions in the house had been handed down from generation to generation. I couldn't remember him being specific about what those traditions were. My mind instantly went to the negative.

He'd probably spent the last weeks thinking about how stupid he was for coming to my room that night. Once he realized what he was jeopardizing, it became quite clear to him what a bad idea a friendship with me really was. I'm sure the traditions include high standards for girlfriends. Without a doubt I didn't measure up to those standards.

I felt a little wave of sadness flash over me. Really? I had only known this guy for a few weeks and I was going to be sad if he didn't want to date me? I understood if that was the case, but the idea of losing his friendship was just as heartbreaking to me.

"Well, every year the brothers of the house, third year and above, are required to 'sponsor' a girl." He flashed a quick look in my direction.

I opened my eyes a little wider, crossed my arms in front of my chest, and nodded my head; wanting him to get on with it. I knew I looked irritated, but dragging this out was excruciating. I could feel a tightness in my chest. If this was the last I was going to see him – he needed to just tell me.

"I'm just going to throw this out there. It's easier to understand if I just get it all out. Every year we have to sponsor a girl, it's a promise to mentor and support her emotionally or financially or spiritually, or whatever that person should need. We do this because, one of the traditions of our house, is to give back to people who may not have been as fortunate in life as we have. Please, don't take this the wrong way, but I would really like to sponsor you."

I could feel the heat rising in my cheeks and my whole face went slack, trying desperately to hide the hurt. All of the *sunny side up* scenarios that Katie and I had talked about—the ones I had secretly held on to, crashed down onto the sidewalk around me.

Tears filled my eyes and I blinked quickly, trying to hide them. I couldn't let him see the disappointment. How could I be so naïve? I thought, or at least I had *allowed* part of me to believe – he'd seen something in me that he could care about.

When I trusted him with my life story, I thought he wanted to get to know me. No wonder he said he needed to "process it". This hadn't been a guy who wanted to know more about a girl he was interested in, it was an interview.

I tried to keep my tone as even as possible. "So that's why you've been hanging around, you want to be my 'big brother'?" I slipped around him and started walking. It felt like it was time to escape this ridiculously uncomfortable moment.

"No, no … not at all". He stepped in front of me, cutting me off. I had no choice but to look at him.

He held onto the upper part of each of my arms, holding me like he was afraid I was going to bolt. I wanted to.

"I knew I wouldn't say this right and that's how you would take it. I didn't want to upset you, I'm sorry. I'm not interested in you in a big brother sort of way. I mean, not in a creepy sort of way either but …" his voice trailed off and he sighed. "This didn't go how I wanted it to." He reached up and pinched the bridge of his nose.

The look on his face softened my heart. He wasn't trying to make me feel bad. It wasn't his fault that I stupidly read more into this than there should've been. He may not have had the same intentions for our relationship as I did, but he had been very kind and sweet to me since I'd met him. The last thing I wanted to do was make him feel bad by being unwilling to hear him out. There were worst things I could think of than having Cale Davis want to be your big brother, even if the thought squeezed at my heart, leaving a lingering sting in my chest.

He stood in front of me, pleading in his eyes, wanting me to understand him.

I composed myself the best I could. "I will make you a deal, you meet me at four o'clock at the library and tell me everything being sponsored is about. I'll decide if it sounds like something for me after I have all the details. Okay?"

"Okay," he said with a smile, his body relaxed and he leaned into me. "Thanks." We walked arm in arm the rest of the way in silence.

~~~

I sat on the floor across from the couch, cross-legged, staring out our window at the gray fall sky. The salad and fries I picked up at the Union sat in front of me untouched.

"Are you going to eat those?" Ryan pointed down at the fries. I shook my head and held them out to him. "I swear I have never seen anyone eat the amount of food you do. It's disgusting really."

He crumpled the wrapper from his third cheeseburger and threw it at me.

"That's because you are like, a fourth of my size. You must come from a mini race. Like those tiny little horses that are so cute. I, on the other hand," he laid his hand on his chest in a reverently. "I come from a race of giants, like …"

"Ogres?" He dropped his hand and we stared at each other, straight-faced for a few seconds until I couldn't hold the laughter in any longer.

"What the Hell Jen? Ogres? I was going to say Greek Gods or something like that."

I gasped for air, laughing so hard I fell to the side holding my stomach. I pointed at him and squeaked out, "Greek God?"

"What? Why is that so funny? I'm hot." He was actually pouting.

I struggled to take in a breath. I grasped at my stomach and rolled over on my back. He got up and stood with one foot on either side of me, looking down at me with a silly smirk. He grabbed my hands, pulling me to me feet.

"It's not that funny. We need to get to class." I fell against his hard chest and took a deep breath, trying to calm down. As soon as the laughter stopped, tears started flowing down my cheeks. Even I was surprised by the sudden change. I lifted my hands and covered my face.

"What's the matter with you?" he asked in a joking tone. He tried to pull my hands away from my face but I wouldn't let him. "Wait, are you really crying now?"

I continued covering my face, trying not to sob out loud. He pulled me in close, rubbing little circles on my back.

"Is this some sort of monthly issue?"

I slapped him on the chest without letting him see my face.

"What? I don't have sisters and if you were a girlfriend, I would've already been avoiding you during this time, so I'm a little out of my comfort zone."

I took a deep rattled breath and stepped away from him. "Cale doesn't want to date me." I said in a little voice.

"Are you kidding me? That's what these tears are for?" I looked up at him and his face tightened like he was in pain. He was really struggling with this emotional stuff.

I nodded my head and more tears filled my vision. He reached out and started rubbing my arms up and down.

"Okay, umm, just quit crying, little one. You're killing me. How do you know he doesn't want to date you? He's with you all the time and he talks about you like, constantly and ..."

"He asked if he could sponsor me."

His face softened. He pulled me to him once more and held me tight, obviously understanding what that meant.

"That's bad isn't it?" I questioned. I just wanted to hear what I already knew.

"Well, no. I mean – there's a very strict policy about not dating the girls that are sponsored."

I took a deep breath and turned my head to the side, listening to his heartbeat, letting the truth of what he was saying calm me. At least now I knew.

"But hey," he pushed me away, not letting go of my arms. "He's Cale Davis. If anyone is allowed to break the rules, it would be him." I smiled and pulled away, wiping tears and heading for the door.

"So, cheer up buttercup."

"Don't call me that." I said as I reached for my bag.

"Sugar pie?"

"Worse." He followed behind me as we stepped out into the hallway. I pointed back toward the door.

"You'd better get that wrapper or Katie will kill you. He rushed back into the room and from inside he yelled, "Honey Boo."

"Stop! You are terrible at this. No wonder you don't have a girlfriend." I yelled as I pushed the elevator button.

~~~

"Okay, spill it. What do you know about being sponsored by one of the brothers in the house?" I frantically asked Ryan as we left our last class. I hadn't brought it up again since lunch but I was dying not knowing what this sponsoring was all about. This was my last chance before meeting Cale and I planned to get as much information as I could before I walked into that library.

"Well," he said as we walked along. "I know it's an honor to get asked, especially by someone with Cale's bloodline." He was serious all of a sudden and choosing his words carefully.

"What do you mean bloodlines, what are we talking about here, dogs?"

"Jenna, these are questions that you need to be asking Cale." His voice was strained.

"I just need to know what to expect. I feel like I'm walking into a world where I don't belong. I just need a little info. Please?"

Obviously waging some sort of internal war with himself, he crossed his arms in front of his chest and began. Butterflies took over in my stomach as I noticed how muscular his arms were. I couldn't lie, he was beautiful. Nothing like an ogre.

"Bloodline refers to the number of generations that your family has been involved in the house. Cale's bloodline goes all the way back to the founding house. Every grandfather or uncle or cousin in his bloodline has been involved in the house in some way."

I stood there like an idiot having no idea what to say. I couldn't imagine having a family tie like that. I didn't even know my father's name.

"And the sponsoring," I urged him on.

Throwing his hands up in front of himself in frustration, he continued. "Isn't this what you're going to talk to Cale about now?"

I pursed my lips together and glared at him. He knew how badly I wanted this information but I didn't want to beg him; although, I wasn't completely against the idea, if he didn't believe the mad girl act.

"I really don't know that much about sponsoring. The house runs on a strict rule of 'need to know' and it all depends on what year you are in the house. First years really don't know much. We are the runners. We serve food, we do laundry, those sorts of things. We earn the right to know what happens in the later years through loyalty to the house. Most of us don't even understand how the business works yet."

"Really?" I was shocked. "I would've thought your dads would've had you in the office learning from the time you could walk."

"No, it's against the rules. You have to make a commitment to the house and that can only be done at age 18. The elders don't want to teach any of the business secrets to someone who hasn't committed. Can't have anyone running off and starting their own business I guess."

This was all so complicated I was almost sorry I asked, but at the same time, there was something so mysterious about it all.

"I don't understand all the secrecy."

"Come on, you're making it way too complicated. It's not like we are some warped group out to take over the school. It's just a way we identify ourselves so we know what level everyone is on. It's just like any other job, you learn as you go. First years, like I already told you, the runners. Second years learn the financial end of the house. They start learning how the house works, from paying wages to the cooks to making sure the lights stay on. Third years, like Cale, get to start learning the business from the ground up. They see how the structure works. Fourth years gets to run a mock business. The top fourth year student though, gets to run the business on a small scale through the house to see what level he will be placed in after graduation. Nolan Mcguire is the Marshall of the house, that's what they're called. He runs things like the faculty banquets that I told you about earlier. The school and the faculty get a lot of perks from the house, due to the Marshall's trying to make an impression on the older generations."

"Run the business through the house? Great, now I'm not only a charity case, I'm a business venture."

"Jen, Stop. It's not like that. I told you, I really don't know that much about the business other than it provides international customer service. So I guess The Marshall runs a small scale of that here in town. Sometimes first years will have to wait tables at big parties or drive someone to the airport. But the sponsoring stuff is something totally separate from that. It isn't part of the business, just something the house has always done because the business is big on giving back to our communities."

"This is harder to understand than any class we've been to today. So you really don't know that much about sponsoring?"

"Nope, sorry. Maybe you could fill me in after you talk with Cale," he said with a wink.

He motioned to me, encouraging me to move my feet as he started to walk backwards, "Come on now, you don't want to make Cale wait, do you?" he smiled as he turned his back to me.

"But wait, I have one more question."

He stopped and looked up to the sky, taking an exaggerated deep breath – obviously done with my interrogation.

"How is it that you're older than Marcus, but you're both first years?"

His face dropped and he gave me a confused look.

"I can't keep up with you, woman." He walked back toward me. "My brother and I have always said we wanted to go through the house together. I waited for him. There's a junior college near where we grew up. I took classes there while he finished his last year of high school." He put his hand softly on my back, encouraging me to move.

"Now, let's go. You really shouldn't make Cale Davis wait."

>CHAPTER TEN<

The library took up an entire block. The historic looking stone front was a stunning cover for the massive building behind it. Trees surrounded the building, and the grounds around it were perfectly maintained. A large grouping of steps lay out in a welcoming fan from the front doors to the side walk.

Even as impressed as I was with the beautiful library, I knew it was not that or the ungodly amount of steps that led up to it, which made my heart pound so heavily in my chest.

I was scared to death.

I forced myself to keep moving. There were multiple ways I could handle this situation. I could be serious and tell him that I would need some time to consider his proposal – or silly and act like either way, if he chose me or not, it was not a big deal. Insulted was another option – tell him I didn't need his charity and walk away.

None of them seemed to be the right answer, so I just kept moving forward.

The inside of the library looked just as you imagined it would. There were staircases everywhere I looked, leading up to different floors of bookcases and study rooms.

What I hadn't expected, was the back wall of the building, to be windows from floor to ceiling. It looked out onto the beautiful gardens the college was famous for. Even though the sun had started its early decent, once again reminding everyone of the changing season, students lounged outside on the benches placed along the winding paths.

I looked away from the windows and my eyes found him. I desperately drank in the sight of him – fearful, that after this talk, the hope of our relationship being more than friendly would be gone. My apprehension melted away and a small smile spread across my face. Even if he wasn't interested in being in my life the way I wanted him to be, I knew there was no way I was ready to let him go. He could be part of my life in whatever capacity he wanted, as long as he didn't leave.

Warmth spread through my body when he looked up and acknowledged me with his eyes. He really was perfect.

He stood as I got closer to him, nervously looking back and forth, between the stack of books in front of him and me. He pushed his hands into his front pockets while he waited. It was the most attractive thing I had ever seen. I sighed to myself, wondering, what I could possibly be doing to have such an effect on him. I wanted to do it over and over.

Simply being near him made my heart pound wildly in my chest, and I was grateful, it was the only thing that reminded me I wasn't floating.

"Hey," he half whispered as he stepped around the table to take my book bag from me. Sitting it down on the table, he pulled out a chair for me to sit in.

"You made it," he teased.

He sat in the chair next to me and laid his hands on the table. I reached over and placed one of mine on top of his. I'm not sure why. I guess I felt like he needed to be centered. I wanted to be that comfort for him. He turned his hand over so he could hold mine.

"Has anyone told you how beautiful you look today?" he whispered.

I tried to maintain some sort of composure, but it was nearly impossible. I was unable to speak. The twisting of emotions, every time he was near, was painful.

"I had planned a speech about all the details involved in sponsoring, but the moment I looked up and saw you coming toward me, my mind went blank. You really are stunning, Jenna."

His words were like a kiss to my heart. I was hopeless for this boy. Whatever or whoever he needed me to be, I'd change it all for him.

"I can't remember being this nervous talking to a girl." He said with a small laugh.

I squeezed his hand softly, "I'm not some girl. I'm Jenna. Just talk."

"I'm starting to understand that. It seems to make this harder." he said as he picked up my hand and gently pressed his lips onto my palm.

Instant desire surged through my body. It mixed with the panic of understanding; this might be my last chance to tell him how I feel. I needed to explain that his presence in my life had changed me somehow in this short period of time. No one had ever made me feel as beautiful, or as wanted as he did, with just a simple touch.

"Cale," I whispered.

He slowly lifted his eyes to mine, I wanted to look away but couldn't. There was something there; a pleading, that I couldn't fully understand, but didn't need to. He had to continue; his choice was already made.

"Why don't we start from the beginning?" I said softly. My heart broke into tiny pieces, understanding that with one sentence, I had given up any hope of making him mine.

"Okay," he said as he carefully laid my hand back down.

As we talked about the possibility of Cale sponsoring me, I couldn't help but get lost in the traditional values it was rooted in. He explained how it came from the desire to give back to the community. The founding brothers of the house felt deeply that this program would help ensure the future of the towns they lived in, and improve the lives of generations for many different families.

He took me step by step through the process. They would first need to get permission from my mom. There would be training and then an interview process with the elders of the house. This included Cale's dad. The final decision would be made after that. If I was accepted, I would be eligible for financial help with items like computers, tuition reimbursement, and even living expenses.

"It's not like you would be expected to wear a t-shirt around that says 'I'm Cale's sponsored girl'," he said with a little sarcastic laugh.

I didn't think that sounded like such a bad idea.

"Well, what do you think?"

"Honestly, I'm not sure I can accept those things from you. I mean, tuition reimbursement and computers, those are high dollar items and I've never really been good with handouts."

"This is not a handout, it's more like a helping hand. And it all comes from the foundation, not directly from me. Besides, if you don't get it, someone else will, and I really want you to have it."

My head spun. It sounded like an amazing opportunity. But I didn't want him to look at me like a charity case. I knew exactly how I wanted him to look at me, but that idea was fading, smaller and smaller by the second. This might be the only way to keep Cale in my life.

"What are you thinking? Your silence is kind of making me crazy right now."

I looked up from my deep thoughts.

"Well, I think it sounds like it's very important to you." I paused, hoping I wouldn't regret this. "I would be honored to be Cale's sponsored girl."

He jumped up and lifted me out of my chair so he could hug me. I squeaked out a laugh. "Thank you, Jenna. Thank you for trusting me."

"You're welcome." I whispered in his ear as I realized that we were cheek to cheek. He pulled back from me just enough so he could see my face. For just a few seconds he stared right into my eyes. I was so captivated by the way he made me feel. I don't think I'd ever felt as connected to another human being as I did with him in this moment. He took a deep breath and slowly put a hand lightly on the side of my cheek.

"This really means a lot to me. I promise I will take very good care of you."

Although, startled by the intimacy of the gesture, I quickly settled into it. I may not be girlfriend material where Cale Davis was concerned, but I was going to take every opportunity I could to feel the way I was feeling right now. "I'm sure you will."

~~~

Cale pulled his car up to the curb in front of the Towers. I reached toward the door handle until I noticed he had put the car in park. I turned toward him, waiting for him to speak, but he didn't.

I sat back in my seat, looking out the front window. The burst of color that barely stretched above the tree tops was the only light the sun could manage at this hour, and that would soon be gone. A light breeze picked up, blowing the fallen leaves back and forth, but not really committed enough to move anything far.

"So you'll let me know when all of the sponsoring events start happening? I don't want to miss anything." I said trying to fill the silence. He spoke quickly, nearly cutting me off.

"I've barely been able to let you out of my sight since the moment I saw you. You can be sure I'll get you where you need to be." He had a smile on his face but there was a flash of something else, maybe frustration.

I sat quietly in my confusion, wondering if I should take that as a compliment or apologize for something. I reached for the door handle again, "Well, I should get going. I have a ton of homework and ..."

"Jenna," this time he cut me off in mid-sentence.

The tone of his voice charged the air inside the closed-in car with heavy emotion. I glanced at my hand, still hovering over the handle, and noticed the slight tremor in my fingers. I struggled to keep my thoughts contained as I turned toward him. He sat motionless, staring straight ahead with his hands on the steering wheel.

"I want to do something so badly," he continued, "something I shouldn't do."

My heart began to race, fear – mixed with excitement – took over. I didn't move, and couldn't have, even if I wanted to. I was so enthralled with the curve of his lips, his flawless skin, and the thick, corded muscles that traced down his neck and disappeared under his shirt.

His chest began to rise and fall with quick breaths and I found myself matching his pace.

"What is it that you want to do?" I asked.

He drummed his thumbs on the steering wheel before letting his head fall back onto the headrest. Pausing briefly, he ran his hands down his face and rolled his head toward me, his eyes wandering down my face until they stopped on my lips. My heart skipped a beat, demanding my body to react to the look in his eyes. I fought the urge to pull him to me.

My mouth suddenly dry, I parted my lips and my tongue slid out between them.

"Oh my God, don't do that," he whispered. "You're so tempting, I can't ..." He closed his eyes and tilted his head, contemplating something. He spoke almost under his breath. "I bet you would be delicious."

I stared at him, unsure how he wanted me to respond.

"Are you?" He paused, opened his eyes and shifted toward me. "Are you delicious, Jenna?"

He reached out and ran his thumb lightly over the wetness on my bottom lip, inhaling sharply like the contact stung. I shivered from his touch and closed my eyes, not so I couldn't see him, but so I could concentrate on the amazing feeling of his skin on mine.

"These lips," he whispered then paused, "No, Jenna, open your eyes."

I obeyed.

His hand slipped to the base of my neck, gently pulling me in close to him. "I want you to see what you are doing to me. I need you to understand the power you have."

Our breaths tangled between us and an urgency flooded into my body like I'd never known. Our closeness was painful, it teased me with desire that my heart demanded; but my soul knew would change who I was. I didn't care. I wanted him, even if it was just for tonight, or the next ten minutes, or for as long as we were in this car.

I reached up and grabbed two handfuls of his shirt, pulling him toward me, wanting him so badly to kiss me. I needed it, needed his hands on me, his skin touching mine.

He lightly moved his cheek down mine, never breaking contact. A touch, soft as silk, yet burning like fire at the same time. The sensation stole my breath, and every thought in my head that wasn't about him.

His lips moved to the sensitive spot behind my ear making my body pulse with need. He began to trace the very tip of his tongue lightly over my skin. I rolled my head to the side, giving him full access to whatever he wanted. He buried his face in my neck, breathing quickly, and the sound of it made every cell in my body tingle with uncontrollable desire.

"You smell so good." His voice was strained and louder than it had been. "I need to stop now, or I won't be able to stop at all."

"Don't stop," I pleaded as I moved even closer to him, pulling his shirt as close to me as I could. The fire in my body continued to build the longer he made me wait.

One quick movement and his hands were on the sides of my face. A small gasp slipped from my mouth, as he leaned in as close as he could without actually touching me.

He used his mouth to touch and nip at the skin around my lips without actually kissing them. The sensations created by his touching my ultra-sensitive skin, caused chaos in my head. I wanted to yell at him for teasing me and slap him for not touching me the way I needed; and push myself as close to him as possible, while demanding things from him that I'd never done with anyone. My body was in complete control and it was ready for more.

He quickly pulled his hands away and put them back on the steering wheel. I froze while my body continued to scream for him, but my head knew exactly what was happening. He was changing his mind.

"I can't do this Jenna. I'm sorry. I ... just need to think some things through – clear my head."

I sat there stunned, trying to calm my breathing, as I suddenly felt like I was hyperventilating. When his eyes turned back toward me, I wasted no time grabbing for my bag.

"Of course. I'm sorry, I shouldn't have ..." I reached for the door handle.

He grabbed my arm. "You have nothing to be sorry about. I'm the asshole. I just, I just don't know what to do with all these emotions. You are so beautiful and I just got carried away." His eyes were pleading with me to understand but I couldn't get out of that car fast enough. There was no way I was going to sit through the 'sorry, not the right time in my life to go slumming' conversation with him.

"It's no big deal. I'll see you ... sometime." I jumped from the car and tried to hold myself back from sprinting up the front steps. Tears streamed down my cheeks. I heard him yell my name.

Just keep going. And this time, I listened to myself.

>CHAPTER ELEVEN<

"He did what?" Katie said, dropping onto the couch next to me, her eyes bugging out of her head.

I covered my face with my hands, shaking my head back and forth. When I'd gotten back to our room, I started with tears but quickly changed over to intense embarrassment, followed by inappropriate laughing. Lifting the pillow from my lap, I smashed it against my face and wondered if self-induced smothering was a viable option out of this situation.

"I know," I said through the pillow, "just kill me now! If you are my friend you will make sure I never have to face him again."

We both giggled nervously. "I can't believe he is such an ass." She said.

I lowered the pillow and took a deep breath. "But he isn't. He was kind and respectful. I was the slut that was grabbing on to him and breathing like a maniac!" I hit myself in the face with the pillow, over and over.

"Please. Kill. Me. Now." My stomach tightened and my heart beat wildly while another wave of embarrassment flooded my body. I shuddered.

"Okay, it's really not that bad." She grabbed the pillow from my hands and threw it across the room. "We just need to figure out how you're going to handle seeing him next time."

"Oh, no! There's not going to be a next time. Call my mom and tell her I'm coming home!" I jumped from the couch and started pacing. I just couldn't sit still while my mind flooded with the memory of what had happened in that car.

"Very funny," she said.

"Not kidding."

Katie took a deep breath, crossed the room and put a hand on each of my shoulders.

"Listen to me. We have to decide what 'Jenna' you're going to be the next time you see him."

I looked at her expectantly, waiting for her to talk sense. She smiled. It made me nervous.

"What the hell are you talking about?"

She released me and walked across the room. "Well, you have a couple choices. You could be 'I have no idea what happened Jenna'. You'd just skip right over it and act like nothing happened after the library tonight. Like he just dropped you off, you said goodbye and left.

"Really?" I hoped she could tell by my sarcastic tone, exactly what I thought about that idea. She started pacing again.

"Okay, you could be the 'screw you Jenna'. Give him the cold shoulder until he comes crawling back, begging you to forgive him."

"He's Cale Davis, I don't think he crawls back to anyone."

"Right, well how about the 'I'm sorry I let it go that far Jenna'. Take all the blame. Tell him you know how hot you are and it isn't his fault that he couldn't keep his hands off you."

"Oh my God! You're killing me. Those are all terrible ideas!" I laughed as I grabbed my shower bag, some pajamas and a robe. She followed me around the room.

I continued, "If you remember, he had no problem keeping his hands off me. It was this girl, right here, that was ready to take him on, in the car, in front of the towers!" I closed my eyes to shake the vision of my humiliation from my head, but it stuck – like gum on the bottom of your shoe.

"I've got it! How about the, 'I'm so sorry I'm a sex-starved virgin, Jenna'. The next time you see him, just jump him and tell him he isn't getting away so easy this time!" I turned and swung my bag in her direction.

She laughed and jumped out of the way just in time.

"Stay away from me. You are not helping," I laughed.

She threw herself onto the couch laughing. "It'll be. fine. This stuff happens. He's probably just as embarrassed as you are."

"I doubt that," I whispered as I opened the door and headed toward the shower room.

The place was empty and the quiet was nice. I missed rush hour by thirty minutes but I was willing to sacrifice hot water for a little privacy. My toothpaste globbed out onto my toothbrush, I started brushing. Auto pilot kicked in, as I reached for my face wash. Catching a glimpse of myself in the mirror, my mind floated back to what happened in the car. The sound of his breathing, the touch of his skin on mine, his voice saying he couldn't; when my treacherous body was clearly telling him he could. I ran my fingers over the edge of my lip – remembering and trying to forget all at the same time.

I stepped into the shower and let the semi-warm water run over my head. Clearing all thoughts, I started to relax. Katie was right. This stuff happened all the time. Never to me, and I doubted ever to her, because who would turn her down, but it happened to other people. And that was the problem. It wasn't supposed to be happening to me. I wasn't the girl that was going to end up with someone like Cale. Both Cale and I knew that.

He needed, no, he deserved, someone like himself ... someone perfect. Not someone who was the opposite of perfect.

In no way would I fit into his world, I wouldn't even begin to know how. I had agreed to be sponsored and I needed to get it through my head that it ended there. He didn't want anything else from me anyway. That was pretty obvious tonight.

I dried myself off as my mind continued to work, putting walls back up, nice and strong and where they belonged. The next time I saw Cale, I would be nice and friendly, but I would keep it under control. No more kissing, no more touching, just friends. It was better that way. It would protect his reputation, and my heart.

The cool air hit my body and I shivered while quickly pulling on my yoga pants and tank top. My pink, fluffy robe helped ward off the cold and I tied it tightly. I wrapped my long hair in a towel and gathered all of my things. The hallway was even colder as I rushed toward my room, wishing I'd grabbed some socks.

"Oh my gosh, it's freezing," I said in a strained voice as I opened the door to my room. My heart dropped into my stomach and my words froze in my throat. Cale turned around and our eyes locked. For a split second I considered running. No good, he had already seen me.

Katie slowly started to make her way to the door. "I'm going to ... I mean, I have to go ..." When she realized neither of us were listening, she slid past me and shut the door behind her.

Cale's eyes slowly trailed down from my face to my robe and a small smirk stretched across his lips. Realizing what I looked like, I reached up and pulled the towel from my wet hair, allowing it to escape as I started to comb through it with my fingers.

"Hey, what's up?" I asked as I walked past him and grabbed my hair brush. What Jenna had I decided on? I couldn't even remember the options. What was it about this guy that reduced me to a hot mess without the ability to form a proper thought?

The *last* Jenna I wanted to be was weak and soft, or worse yet – stupid and mute. Those were the only two options I was able to come up with at the moment.

"I came to apologize for my behavior in the car." An awkward silence followed and I knew it was crunch time. I had to decide now. I prepared myself to pretend to act anything but embarrassed about what had happened. Whatever Jenna decided to come out, she had to act like she had things under control.

But when I looked at him again, I noticed something I hadn't before.

He stood with his hands low on his hips, his shoulders slightly hunched over and he shifted his weight from one foot to the other. He was just as embarrassed as I was, and not only that, but he was nervous.

Once again, I had a little bit of control over Cale Davis, and I liked it. He had said it in the car – he needed me to know the power I had. I cleared my throat and set my eyes on his face.

"Listen Cale, neither of us really knows where this is going or where we want it to go." That was a total lie. I knew exactly where I wanted it to end up and I had started it in that damn car.

"Let's just give each other a pass for what happened, okay?"

"A pass?" He looked at me, questioning my words.

"Yes, like it never happened. You act like you didn't just cross some invisible line that you have drawn and I will act like I was not completely willing to let you cross it."

He let out a small laugh and I smiled at him. He walked over to me and pulled me into a tight hug.

This was totally counter-productive to my whole idea of keeping my distance. I would worry about that later. I took a deep breath and let him hold me. I didn't want to admit what this boy was doing to me. Warmth started in my chest and it wasn't just because his arms were around me. I was starting to have feelings for him, real feelings.

"Okay, I'll take a pass," he whispered.

My heart dropped, even though I had offered it; there had been a little part of me that was hoping he had come here to finish what we had started. He dropped his arms and picked up a bag from the couch. "This might not be the right time, but I really want you to have this tonight. I hope you like it." He pushed the bag at me. "Come on. It's just a little something that you need."

I reached inside the bag and pulled out a new cell phone, still in the box. I couldn't contain my excitement. I had never had one before.

"Oh my gosh, Cale. This is amazing. I don't even know how to use this thing," I said as I ripped into the packaging and pulled it out. I flipped it around in my hand, trying to figure out how to turn it on.

"You are a smart girl and the directions are in the bag."

"Thank you. I feel like I shouldn't take this from you, but I'm going to anyway!" I laughed as I hugged the phone to my chest.

"Since you agreed to be sponsored, this is the first thing I felt like you needed. I have to be able to get a hold of you."

"You do?"

"Yes. There are things we're going to have to be in contact about. First things first, my dad is coming into town in a few weeks and he's going to want to meet you."

"What? Oh no. What if he hates me?"

"Are you kidding? He will love you."

I could feel a tornado of out of control emotions twisting inside me, as he rubbed his hands softly up and down my arms. The contrast of the two was overpowering rational thoughts.

"You are going to be fine. I've already told him about you. He's very excited to meet you."

"He is?"

"Yes. Now, do you have any dresses?"

The question took me off guard. I shook my head.

"We'll have to get you a nice dress before he gets here. Oh, and some heels, he likes heels."

I just continued to stare at him. I would have to get a nice dress? I guess my clothes were probably not nice enough to meet someone like Cale's dad. I didn't mind wearing dresses – I just never had a reason to wear one.

"I've got to get back to the house, we have a rules meeting with some of the younger brothers tonight. I will text you later." He tapped my nose with his finger and it made me smile.

"You look scared. It's just my dad, Jenna. I know it's weird but he thinks girls should look a certain way, conservative, I guess. I just want you to be as comfortable as possible and not have to worry about anything. So let me take care of the little things okay?"

"Okay." For some reason it came out as a whisper.

He headed toward the door, stopping just as he cracked it open. "You should call your mom and let her know about all of this. She is waiting to talk to you." Flashing a beautiful smile at me, he slipped out the door.

Seconds later the door flew open and Katie came running in. I couldn't move. I stood staring at her. She covered her mouth with one hand while pointing at the cell phone with the other. I could see the smile forming as she dropped her hand.

"Everyone wants that phone. I didn't even know you could buy them yet!" She squeaked before running over to me. She picked up my hand that was holding the phone. Her face looked like I had just won the lottery.

She shook her head as she snorted out a loud Katie laugh. "I don't know what Jenna you decided to pull out, but well played, my friend, well played." She patted me on the back as she fell onto the couch. "Come and tell me all about it."

"I need to call my mom first. I think I need to talk to her about everything that's going on. I stared at my new phone, flipping it over a couple times, before looking back at my roommate. "Can you help me turn this on?"

>CHAPTER TWELVE<

I walked into the hallway trying to figure out how to explain all of this. Since I was confused by most of it, I had no idea how to begin to explain it to my mom. My stomach knotted into a ball and I rubbed my temples, trying to ward off the pain this kind of stress always brought on.

Tension rolled through my body. I needed privacy, somewhere I could sort through everything that had happened. But where do you go for privacy in a tower full of girls? The stairwell was the only place to go.

I pushed through the door harder than I meant to. It swung open hard, slowly clicking shut behind me. Silence took over. My reflection stared back at me from the panes of glass that lined the stairwell, the outline of the city behind her.

I stared back, unflinching, unable to look away. Where was the girl that came to this school only a month ago? I looked at myself but nothing seemed familiar.

"Why me?" I wondered out loud, "Why would he want me?" I was nothing.

Without thought, I sprinted up the stairs. I wasn't sure what I was running from, but it was real and terrifying. I somehow knew I could never outrun it – even though I tried. Every time I looked at my reflection, it would be there.

My robe flowed out behind me as I ran, sometimes taking two steps at a time. I frantically looked over my shoulder, as I fought off the feeling that something was right behind me – leaning heavily onto my back – breathing down my neck.

Every cold metal step my bare feet pushed off, sent painful sensations surging through my legs. I gripped the railing, pulling myself upward with all of my upper body strength as I commanded myself to keep going, keep fighting, keep running. Run from your insecurities, run from the negative thoughts, run until exhaustion takes over.

I climbed until the burning in my lungs was too much to ignore. I stopped, letting the silent tears flow down my cheeks. My arms hung at my sides like heavy weights, my legs shook – Warning me they no longer could hold my weight. I collapsed onto the steps, resolved to the fact ... fear had won again.

The cold metal railings were perfect to press my sweaty forehead against. Rapid breaths echoed up and down the empty stairwell and my feet throbbed, trying to regain normal circulation after the unfamiliar surge of exercise. I swallowed against the burning in my throat.

Although the sky had already begun to darken, a storm threatened with a looming black cloud in the distance. I watched as it hung, lingering, just waiting for its chance to move over the city and unleash devastation.

The lights of the city began to pop up across the skyline like fireflies. I wondered how just a few sparkling lights could make the impending darkness seem less frightening. The storm would still happen, but the lights would make sure it wasn't all-consuming.

I thought of my mom and a tremor started at my core. Trying to calm the turmoil myself was useless. She had never hurt me personally, but when someone allows violence and pain to be part of your life, you learn early on that fault doesn't always lie with the person who is doing the actual hurting. You become cautious when other people have been so careless.

My mom wasn't an unreasonable person, but she was very independent. Unless there was a man involved, then she became disgustingly submissive. I shuddered, as I remembered the faces of the ones that didn't like little girls, or worse yet, the ones that like little girls too much. Staying safe was always a balancing act of when it was okay to be seen and when it wasn't.

I had no idea if I would have a battle on my hands or not. I prepared myself just in case.

Cale was important enough. I pulled out my new phone and dialed the numbers. I heard the first ring, my heart nearly pounded out of my chest, then the second ring ...

"Jenna! I've been waiting for you to call. What took you so long?"

"I know mom, I'm sorry, it's just, I've been really busy getting settled and ... wait, how did you know?"

"Did you get picked yet?"

"What?"

"For sponsorship, did you meet Cale's father yet? Cale, by the way, is extremely well-mannered, makes a very good impression."

"You talked to Cale? But ... when?"

"Yes I talked with him, he called yesterday. He gave me the number to your new cell phone. I bet you were so excited to get it. I'm so happy for you, honey." She sounded like she might actually be jumping up and down.

I was speechless.

"Wait. Stop. You're happy for me? You're fine with all of this?" I pulled the phone away from my ear and glanced at the numbers on the screen, making sure I'd called the right number.

"Well, I'll admit that at first I was a little freaked out by it. But after talking with Cale for a while, and then talking with William," she paused like I should know who that was.

"Who's William?"

I heard her groan on the other end. She always made that noise when she was frustrated with me.

"William is Cale's father. Really Jenna, you're going to have to pay more attention if you want to be sponsored by them."

Speechless again.

"Jenna?"

"So let me get this straight. You've talked with Cale?"

"Yes," she drug the word out dramatically.

"And you've talked with Cale's father?"

"Yes, and they both took time to explain what an amazing opportunity this would be for you. Did you know there are ways you can actually earn points so the foundation will pay your outstanding tuition? All you have to do is help with volunteer projects in the community. Also, they guarantee job placement within their company after graduation. They guarantee it, Jen!"

"No, I didn't know any of that. So, tell me again, when did you talk to them?"

"Yesterday, why?

"Well, I guess it's no big deal, but Cale didn't even ask me until today. Don't you think it's a little strange that they would talk to you before they asked me?"

She groaned again. I was instantly irritated. "Don't make this creepy. You are always so cautious. They called me first because they said they feel it's important to have the families involved. That's all it is."

"I'm always cautious because you never are." The words spilled out before I could stop them. I couldn't think of anything to say to soften them. I sat on the cold step, staring at my toes, wondering why none of this felt right to me; and my words hung in the silence between us. I could hear her breathing on the other end of the line. A tear spilled over and I held in a sob, I never liked hurting her.

"Listen sweetheart," her voice was soft. "I know that you've had a really hard time trusting people. I also know that I'm probably to blame for that. You were with me or working when you should've been learning how to form bonds with other kids. I brought a lot of people into our lives that I shouldn't have. But please, don't let my shortcomings as a mother be the reason that you turn down the biggest opportunity of your life. This is your chance to change the entire direction of your future."

My throat constricted, holding back the words that I wanted to speak, but couldn't. We'd never talked about any of this. How could she just throw all of it out there, like it was history, and I wasn't still dealing with the aftermath every single day? Years of pent-up frustration surged but I shut it down quickly. This day had already been too much to add in a discussion about my mom's parental choices.

"Okay mom," I finally whispered into the phone.

"I have to get back to the restaurant. I picked up an extra shift tonight. I love you, honey. Now that you have your fancy new cell phone, I expect you to call me and tell me everything about your life at college. Talk to you later."

The other end of the line went dead.

The phone suddenly seemed very heavy in my hand so I dropped it into my lap. I laid back onto the cement, welcoming the coolness. Staring into the never-ending maze of the staircase, the craziness of today bounced around inside my head, flashing images of the events. None of the memories stuck around long enough for me to process anything. I was okay with that.

Willing myself to stand, I started back to my room. I needed to talk this all out with Katie. Cale had told me that they'd need permission from my family. I just thought that would come after I had agreed, not before Cale had even asked.

I cracked open the door to my room and heard the muffled voices.

"Hey Marcus," I said and threw him a quick wave. The fire escape was really coming in handy for them.

"I think I'm going to go for a walk," I said as I fumbled around the room, hoping they couldn't tell I had been crying.

"Don't leave because of me. I just stopped by to say goodnight." Marcus said.

"No, its fine...I need the air." I shed my fuzzy robe for a hoodie and fake Ugg boots. My hair was still wet, so I pulled it up into a messy bun and headed out the door.

>CHAPTER THIRTEEN<

The night air was chilly and the darkness of the storm had moved over the city. A light mist of fall rain fell silently. I pushed my hands into the pockets of my hoodie while focusing on the sound of my boots crunching the fallen leaves.

The rain shimmered off of the oncoming headlights, encircling the beam of light with a blur of rainbow colors. A shiver ran down my spine as rain droplets rolled down my exposed neck. I pulled my hood over my damp hair but it was useless, the damage had been done.

I'm not sure if there were other people out or not, I kept my eyes locked on the sidewalk. I needed to disappear, to be invisible.

The same questions as before took root in my brain and spun endlessly over and over.

"Why me and why do I have such a bad feeling about this?" I whispered to myself.

Was this some sort of leftover childish thing against my mom? She thought it was a good idea so now I have to think it's a bad idea? Shit, I hoped I was past that.

"Please don't let my shortcomings as a mother be the reason that you turn down the biggest opportunity of your life." Her statement echoed over and over in my head, clashing and meshing with my own self-doubt.

Is that what I was doing? Allowing my screwed up childhood to ruin an opportunity? The word didn't sound right to me. Was I using Cale as an opportunity – is that why it didn't feel right? Or, was he somehow using me as one?

I walked and walked, trying to clear my head, paying no attention to my surroundings. Only noticing when the noise around me changed; I was far enough away from the dorms that sounds were now more city than campus.

The sidewalk led me onto a bridge. I stopped and turned toward the water, hoping to come up with the answers I desperately needed. Instead, the breathtaking beauty of it overtook me.

The river drew out like a long road ahead of me, rolling its waves and reaching desperately toward the moon that hung low at the end. It was a lonely sight. The sporadic raindrops of the mist fell onto the surface of the water, interrupting the connection between the water and moon, giving it a sparkling appearance. A thick intertwining of trees and brush ran along the banks making it impossible to get to the water. Untouchable and protected in the middle of the city, it struck me how out of place this was...I felt a connection. My eyes were drawn to a spot where the water seemed motionless while the moonlight gently covered it as if it was precious. That's where I longed to be, in the calm. All around it the water spun and twisted, jumping over rocks and disappearing into itself. But this spot was steady and strong; unchanged by the chaos around it. I stared it – letting its quiet strength invade my mind. I desired peace, but it was foreign to me – I had no idea how to achieve it. I closed my eyes and inhaled deeply, lifting my face to the sky. The rain ran over me as I prayed for a cleansing. I begged the water to wash away my insecurities, all of my cautiousness and fear.

My heart knew it wouldn't happen tonight or probably any time soon. Visions of the day replayed in my mind like snapshots. I reached for the railing to steady myself as my head spun. My stomach twisted and my chest was too heavy to take in air. I turned toward the road. Panic started to creep up as I frantically looked for help.

The sidewalk had narrowed once I was on the bridge – I hadn't noticed it before. The cars passed by only a few feet from me. They sped by through the developing puddles, spraying me with a torrent of water. I gasped for air, my lungs burning with need, as the cold water hit me. I pled with myself as the anxiety mounted. "No, please. Not this ... not now."

That's the bad thing about anxiety, it alters your ability to move past the walls you've built and the reasons you did. Anxiety hides all the goodness while parading all the shit of your life in front of you like that's your only choice for reality. You stay safe and warm within the Hell you've created – with all your personal demons as best friends. It's a fucking monster, one that stays around much longer than the boogeyman.

Spots dotted my eyesight, as I eased myself back against the railing, then lowering myself to the ground. I pulled my knees to my chest and held on tightly. There's a point where you have to give up hope that there's salvation from it, and accept what's about to happen.

My hands began to tingle and tunnel vision took over. My whole body shook as I gave up and let the panic ravage me.

Sounds were vague and my breaths came in labored pants. The pain of knowing that my life would never be worthwhile burned in my chest. Thoughts of self-loathing consumed me, as if someone was whispering them directly into my soul.

Each blink of my eyes lasted longer and longer. Soon, the heaviness would make it impossible to open them. I prayed I would pass out. I was no stranger to this, but this time – I wasn't sure I wanted to wake up. I relaxed and called to the nothingness to take my pain, take my doubts … take me.

The noise around me spun, a twisted vacuum of sound, fading in and out each time I opened and closed my eyes. My eye lids continued to get heavier and heavier.

"Jenna!"

I forced my eyes open but everything was lost in the rain. I let them close again.

"Jenna! What the hell are you doing out here?"

I felt … weightless … I was floating. This happened sometimes. I smiled as numbness took over, I liked this part.

I forced my eyes open one last time, "Ryan?" I whispered.

"Keep your damn eyes open, Jen. I mean it, don't close them again." He crossed the street with me in his arms, opened the car door and placed me inside.

Once out of the rain, the cold took over. A wave of tremors attacked my body as I held onto myself tightly. My toes and fingertips ached as streams of water ran down my face.

I struggled with the fogginess in my mind. It often took some time to think clearly again. There was nothing I could do about it. I barely registered the driver's side door opening. He turned the heater on high. "You're freezing." His voice was a mixture of frustration and concern.

He maneuvered his car off the road and into a roadside park near the river. In a frenzy, he reached behind my seat and pulled out a gym bag.

"You need to get out of those wet clothes. My workout stuff will be huge on you, but it's better than freezing to death."

I laid my head back against the headrest, fighting to make my teeth stop chattering, and watched him. He frantically dug around his bag and pulled out a sweatshirt and a small towel.

His blue eyes met mine. His voice barely a whisper, "Jenna, please."

Even the slightest movement was painful – my mind too clouded to fight against the pain. All I could do was stare into his eyes.

His large hand cupped my chin, hesitantly dabbing the rain from my face. I closed my eyes, fighting the tears that threatened to spill out. He paused for a second, but then continued, moving the towel from my cheek, gently down my neck.

I almost opened my eyes, but shame stopped me. I couldn't look at him. Shame was an emotion that tore you down. It ripped to shreds the dreams of who you wanted to be, and made you believe other people saw you as disposable. Ryan had seen almost every fault I had, and never asked questions. He never needed explanations. But this was the first time I couldn't hide the shame of who I was. He had seen it, all of it. After this, I would be disposable to him. I wasn't ready to see that.

I felt a light tug on the zipper of my hoodie. He slipped the wet fabric down and slowly wiped my shoulders dry.

"Jenna, you need to take this off and your tank top too".

I nodded my head and opened my eyes.

He was just as wet as I was. Droplets fell from his hair onto his flushed cheeks. He reached out toward me, intending to stop rain water from falling onto the areas he has already dried, but I gently stopped him. I wrapped my hand around his wrist and took the towel from him.

There was a split second I thought he was going to resist me. But his body relaxed as his eyes searched back and forth between mine.

I ran my hand up the back of his neck, and through his wet hair, leaving my hand intertwined in there. I laid the towel against his temple, looking one more time into his eyes for permission. Slowly, I moved the towel along his hairline, following it all the way to the back of his neck.

A droplet of water hung off of his lip. I moved the towel over his mouth, lightly wiping the soft skin dry. I lowered the towel, looking away from him.

"Thank you," he mumbled and handed me his sweatshirt. He turned away in his seat while I slipped off my hoodie and tank and put on his huge sweatshirt.

"There's a pair of sweatpants in there too."

"Okay," I whispered. I drew my feet up onto the seat and all of the extra clothing draped around me. He let out a strained laugh. "You look even smaller in my clothes."

I forced a smile and nodded my head. A strange buzzing noise went off inside of the car. Ryan made a face as he reached inside his pocket. "That wasn't me. I thought you said you didn't have a cell?" he asked.

"I just got it tonight." I dug through the pile of wet clothes that were on the car floor and found my new phone. A tinge of guilt hit when I realized how poorly I was already taking care of it. The screen lit up with Cale's name.

"Press on his name." Ryan said. I followed his direction and read the text.

"What are you doing?"

I shoved the phone under my leg. I didn't know how to reply to him and right now I didn't want to. I still had a lot of thinking to do. Ryan gave me a sly smile and cleared his throat.

"Are you going to tell me how you got all the way out here and why you were trying to freeze yourself to death?"

I didn't know how to sort it out for myself; I certainly couldn't do it for someone else. It was none of his business why I was out there anyway. Defensively I snapped, "I could ask you the same question. What are you doing out here, stalking me?"

I instantly knew that was the wrong attitude to take but I'd already thrown it out there.

"No, I work out in a gym in the city and I was heading there, until I saw a pretty little, suicidal girl sitting on a bridge."

Well, shit … he had a valid reason.

"Do you have any idea how close those cars were coming to you? If you had passed out, you may have fallen into traffic and then …" A buzz came from under my leg. I reached for it and pushed on Cale's name again.

"Where are you at?"

I tucked it back under my leg and turned toward Ryan.

"Where did you get the phone?" he asked in a calmer voice.

I shifted uncomfortably in my seat. For some reason I didn't want to tell him.

"Did you steal it?"

"What? No!"

"Okay, just checking. You're a little out of your element here. I thought maybe there was some sort of 'Shady Jenna' hiding inside there that likes to hang out in the bad parts of town and steal cell phones." He flashed me a smile.

He had no idea how many versions of "Jenna" had been thrown around tonight.

"Cale gave it to me," I said.

"I'm guessing the sponsoring thing went well then?"

"Yep." I said, drawing out the word in a sarcastic tone. I sounded like my mother.

"What does that mean?"

I jumped as another buzzing went off under my leg.

"I am worried; please tell me where you are"

Emotions started to swirl like a hurricane inside me. I knew I was at risk of having another full-on anxiety attack if I didn't work this out. I began to shake again and Ryan reached for the heater. I gently laid my hand on his. My voice was low, "I'm not shaking because I'm cold."

"Okay ..." It wasn't a statement; it was a question needing more information. We dropped our hands but I kept hold of his. I was going to need something to ground me through all of this.

"My dad left as soon as he found out that my mom was pregnant."

He didn't speak, but gripped my hand tighter, encouraging me.

"It was just me and my mom. She was lonely." My heart started racing as I realized what I was about to share with him.

"She had a lot of guys in and out of our apartment. Some stuck around for a while, some for one night." I took a deep breath and continued. "Every time one of them would leave, she would talk about how he wasn't her Prince. Then we would watch love stories on TV, and read the entire princess book series over and over again ... until another guy showed up. Every time I would meet one she would say, '*I think this is the one, Jenna. I think this is the opportunity we've been waiting for*'."

A look crossed his face as he realized where I was going with all of this. "Jenna, I..."

"Wait, please hear me out. As I grew up, while more men came in and out, I found out the hard way that desperate people have a way of letting evil in. And that's what she did. She let evil men into our lives Ryan, all in hopes that he might be the one, an opportunity out of her shitty life."

I swallowed the bile that rose in my throat and squeezed his hand tighter.

"There were a lot of men out there that wanted my mom, but not me." He turned in his seat so he was facing me.

"Let's just say I had a lot of accidents as a kid, lots of black eyes and bruised ribs." I glanced up at him but his eyes were focused on our hands; he shook his head and he raked his teeth over his bottom lip.

"The reason I freaked out about that fight was because in my life – when I was that close to violence – I was the one getting hit."

He reached out and grabbed me around the shoulders, crushing his chest against me.

"I'm so sorry you had to go through all of that," he whispered into my hair.

I gasped, "Can't really breathe," I choked out.

He released me quickly, "Oops, sorry." We both laughed awkwardly and it felt okay, like telling him my life's secrets was the right thing to do. I leaned back into my seat, a little more at ease.

"Honestly, I was kind of shocked that I reacted that way. I think when I got here, I wanted everything to be so different. I clouded myself in a false sense of safety. I need to remember that I'm not really safe anywhere."

Ryan reached over and squeezed my knee. "You're safe with me, Jenna. I can promise you that."

My phone buzzed again.

"Katie said you went out for a walk 2 hours ago and she hasn't heard from you. TEXT ME BACK AND LET ME KNOW YOU ARE OKAY! OR CALL, PLEASE!"

Holding the phone tightly in my hands, I stared at the screen. "Tonight my mom called him my 'opportunity'. What if I'm letting something into my life out of desperation and I can't see it for what it is?"

He reached out and covered my hands with his, blocking my view of the screen. "Whoa, wait right there. First of all, you are not your mother. I've never met her, but it sounds to me like she was very confused on what the first rule of parenting is. Even I know you protect your children at all cost."

"It's not like that ..."

"Don't defend her to me Jen, not right now. Not after what you just told me. Maybe somewhere down the road, I can listen to you tell me that she was a good mom, but not now."

I nodded at him.

"And secondly, Cale is not those guys. He's good and has a big heart. He obviously has feelings for you because he hasn't been able to stop talking about you since you met."

The phone buzzed again.

"*I am going to give you fifteen minutes to text or call me or Katie before I contact the campus police*"

I held the phone at eye level for him to read it. "You don't think that is a little creepy?"

He gently pushed my hand down, looking me in the eyes. "No, I think that is a guy, who is used to being in control of every part of his life. Now he's met you, and you're making him crazy."

"How?" I was completely confused.

Ryan rolled his eyes and shook his head back and forth. "You are so bad at this." He held both hands out in front of him, making sure I knew what he was about to say was important. "Any other girl on campus would've been so thrilled that Cale Davis was texting her, they would've replied back … immediately." He dropped his hands in defeat, "And now you've made me sound like a chick."

I thought about this for a few seconds. "Should I text him back?"

He looked at me with a funny face. "Yeah," he said with a small laugh.

"What should I say?"

"The truth. Tell him you got lost. It's not a lie and he'll believe it coming from you."

I scowled at him, he didn't care.

"Tell him I found you walking downtown and picked you up and that you are almost back to your room now."

Ryan started up his car and headed toward campus. I responded to Cale's texts, typing exactly what Ryan told me to.

We pulled up in front of the towers. I gave him a quick hug, thanked him and jumped out of the car. I could hear him laughing as he watched me struggle to get up the steps in his clothes.

I opened the door to my room and Katie jumped off the couch. "Where have you been? Cale almost had the FBI looking for you!"

"I went for a walk and got lost."

Katie folded her arms across her chest, shifted her weight to one side. "Really ... and did your clothes get lost too?"

I put my hands up in surrender and then had to grab the waist of the sweatpants quickly before they fell to the ground.

"They're Ryan's clothes." Katie just nodded her head like she already knew that.

"What? I really did get lost."

We both jumped, surprised by the frantic knocking at the door. Cale's voice boomed from the other side. "Katie! Is she back?"

Katie's face went from surprise to panic. She reached into my drawer and threw some of my clothes at me, whispering, "Change."

I scrambled to change as she yelled, "Yes she's here, just a second I, um … I'm just getting changed."

I shoved Ryan's clothes under the couch, we gave each other a reassuring nod and she turned the door knob.

I held my breath as the door opened. I had no idea what to expect. I knew he would be upset by the tone of his texts, but just how upset, I didn't know.

His eyes met mine. My heart jumpstarted. It felt like it would beat right out of my chest. His cheeks were flushed and his hair was a sexy kind of messy. He had been running his hands through it, worried about me. I walked over to him in silence and wrapped my arms around his waist. He let out a long breath and leaned into me. He pressed me against him with one arm while holding my head against his chest with the other, leaned into me and whispered into my hair, "Are you okay?"

I had never felt so completely cared for than I did in this moment. I nodded. I wanted to talk to him, but I couldn't. A nod was all I was good for right now.

He kissed the top of my head, again whispering, "Okay." He released me and my hands fell to my sides as I watched him walk away. Shame crept back in.

>CHAPTER FOURTEEN <

My head pounded. I'd spent the last two weeks learning what it really meant to be sponsored. Things had been so crazy since I accepted the sponsorship nomination from Cale. There'd been classes for myself and all the other prospective sponsored girls. It may have been easier if I could've bonded with the others, but because there were only four slots available and twelve girls vying for them, interaction was not recommended or encouraged. It was a competition, and they made sure to remind us of that every chance they got, making it a very lonely process.

Nolan Mcguire taught the classes and they were miserable. There was table etiquette, proper English, conversation etiquette, written letter etiquette and a whole bunch of other *etiquettes* I had never heard of before. He made it very clear that being sponsored by one of the brothers made us a representative of the house by proxy. It was his job, as the Marshall of the house, to make sure we represented it well.

The worst part was, it became even more obvious, being me was not going to be good enough. I needed to change everything. The last thing I wanted to do was make Cale look bad, but this shit was hard.

With all the sponsoring classes, finding time to spend with Katie was nearly impossible. Cale insisted that we have dinner together every night so we could review the things I'd learned that day. Then there was studying at night with Ryan who, except for today, had been acting weird since our night on the bridge. And dealing with my mom, who thought she needed nightly updates on my sponsoring status – my life had been turned upside down.

"I'm done! I can't do this anymore," I whined as I pushed my "Cale gifted" laptop to the side and rolled over, hiding my face in the back of the couch. It was Saturday and Ryan and I had been studying most of the day. "I hate this stupid class anyway."

Ryan laid flat on his back in front of the couch. He'd been down there for the last few hours, rolling around on the ground as we tried to study. He said it helped him think better.

He let out a small sarcastic laugh.

"What are you laughing about?"

"We have been studying for 6 hours and I don't feel like I know any more than when we started." He giggled a very unmanly giggle.

"You giggle like a girl; and why does that make you laugh? This is serious stuff Ryan. Do you want to fail?"

His laughter started to build and he rolled toward the couch.

"If you would pay attention and stop acting like an ass we could get back to work."

I wanted to be serious, but watching him laugh was contagious. A smile started to spread across my face and he spotted it right away, pointing at me and laughing even harder.

"No, stop it!" I scolded. "This is not funny."

Before I knew it, I was laughing along with him. It wasn't long before it morphed into a crazy, out of control, 'I have finally lost it,' laugh. I tried to calm myself down. I took some deep breaths and even got off the couch to pace, shaking my hands – thinking that in some way it would help stop the laughing – but I couldn't keep it together.

I continued laughing – having not slept in days I was ready to forget about all of it. This mess that had become my life was ridiculous. I fell back onto the couch in another failed attempt to regain some control. But every time I did, Ryan would start all over again.

"Stop," I snorted, just before another wave of hysterics rolled through me. I reached over the side of the couch, grabbed a handful of his shirt – twisting it, and pulling him closer to me. "Please. I. can't. Breathe." I begged. He pulled me to the floor next to him – I landed with a thud. I was stunned silent but it made him laugh even harder.

"That hurt, you jerk." I made a sad attempt to hit him on the chest; he grabbed my arm and held it tight, so I couldn't try again. We lay on the floor, trying to catch our breath as the memory of what was so funny faded.

His hold on my arm lessened. I rolled up next to him, my body fit perfectly to his. He had become important to me in the last few months. We spent as much time as we could together. He was: my study partner, my stress reliever, my oasis – my best friend. He stared at the ceiling, looking relaxed and rubbing my arm lightly; leaving goose bumps wherever he touched.

"How do you do that?" I asked.

"What?"

"Make all the craziness melt away."

He lifted my hand to his mouth and kissed it quickly. "There isn't anything," he laughed, as he swept his hand in the air over me, "that can make all this craziness go away." I hit him on the chest – again.

"Woman, I swear, you are too much to handle sometimes." His big smile reached all the way to his blue eyes.

I sighed. "I'm trying to be serious with you right now."

"Oh no." He covered his eyes with the palms of his hands. "We're about to have another girl talk aren't we?"

"Yep."

He rolled over onto his side and propped his head on his hand. "Okay, tell me; what do you mean?"

"Just … everything with the sponsoring classes. I had no idea what I was in for. Nolan is telling me I've got to change everything about myself."

He grunted and scrunched his face. "What do you mean? You're perfect."

"No really, he says I talk wrong, I walk wrong, I need to work on my manners, and a whole bunch of other shit. I wish I could just quit."

The room was silent. His expression seemed to harden, the smile was gone.

He sat up and I groaned at him, because that meant I had to move too. "You can't quit."

"Why? What do you mean I can't?"

"Don't even try to. I mean it. You cannot quit." His voice had a sharp edge to it. It surprised me, and pissed me off.

I glared at him, "What's your problem? I didn't say I was going to quit. I just said sometimes I would like to."

"This is big stuff, important stuff. You're acting like it's no big deal Jen. If you quit, you'll make Cale look like an idiot. And you'll upset a lot of important people."

I stood up, continuing my glare. "Important to whom? I'm not going to quit, I already told you that. I was just trying to share with you how stressful this is. And I don't really care who I piss off. There are a thousand other girls at this school. Can't he pick one of them?"

He reached up to grab my hand but I pulled it away. He was instantly on his feet. "Hey, I'm sorry, okay? But you really need to think before you speak sometimes." he said softly.

"No, Ryan, it's not okay. I thought you were a real friend and now there are things I need to change for you too? I didn't realize I needed to censor what I told you. I guess I'll just add it to my list." Shrugging my shoulders as I spoke, "I don't have to do anything I don't want to do. I don't care what you, my mom or Cale says. If I want to quit, I am going to quit."

He tilted his head and shrugged back at me, "Okay, quit."

I was stunned. What the hell kind of game was he playing? "What? You just said I couldn't quit. Now you're saying the opposite." I grabbed at each side of my hair. "Ugh! And guys are always talking about how confusing girls are." I started pacing back and forth.

"Girls *are* confusing Jen, especially you." He put his hands up between us in a surrendering way when I whipped my head in his direction. "Now hold on and hear me out."

I pushed my finger up against his chest. "Screw you, Ryan. I'm so sick of all of this. I'm tired of everyone telling me what I can and can't do. Everyone thinks they know what's best for me. Where have you been my whole life when no one has given two shits if I was okay? No one came to my rescue when I lay in my bed at eight years old, crying myself to sleep. Or when I was fourteen, in the emergency room, alone with a broken arm because my mom thought it would look less suspicious if she stayed at home with *him* instead of going with me. How about after my graduation ceremony, when everyone else was going to their own party and I was going to work? No one ever rescued me then – not ever. Why do you think I need it now? I've done just fine without any of you up until now, and I'll be just fine without any of you from here on out." I turned to grab the door handle.

His hand was over mine before I could get it open. He leaned his chest against my back, pushing me up against the door.

"I won't let you run this time." I fought against his body weight pressing against me.

"Get off me." I knew there was no way to fight him, but that wasn't going to stop me. I arched my back and pushed away from the door. He snaked his other arm around my waist as he spoke into my ear. "Hold on, let me talk to you." His warm breath spread across my skin.

"Get off me." I growled, fighting against his grip.

"You're okay." He whispered. I grabbed at his hand, trying to pry it away from me. I twisted and pushed against his hold. He continued to whisper softly in my ear. "I'm here, I'm not going to let go."

Panic took over and I pounded on the door, yelling against the tightness in my throat, tears streaming down my face.

"No one came before ... no one rescued me then." Didn't he know I needed to get away from here? I needed to be invisible. I thought he knew these things, I thought he understood. Finally I couldn't physically do it anymore. No one was coming to help me now either ... no one ever came. Defeated, I dropped my head back against his chest, the sobs overpowering me.

He kept his hold on me but dropped his face to the bend of my neck. I cried out every tear I had ever held in. Tears for the little girl I'd never been allowed to be – for the all the times I had been lonely and afraid. I cried for all the times I should've told someone, anyone, but didn't because of fear. I cried for my mom, who never felt good enough for anyone either, and for the life I didn't want to live – but seemed destined to have. The tears had stopped, but my body continued to shake from the after effects. I took several deep breaths to steady myself.

"I would have," he whispered.

I drew in a ragged breath. "You would have what?"

"I would've come for you – I would've rescued you." He spoke in a breathy, broken voice. My heart swelled with emotion. I laid my forehead on the door and he held me up. The fight was gone. I believed him; he had rescued me in so many ways already.

When I felt I could finally stand on my own, he loosened his grip. I took hold of the hand around my waist, and moved it away from my body. He placed it on the door next to my head and lifted his weight just enough that I could turn and face him. His head hung down – I raised his face so I could see his eyes. My heart broke into a thousand pieces to see the trails of tears. Tears for a Jenna he'd never known. I traced a finger down his cheek as I leaned back against the door. I couldn't stand the fact that I had put that look on his face. The only thing I was good at was ruining everything.

His lips parted slightly, but then closed again. "What is it?" I whispered. He hesitated, but then reached out, wrapped his arms around my waist and leaned into me.

My body reacted to him with instant desire. He leaned in close enough that our lips could almost touch. His look was desperate and needy. I could feel his heart beating against my chest. I ran my fingernails softly up his back, making him pull me even closer.

"I'm going to kiss you now." His voice was low and raspy. "I know there are a million reasons why I shouldn't, but I don't care. I'm going to kiss you like you're mine, like you belong to me. Are you ready, Jenna?"

His eyes stayed on mine until the very last second. I closed my eyes when the delicate touch of his lips joined with mine. Every wall inside of me shattered for him. His lips moved slowly at first and then with more need. I ran my fingers through his hair, trying to get him even closer. His tongue teased my lips and I instantly opened up for him. He groaned as he grabbed both sides of my face and kissed me even more deeply, claiming every bit of me. Ryan was the healing that I had desperately searched for my entire life. He was my acceptance, my shelter from the fear. Everything else was lost to me but him. It was suddenly so clear; he was all I wanted, all I needed. It had always been him.

His kisses began to lighten so I tightened my grip, afraid to let go. His weight lessened against me, and my heart began to panic. He stepped back, putting some distance between us. I was breathless and broken without his touch.

"If you were mine, that's how you'd feel all the time – safe, wanted, loved." He reached out and ran his fingers down my cheek, "… perfect the way you are."

He backed away from me, "But we can't do this anymore, I mean … I can't do it."

He ran his hand over his mouth and I felt a tear escape. He was wiping away the feeling of my lips on his. It was too much for him, I could tell. This had been a mistake for him.

He turned away from me and crouched down to grab his bag. He stayed there, with his head hung down. As he stood, I moved away from the door and my fingers touched his back. He stiffened at my already unwelcomed touch.

"Wait." I pleaded. "Can we talk about this? I need you … I need us."

His shoulders rose and fell slowly and then he turned toward me. "No. There can't be an 'us' Jen."

I took a small step back, my heart trembled in my chest, my head racing back to just minutes ago.

"But, why?"

"Because, you're already his." His eyes fell to the ground as he stepped around me and toward the door.

"No, no I'm not." I grabbed his arm as he passed. He looked down at me. "I'm not." I reassured him.

He gently moved a strand of hair from my face. "Yes you are. From the moment you said yes to sponsoring, you became his." He leaned down and placed a kiss on my forehead. It felt final and my world tilted.

"No, I won't let you leave." I ran around him and stood in front of the door. "Not after ..."I whispered as my fingertips touched my lips.

He watched me, his eyes sad. "You have to let go of me."

I stood my ground, shaking my head.

"Jenna, stop it. Don't you think this is hard enough for me?" He spread his arms out wide. "I can't give you what he can right now."

"What are you talking about? I don't care about all that. I don't care about him like that."

"The fuck you don't! Now, I know you're lying." He shook his head and spoke through gritted teeth. "I see the way you look at him, everyone sees it."

"What are you talking about?"

He placed his hands on his hips and looked down. "Would you leave him, Jen? Would you walk away from Cale Davis to be with me? We'd have to leave school; you would have to give up your scholarships. I'd have to leave The Brotherhood. That means no money. No trust fund – just me and you."

I let his words hang in the air while dread rose inside of me. I ran my hands over my eyes. He would have to leave The Brotherhood. The only thing he ever wanted to do. The thing he and his brother had talked about doing together since they were boys. Traditions he had been raised to be part of – that he needed to be part of.

The money meant nothing to me. I'd lived my entire life with nothing. But Ryan – his life had been different than mine. My mind locked into a heated battle with my heart and soul. Yes, without a doubt, I would leave everything for him. But what I wouldn't do is take everything from him.

"I'm ready; just say the words right now and I will leave everything. I've thought this through since the moment I met you. I didn't plan on doing this tonight, but now I have to know because that kiss killed me, Jen. You just stole my fucking heart, so tell the truth. I think you are his," he reached his hand out to me, "prove me wrong. Tell me one more time that you belong to me and I'll take you away from all of this tonight."

My mouth fell open and I stared at his hand and then back at him. He was breathing like he had just run a marathon and his eyes snapped with some emotion I had never seen from him before. I tried to speak but the words stuck in my throat. I knew what this looked like to him, but it had to be this way. He needed to believe me.

He began to shake his head before dropping his hand slowly. "I'll never be Cale. I'll never be good enough." He stepped around me, but stopped and took something out of his back pocket. He walked over and laid it down on my desk. Staring at it, he tapped his finger on the envelope several times, before he spoke. "Cale asked me to give this to you. I would have *never* thought this of you before tonight, but now – I think this will ease your guilt of what just happened between us."

He paused at the door, and I thought he was going to turn around, but he pulled the door open and said "Good bye, Jenna." as he walked out.

My body began to shake as his words echoed in my head. My future started to become clear. And nowhere in that future was Ryan Kitson.

My emotions were in protection mode – I was numb. I felt nothing at all – so when I picked up the envelope and read the words printed on the paper –

nothing changed inside of me. No emotion at all. I watched as if this was all happening to someone else. As the paper fell from my trembling fingers onto the floor, I read the bright red letters stamped on it one more time … Tuition: PAID IN FULL.

>CHAPTER FIFTEEN<

The heavy beat of the Dubstep music could be heard from down the block. Katie twirled around in front of me, dancing on the sidewalk.

"This is going to be so much fun. I can't wait to get inside and dance." She threw her arms in the air and twirled. I shook my head at her, like she was being silly, but truthfully I was just as excited. I had never been in a club. She was right; it was going to be a blast. I wasn't so sure about dancing in the high heeled, brown, suede boots she demanded I wear though. I pulled at the bottom hem of the form fitting, nude-colored mini dress she said the boots matched perfectly with. Katie bought this dress for me on one of our many outings to find appropriate dresses to meet Cale's dad. Although we had both agreed that this was definitely NOT appropriate for that, it was exactly what I wanted to wear for a night like this. My long hair was in a loose braid and lay over one shoulder.

"Stop fussing, Jen, you look frickin' amazing!"

I'd spent a couple hours feeling sorry for myself after Ryan had left. The numbness helped; as dysfunctional of a coping skill as it was, there were times it came in handy. The thought of not having him in my life was excruciating, but the idea of him leaving everything behind for me was even more painful. So I shut it all down.

When Katie had returned, I filled her in on most of what had happened. We sat on the couch and ate chocolate. I cried, she talked, "Boys are stupid, well except Marcus. You don't owe those two anything and if Cale is too stupid to see what he is missing out on and Ryan too big of an idiot to fight for you, they don't deserve you. We're going out!"

We stood in front of Midnight, the hottest club in town according to Katie. She dug around in her purse to find her phone. Cale had sent me a text earlier asking what I was doing tonight. I sent him a quick text back,

"I need some time and space, please give it to me. I am fine, I will be with Katie."

As soon as I'd hit send, I turned it off and threw it in my drawer. I wanted to be me tonight, with no one wondering where I was or what I was doing. I didn't want the watching eyes to make sure I was representing someone well or behaving appropriately. I had one goal tonight – have fun.

It only took Marcus a few minutes to appear at the door. A quick word to the door man and we were ushered into the club.

Our first few steps were in total darkness. I grabbed for Katie and she took my hand. Suddenly the music stopped, everything was quiet … then, all at the same time, the beat dropped and people went crazy. Lights from all over the club shot straight onto the dance floor, lighting up wall to wall people. The whole building shook as the lights began their elaborate show. People jumped to the beat and threw their hands around, as lasers and spinning lights of color quickly touched every area in the club, but for only seconds at a time. I moved my head to the beat as I danced behind Katie and Marcus on our way to the dance floor.

We stopped and I continued to dance in place. There were so many people, I really couldn't see farther than Katie in front of me. Marcus handed me a shot glass with something red in it. I tried to ask him what it was, but he just smiled and motioned for me to drink. I put the drink to my lips and tilted my head back. The strong taste of alcohol hit first, making me cringe, but it was quickly followed by a fruity aftertaste. He and Katie both stared at me, waiting to see how I reacted. I handed the glass back, smiled and mouthed, "More please." They both cheered and

Marcus turned back and motioned toward the bartender.

We took two more shots before starting back toward the dance floor. My entire body was warm. I could feel the alcohol working through my system, helped along by the spinning lights.

Marcus easily found us a spot on the crowded floor. It looked like people parted to let him through as he walked. I must've been drunk already. I really didn't care how we got out there, only that we were here.

At first, the people surrounding me made me nervous. My eyes darted around me, trying to see who was next to us. Every time someone would bump me, I would turn and look, trying to move out of their way.

"You have to relax or this will be miserable for you," Katie yelled into my ear. I stopped and looked around slowly. The music continued its beat as the sea of people melted together. People seamlessly moved from one to another, their bodies moving to the music without caring about anything else. It was then I realized that I was just another person. No extra attention was being given to me, no one needing me to be anything other than what I was.

So I let go … really let go for the first time in my life.

I closed my eyes and swayed my hips, raising my hands in the air and letting the music dictate my moves. It began with small bumps, then finger tips, then hands on my body. I danced with whoever was around me … girls, boys, singles, groups, I didn't care. The music had taken over my body and the alcohol my mind. I had no inhibitions – I was free.

I faintly heard my name being called but didn't open my eyes until I felt a tug on my dress. Katie pointed toward the bar, "Want to get a drink?"

I nodded my head and grabbed her hand as she led me to the edge of dance floor. "This is the most fun I've ever had."

She smiled at me over her shoulder, "You're an amazing dancer. Everyone was trying to dance with you." She shot me a huge smile. I was suddenly embarrassed. It must have flashed on my face because she laughed and said, "Oh stop it, you looked beautiful." The smile returned to my face.

Marcus led us in front of the booths that lined the dance floor on our way to the bar. He stopped suddenly and leaned down toward someone that was sitting in a booth. Katie turned back toward me and hugged me tight. We stood there swaying to the music as we watched everyone dancing. I heard Marcus's voice above the music, "Don't be a dickhead." I looked over my shoulder as Katie grabbed my hand and pulled me along.

Ryan was in the booth with a bunch of people I didn't know. He glared at his brother as we walked by. I stopped, but when his eyes met mine – I knew I wanted to keep going. Katie tugged on my hand and I followed. Before we could get past, I heard him. "Jenna. Jenna." I stopped. Katie gave me a pleading look and shook her head no. I turned toward him.

He had one hand wrapped around a beer bottle on the table, the other was draped over the back of the booth. He picked up his beer bottle and used it to point at me. "You look beautiful."

By the tone of his voice, it wasn't a compliment. I just stared at him. He took a drink from his bottle then pointed it toward the dance floor. "Sure seemed like you enjoyed the way everyone was touching you out there." He flashed a cocky smile. "Did you? Do you like having a bunch of strangers fondling you like that?" The other guys at his table started laughing at his comment. But he was not laughing, his eyes locked onto mine. This wasn't the Ryan I knew. His eyes flashed with some sort of emotion that made me uncomfortable. He was drunk. I had seen that look in men's eyes my whole life, but there was more to it than that.

"Shut the fuck up, Ryan," Marcus yelled from behind me. Ryan didn't acknowledge him at all, keeping his eyes on me. Katie pulled on my hand, "Let's go." I stood my ground.

"Everyone is dancing like that." I said.

He just nodded his head slowly at me while he took another drink from his bottle, his eyes never leaving mine.

From my side vision, I saw her walking up, but didn't realize who it was until she slid in under Ryan's arm. She turned slightly toward me, set her drink on the table, and then looked at me from head to toe with a disgusted look. She turned back to him and whispered something in his ear—he smiled. "Dana, aren't you going to say hello to my brother and his friends." My gut twisted.

"I don't think so." She leaned into him and kissed the side of his mouth. He turned toward her, giving her his full attention. She attacked his mouth and he reciprocated. I stood there, unable to turn away. I could feel the anger burning inside of me. My heart felt like it was crumbling. Once they were done, he reached out and smoothed a piece of her hair out of her face, just as he had done only hours earlier...to me. She turned to me as he hung his arm over her shoulder and pulled her closer, burying his nose in her long brown hair. She smirked at me. "I'm sorry Jenna, it's just ... girls like me don't associate with girls like you."

Katie pulled on my arm, "Let's go." I shrugged her hand off.

"Yes, you really should move on, Jenna." He motioned in the direction of Katie. "I clearly have," he said as he tightened his hold on Dana. I heard Katie gasp behind me. I ignored him, focusing on Dana.

"And exactly what kind of girl do you think I am?"

Obviously irritated, she turned toward me and crossed her arms in front of her. "One who happened upon a nice guy like Cale Davis, and for whatever reason, he took pity on you. And now you think you have the right to spend time with people like us." She motioned around the booth to the other people. "You are nothing but a charity case and when Cale is done with you, you'll go back to whatever trailer park you came from and he will come back to us, looking for someone who is actually worthy of him." Ryan leaned back against the booth, she leaned closer into him and with a flick of her hand said, "That's all, you can go now."

I grabbed her fruity drink from the table and threw it at both of them. She shrieked and made a pathetic attempt to block her face as the liquor hit her. My other hand slid across the table toward them, clearing it of every beer bottle that had been sitting there. Ryan's arms flew up in the air and he almost tipped the table as he tried to escape the beer that ran across the tabletop toward him.

"What the hell ..." he yelled, but didn't get to finish what he was going to say, because he had to duck as I threw the empty glass that was still in my hand. The glass shattered as it hit the wall behind him and he cursed again. Everyone scattered away from the booth as I picked up a napkin and threw it in Dana's direction.

"You don't get to dismiss me like that, you bitch." I screamed. Ryan just stared at me, eyes wide with shock.

I smirked at him, "I guess you're right, asshole. Nothing can control all of this craziness."

Strong hands grabbed each of my arms and I tried to struggle against them. Cale's voice was forceful and pissed. "I think you've drawn enough attention for one night, let's go." He pushed me through the crowd, making our way to the door. People stared as we walked past but I kept my eyes on the floor.

The cold air hit my body as soon as we got to the parking lot and I shivered. He took off his jacket, put it around my shoulders and took hold of my hand. He walked in front of me – leading me to his car. I looked back, Marcus and Katie stood in the doorway. Katie flashed me a helpless look and I gave her a little wave.

The car was already running. He opened the car door for me, but looked over my head, saying nothing as I slowly climbed in. He hesitated outside of the car, one hand leaning against the roof, while staring off at nothing. After what felt like an eternity, he pushed himself off the car and walked around to the driver's side. He slid into his seat, inhaling deeply as he did.

The silence was heavy. A million things ran through my head. I needed to break the tension – it was killing me. I started simple.

"I'm sorry if I embarrassed you." My voice was small, like a child's.

He pulled his lips into a tight line, but then turned away from me, looking out his side window.

I sat in my seat, staring at my folded hands in my lap. I spoke one more time, "I understand if you don't want to sponsor me anymore."

He shook his head and shifted in his seat toward me. "Jenna, that's not it at all. You didn't embarrass me, you embarrassed yourself. I care too much about you to let you do that. I don't care what any of those people think of me. But you do, and that's what worries me."

"What do you mean?"

"Listen, Dana is a bitch – that is no secret. I can only imagine what she said to you. But the truth is, if you are going to be sponsored by me, you have to learn to deal with women like her."

I dropped my head back against the headrest. "I don't know if I can."

"Of course you can," he said. It was a matter of fact; he didn't question it at all.

"How do you know that? Is Nolan going to teach a class on it?"

He let out a small laugh, "No, but he will want to talk to you about this."

I slid down a little bit in the seat and pulled his jacket tighter around me. That would not be a fun conversation.

He drummed his fingers on the steering wheel awhile and then asked, "Why did you shut off your phone?"

My stomach dropped. I'd been acting so childishly. "How did you find me?"

"I was worried so I sent Katie a text. She told me where you were going."

"It's nothing personal, Cale, I just wanted to be myself tonight. I didn't want to be watched or analyzed. I didn't want to be anyone's … anything."

"So, that was the real you in there tonight?"

My cheeks burned as I thought about what I had done. I pushed the pain of Ryan's rejection away. "No, not really." I whispered.

"And as far as people watching you … you are beautiful, I don't know where you can go to avoid that." I looked up and he smiled at me. I rolled my eyes and smiled back.

"I'm coming to terms with the fact that you're not interested in me the way I'm interested in you, but I thought we were at least friends."

I froze in my seat. "Wait, what you are talking about?"

"I don't want to sound arrogant, but I'm not really used to showing interest in a girl and having her not reciprocate."

My head started to fire off all sorts of questions. All I could squeak out was, "You like me?"

"Of course I do."

"And you think I'm not interested in you?"

He looked back toward his steering wheel. "It's okay, I'm getting used to the idea."

Ryan's face suddenly flashed through my mind. I looked out my window, closing my eyes tightly to keep the tears from falling. My body tingled at the memory of his lips … my heart broke at the memory of what had just happened.

"Please don't." I whispered.

"Please don't, what?" he questioned.

"Get used to that idea."

>CHAPTER SIXTEEN<

Cale and I decided to take our relationship slow. Well, Cale decided, and I tried to ignore the fact that I knew he didn't want to become too attached, until he found out if I was chosen for sponsorship or not. Being a man true to his word, we had not progressed past holding hands. It was endearing and maddening all at the same time. Honestly, it made me crazy, along with everything else that had been happening.

Except from across our classrooms, I had not seen Ryan at all. He stopped meeting me before class, stopped coming over for lunch, and refused to text me back. It was miserable. I knew I had made a mistake freaking out like I did, but I couldn't say I wouldn't do it again. Dana was a bitch.

My nights since the club were spent in my dorm room with Cale. We never went anywhere else and I was okay with that. I liked having him to myself. I couldn't imagine the stress of actually going to a social situation with him. I needed more practice before that happened.

There was no down time, or fun time, every second was used to "prep" for the sponsorship evaluation. He quizzed me on current events, the history of The Brotherhood, or whatever other ridiculous topic he had given me the night before to go over. I struggled balancing all of it with my schoolwork, especially since my study buddy was acting like I didn't exist.

I would never tell Cale that though. Studying by flashlight into the late hours of the night became my normal. I would admit, however, my lack of sleep may have played into my absolute refusal to see the day as anything other than a pain in the ass.

"Yes, Mom, I'm here now." I paused to let her talk as I slipped another dress over my head. "No, he picked some out for me to try on." I tugged on the bottom hem, wondering if there was more to it. "No, I'm not having fun."

"Just come out or I'm coming in," Katie yelled through the dressing room door. I took a deep breath, raising my shoulders up to my ears and exhaling in exaggerated defeat.

"I have to go, Katie is waiting." I pulled the dressing room door open and walked out like a pouting five year old, and over to the wall of mirrors. Katie and the sales clerk whispered back and forth.

I glared at myself in the mirror while Katie and her side-kick clerk circled around me, inspecting every inch. What had I gotten myself into? This was ridiculous. I had no business standing in this swanky dress shop, no business wearing this god awful expensive dress and certainly no business meeting Cale's father.

My whole body tightened as if rigor mortis had set in. Cale's father was coming here to meet me and it was my worst nightmare. My stomach twisted as the thought ran through my head.

Technically he wasn't coming to meet only me; but all the proposed sponsored. Maybe I would've been less tense if I'd gotten the chance to meet him before now as planned, but unfortunately, business hadn't allowed it. And who was I kidding; the sponsorship evaluation would suck either way.

So now it wasn't just Cale's father I would be meeting, apparently there was a panel of elders that did the judging. It kept getting better and better. Maybe they could throw Dana on the panel, you know, just to make things more interesting.

"Are you feeling okay? You suddenly look green." Katie whispered.

"I'm not sure," I mumbled under my breath, stumbling toward the dressing room door. I grabbed the handle but it was locked. I shook it a few times, trying to will the damn thing to open. The sales clerk hurried over to unlock it.

She timidly spoke to me, "Miss Clausen, Mr. Davis wanted you to pick three dresses, do you know which ones you would like?" I just stared at her, unable to really form a thought.

"Let her pick." I pointed over my shoulder to an obviously annoyed Katie.

My purse was buzzing as soon as I shut the door.

"How's it going? Are you and Katie having fun?"

I closed my eyes and squeezed the phone in my hand. He wanted to know how it was going and if I was having fun? I could think of so many ways to respond to that right now. None of them being very nice, so I went with sarcastic that could be confused for nice.

"YEP, can't text right now, trying on all these beautiful dresses!"

I threw the phone back into my purse.

Katie barged into the tiny dressing room and closed the door behind her. "What is your problem?"

"What?" I asked innocently.

"That was miserable. A lot of girls would love to have their boyfriend send them into this over the top, expensive shop and tell them to buy whatever they wanted."

I held up a finger with each point I was trying to make. "One, he is not my boyfriend. Two, he picked out the dresses, not exactly 'anything' that I would want. Three, I have to meet his dad in one week and I have no idea what to expect." My phone buzzed so I grabbed it. "And four, he won't stop texting me! You know how crazy he gets when I don't text him back."

She knew I was referring to a couple weeks ago when I'd gotten lost and Ryan found me. Time had moved forward since that night and I groaned when I realized how much had changed. This is my life now. Ryan was with Dana, and I was standing in a tiny dressing room with Katie, trying to buy a dress that would fool a powerful man into believing I was worthy of his son.

But there was something even my growing feelings for Cale couldn't get past ... his need to know where I was at all times. It drove me crazy.

Katie snapped her fingers in front of my face, dragging me back to reality. "You need to get over this paranoia." She grabbed my hand holding my phone and lifted it so it was eye level between us.

"This is what people do, Jenna. They text, a lot, especially, when you're interested in someone. He was right to be worried about you that night. I was worried too." She paused as her eyes searched my face. "He didn't freak out when he came over, he was checking to see if you were safe."

Her voice softened as she reached up, rubbing each of my shoulders. "If you don't want to do this, then you need to let Cale know. But if you do, then you need to start acting like someone who's worth being sponsored." She gave me a small smile and turned toward the door. "You can take that one off; I picked the black one with the slit, the pink with the striped skirt and the red one."

~~~

Katie and I walked toward the nearest coffee shop in a comfortable quiet. I knew she was already done being upset with me, but still I wanted to find the right words to explain why I was terrified of what was happening.

In my head I knew the sponsorship was a huge turning point in my life. It would open a world of opportunities that would've never been available to me without it. I also knew there was no room for Ryan in that world. Moving forward with Cale meant Ryan's goodbye would be permanent. I wasn't ready to face that yet.

"I'm sorry, Katie. I didn't mean to get so upset with you. It's ... well, I really don't know what it is."

"I think I know why you're so crazy about all of this."

"You do?" I hoped she could give me some insight to my crazy thoughts.

Katie nodded her head. "Well for one, you are getting no sleep at all. You are completely overwhelmed and you are so worried about letting Cale down that it's making you act like a crazy person."

My heart sunk just a little bit.

"If you don't get picked for sponsorship, you are worried that he won't be interested in you anymore. You think that's the only reason he's hanging around, don't you?"

I couldn't respond to her. How could she be so right about this and so wrong at the same time? Every word she said was true, but there was an entire side of it she was missing.

Even though the thought of not being picked up for sponsorship scared me to death, there was a part of me that wondered if it wouldn't be a relief. I didn't want to lose Cale, but I also didn't want to be constantly watched and worried over. It sounded so refreshing to just be Jenna — walk to class by myself, worry about myself, go back to invisible. I was so screwed up; I wanted the attention, but at the same time I wanted it to go away.

"Hey Katie." Ryan said from behind me. My blood turned cold. I wanted to run away and never look back. I searched the store fronts frantically with my eyes, wondering if I could casually walk into one. It was no use, I was caught. I turned, Katie stepped protectively between us.

My eyes met his for a split second and the pain was crippling. The lie I'd told myself about being able to move past him violently unraveled inside of me, allowing my wounded heart to bleed pain all over again. The aching breached my defenses. I visibly flinched, trying to remain in control. I looked away, biting my bottom lip until I tasted blood. An emptiness opened inside of me. It was the space that he'd left. It reached out from my soul, wanting him back. I shut it down fast – I had no choice. He'd chosen her; I needed Cale. This was the end of our story together.

Still, the sight of Dana hanging on his arm like some sort of leech made me sick. It was exactly what I needed to get my strength back. If that bitch was what he wanted, then he wasn't the person I thought he was anyway. The only power the two of them had over me was what I gave them. I wasn't planning on feeling powerless in front of Ryan, or anyone, ever again. Katie's eyes flashed to my face before looking back at Ryan, giving him a cold, hard stare. "Hey," she said.

"Let's go, baby," her voice was sugary sweet. "It's cold out here."

There was an awkward silence that seemed to engulf every noise that had previously surrounded us. I pulled my shoulders back, and looked directly at him. She tightened her hold on his arm.

"Hey Jen." His voice was strangely soft and he looked beautiful – another crack in my heart. His eyes were distant, almost hesitant as his gaze shifted nervously between Katie and me.

Several days of scruff shadowed his face, but it only made him sexier – and I hated that. His gray beanie was pulled down to barely above his eyebrows. He put both of his hands into the pocket of his black leather jacket.

My heart raced like crazy in my chest. I wanted to throw my arms around his neck and tell him how much I needed him – and then punch him in the face.

Instead, I tilted my head and looked directly at Dana, giving her a long drawn out smile that made her shift uneasily, and then I slowly looked back at him.

"Really, Ryan?" I chuckled sarcastically. And as my heart broke, I held my chin high and walked past them.

Katie scrambled up behind me and fell into step. I continued walking until she grabbed my arm and made me stop. Her face was hard at first, until she saw the streaks the tears left on my cheeks. Her face instantly softened and she pulled me into a hug. The tears continued to run down my face. I half chuckled-half sobbed when she partially released me and gave me a smile.

"He is sorry, you know."

I wanted to speak, but I knew if I tried it would only come out as a sob. I composed myself as best I could.

"I don't care," I whispered. It was the second lie I told myself about Ryan Kitson.

>CHAPTER SEVENTEEN<

The soft music playing in the background irritated me. I wanted to purposely spill my lemonade all over the white table coverings. The black dress that Katie had picked out squeezed me in the wrong places, making it impossible to take a full breath. The stupid heels made my feet ache.

"You look beautiful tonight." Cale stared at me from across the table.

I used the fork to move food around my plate, ignoring his compliment. The few bites I'd taken tasted wonderful but my stomach was in knots. I needed to be cautious about how much I ate, in case I happened to see it again later.

It was crunch time now.

The sponsorship evaluation was the next day and every cell in my body was on high alert. My stomach lurched and I dropped my fork onto my plate harder than I'd intended. I looked around and locked eyes with the well-behaved people in the room. They knew I didn't belong.

He reached across the table and laid his hand over mine. "Why do you look so uncomfortable?"

The simple kindness in his gesture put a huge crack in my already fake image. Tears stung my eyes. A fountain of emotions erupted inside of me and I struggled to keep it under control. I wasn't sure if he wanted to hear the truth or not. What I really wanted to say was, *"What am I even doing at this type of restaurant? I'm not even qualified to wait tables here. Why the hell didn't you tell me that this sponsorship thing would take over my whole life, consume my every second and make me lose the best friend I've ever had? And ... don't look at me like that because when you do, you can get me to do absolutely anything."*

What actually came out of my mouth was, "I'm just tired and a little overwhelmed." It wasn't a lie.

Cale intertwined his fingers with mine and brought them to his lips. He pressed a light kiss on the top of my hand. My shoulders relaxed a bit.

"Jenna, I know you're worried about what's going to happen tomorrow, but you're so amazing, there's no way you won't get picked. You have learned so much over the last month – it's been impressive to watch you come so far."

My heart pounded. I wanted this so badly for him. No one had ever had so much confidence in me. He really cared if good things happened for me or not. I squeezed his hand, "I guess I'm a good student." I said.

"And remember tonight is a night off. We are supposed to be relaxing and not thinking about what's happening tomorrow."

I smiled and nodded my head slightly.

"Now eat." He motioned to my plate. I felt a little more centered after his little pep talk. He settled his back against his chair and focused on me.

"I do have one question for you though."

"Okay."

"What happened that night on the bridge with Ryan?"

I stiffened at the sound of his name as Ryan's face flashed in my mind. Heat rose in my chest, twisted up my neck and it was suddenly hard to breathe. The absence of him in my life was still so raw. I wondered if there would ever be a time that his memory wouldn't affect me this way.

Cale hadn't asked a single thing about that since it had happened. Why now? My heart beat wildly at the thought of the conversation that happened between Ryan and me in the car that night. It was the only time that I'd questioned Cale's motives out loud. I'd been terrified that in the midst of our fight, Ryan would betray me by going to Cale with my doubts. I didn't think Ryan would do something that horrible, but I never thought Ryan would hurt. He'd already proven me wrong in a big way. I laid my fork back down.

"It's like I told you, I got lost walking and Ryan happened to find me."

"Did Ryan know you were going for a walk?" His eyes were steady on mine. I didn't really understand what he was asking. Was he questioning if I had left alone? If I had called Ryan and told him where I was going? If we had gone together?

"No." I couldn't seem to get any other words out. The mood between us changed. It was charged with something unfamiliar – it made me nervous.

"Has he ever touched you ... inappropriately?"

This damn dress was too tight and I couldn't breathe. Memories of Ryan slammed back into me with a crushing force. I could feel his arms around me, his lips on mine.

"No." There was nothing inappropriate about the way Ryan had touched me—it had been perfect. But he wasn't mine, and that would never happen again. I wrapped my arms around myself, trying to fight off the sickening feeling that he was probably touching Dana that way right now.

He lifted his napkin and patted his mouth before setting his hands down on either side of his plate. "Good. I know I don't have the right to ask you who you spend time with, or who not to. You're smart, I'm sure you understand me."

"Are you asking me not to spend time with Ryan?" He was obviously unaware that Ryan and I were not associating with each other.

A small laugh escaped his lips and he shook his head. "No, not at all. I 'm just asking you to please be careful how much time you spend with any man, but especially Ryan. I introduced you to him because I know he's a nice guy. But you are a stunning woman, Jenna. Even a man with the best intentions can be swayed by your kind of beauty. Believe me, I know."

His eyes connected with mine and electricity surged through me. I desperately needed to touch him. He hadn't crossed any lines since the night in the car, always being the perfect gentleman and leaving me wanting more and more from him every time he was near.

He frequently talked about the control I held in my beauty, and the power I was unaware of. I decided it was time to test those theories.

"You do?" I asked. I reached out and ran my fingers over his hand. His stare turned intense. I continued to softly rub my fingers over his knuckles, never breaking our stare. Boldness was not usually in my character, but I had also never had Cale Davis in my life, and I wanted him to cross that stupid line again. I needed to feel my sacrifices had purpose.

His voice was a throaty whisper, he answered, "Yes, you can be very hard to resist."

"Why do you have to resist anything?" I asked quietly.

"I'm not sure why, I just know I do. And that makes me ..." He shook his head slowly and gave me a smirk. "You have no idea the thoughts I have running through my head about you. The things I want to do to you, to teach you."

"Well, Mr Davis," I bit my lower lip and flashed him a smile, "We've already established that I'm a great student."

He grabbed onto my hand and was quickly out of his chair, pulling me behind him. My heart beat wildly in my chest. He stopped just long enough to pay the hostess. I stood restlessly just behind him, rubbing my hand softly on his side but it wasn't enough. I leaned into him and wrapped my arms around his waist, letting my body press against his. A small smile lifted the corners of his mouth as he stole a quick glance over his shoulder at me. His eyes flashed to my mouth, and quickly we were moving again, out the door and across the parking lot toward his car. I was nearly running to keep up with him, surprised when we kept going past his car.

"Where are you taking me?" He didn't answer, just kept walking toward the alley that ran between our restaurant and the building next to it. I slowed a bit but he continued to hold onto my hand. Something inside of me cringed.

We reached the shadows the tall brick walls of the buildings provided. He dropped my hand and walked a few more steps. With his back to me, he ran his hands through his hair slowly.

I trembled as a chill ran up my back. Darkness surrounded us; I looked over my shoulder toward his car sitting in the lighted parking lot. I had a sudden urge to run into the light. No one could see us here, and I suspected no one could hear us either, unless I was screaming. I really hoped it didn't come to that.

He started pacing. I tried to swallow but my mouth was dry. I kept my eyes on him, trying to anticipate his next move.

"Cale," I whispered.

"You just don't understand the kind of pressure I'm under," his voice was tight, "My father … he is a very powerful man and has high expectations for me." He stopped and looked right at me. "He expects me to be running our part of the business within the next two years, Jenna … two years. I never asked for this. I never wanted this." His pacing increased and he ran his hands down his face.

I stood still and silent. I had seen people like this before. It was clear that Cale was not in his right mind. I knew a sudden movement might make him lose it, and from my experience, that never ended well for me.

The dampness of the alley crawled up my bare legs and I started to shake. I wanted to wrap my arms around myself to try and hold it together, but that would bring attention to myself.

His eyes locked onto my face but he looked through me. I gasped at the sight of his face. His eyes were changed ... emotionless. He was completely inside his head right now, fighting whatever internal demons lived there.

My body's instinct to get me out of this situation overtook my level head that was screaming to stand still. I took a few small steps backward toward the parking lot.

He rushed toward me – a predator closing the distance on his pray. I held my breath and closed my eyes, stiffening my body to prepare for whatever he had planned.

He gripped tightly around my neck as he backed me up against the rough wall, forcefully pushing himself up against me, making me straddle his legs. His breathing was heavy on my neck and I struggled to control my own. Confusion coursed through me. I wasn't supposed to like this, but I could not deny the pleasure I was feeling. Tears flooded my eyes as the confusion of these feelings swirled around me. I flattened my hands against the wall, surrendering. He ran his free hand up the side of my body, cupping my breast and pushing himself even harder into me while tightening the grip on my neck.

"You make me crazy. I can't fucking think, Jenna. I crave you, I can't get enough." He pressed a hard, passionate kiss onto my lips. There was nothing careful or gentle about it. It tasted of pure lust and his intent was to consume me. When he finally pulled away, my lips throbbed from the assault. "My father would call you a distraction," he growled.

My mouth dropped open as a rush of heat surged through my body. I moaned and pushed back against his leg, trying to get some relief from the intense desire that controlled me right now. A frenzied look crossed his face. I didn't know what to do, nothing made sense. I should be terrified, I should fight back, but I wanted him, I didn't care if he hurt me. I deserved it, needed it … wanted it.

"Cale, please." I reached behind him, twisting my hands in his shirt, trying to get him as close to me as I could. "Please, do something … anything …" Suddenly his hands were all over me, rough and aggressively attacking me. It was painful and shocking and I loved it…and wanted more. He lifted me off the ground and I wrapped my legs around him. I pulled his mouth to mine, taking his hungry kisses over and over until I had to break free to breathe.

He buried his face in my neck and held onto me, still pressing me between his body and the brick wall. "Damn it," he whispered forcefully. The air between us changed and I knew that it was over again.

He took a deep breath and whispered, "I'm sorry. I can't do this." He lowered me down to my feet, still pressing his weight against me. I put my hands flat against his chest as I closed my eyes and took a deep breath, begging my body to calm down. I tried to push against him, wanting to get some space between us.

"No, wait." He begged holding on to me. I pushed harder and harder until I was pounding my fists against his chest. He stood there motionless until I had exhausted myself. I pressed my forehead against his chest and let the tears come.

"Please move," I sobbed. He shifted slightly and I slipped past him, running toward the parking lot. I tried to regain my composure and the tiny shreds of dignity he'd left me; while the word 'distraction' swirled in my head.

>CHAPTER EIGHTEEN<

I stood in the darkness of my dorm room, trying to slow my breathing. White dots speckled my vision while I held myself, trying to stop the uncontrollable shaking. The memory of Cale's hands touching me made me feel dirty and disgusting. I thrust my hands into my hair, squeezing my temples to relieve the throb in my head, trembling as I realized what I'd been willing to do to fill the void Ryan had left.

Who had I turned into? I braced myself against the door and slid down until my knees were against my body. Resting my head back and rolling it from side to side, I wondered how I'd become this person. My life was filled with lies.

I pictured Ryan's face – it always came back to him. My heart began the slow ripping that only happens when you realize you've betrayed someone you love. I gasped from the pain, covering my mouth with one hand while pushing the other against my chest.

I was breathless … needing to cry out to relieve the agony. But this type of pain refuses to be comforted. It consumes everything, staying inside and reaching into the places where only the worst kind of damage can be done.

Fear was nothing new to me. But I'd always fought to keep away the destruction someone else was capable of. Now, I fought the fear of what I'd become because of the damage I had inflicted upon myself. I didn't know how to change things back.

A numbing washed over my body, an unnatural calming that can only happen when pain wins and leaves you broken. I straightened my legs in front of me as my arms fell to the side – the tears slowed. Not because I felt better, but because my mind had developed a shut-off switch to save me from falling into real depths of darkness … The kind I could get lost in for a lifetime.

Once this fake calm took over, I noticed the shadow sitting in the dark by the window. His long legs were bent up in front of him. Muscular forearms hung over his knees, holding a bottle of something. His black baseball cap was turned backward and his head hung down. The moonlight shone in the window throwing a shadow on his face, but I wasn't afraid – I knew exactly who he was.

I should've been embarrassed about what he'd seen, or pissed he'd come here at all. But I didn't have enough energy left for extreme emotion like that.

"Hey, Ryan," I whispered, wiping tears off my cheek.

"Hey," he said softly. He took a long drink of whatever was in the bottle and wiped his mouth. Turning the cap around on his head he pulled it down low and squeezed the bill.

"You okay?" he asked.

I looked away from him, "I'm not sure."

He took another drink. His voice was laced with anger this time, "Did he hurt you?"

My chest constricted. He had no idea my misery came from *his* absence, and I wasn't sure what it would do to him if he did. I wanted so badly to tell him the truth. But I couldn't, he had too much to lose. My throat tightened, making my voice crack when I responded to him. "Not in the way you think."

He nodded slightly nodded, thinking he understood.

"What are you doing here?"

He slowly shook his head while taking a quick deep breath, "I really don't know. I guess I'm kind of lost."

"You and me both," I whispered.

"Yep, me and you, best friends – both lost." He brought the bottle up to his mouth one more time. "Yet somehow we found our way back to each other."

"I'm sorry you had to see …" He cut me off with a wave of his hand.

"It's no secret what he does to you, Jen. It's written all over your face whenever he's around." He took another drink from his bottle.

"That's why…" He pushed himself up.

"That's why, what?" I asked.

"Nothing, never mind."

I struggled to my feet, exhausted from everything I'd been through. His gray t-shirt stretched across his body tightly. He lifted his cap, ran his hand over his hair, then pulled it back on. Noticeable swelling under his eyes made my heart ache. His facial hair was longer than the day I'd seen him and Dana on the street – he was a mess. Hiding his face with his cap, he kept his eyes to the ground.

"That's why, what?" I whispered.

His stance was ridged as he pushed his hands into his pockets. Something inside of me broke loose, a longing for my soul to be reconnected to his. I hesitated, but then rushed to him, sliding my arms around his body. My heart pounded with joy at his closeness. He'd been gone for so long and I missed everything about him. I pressed my cheek up against his chest and took a deep breath, listening to his heartbeat. It was the most beautiful sound in the world.

"Jen," he whispered as he wrapped his arms around me, "I've missed you." I rested in his comfort as he held me close with one arm and ran the other slowly up and down my back.

"I've missed you too," I cried as I looked up at him.

A tear slipped down his cheek, I brushed it away. With my touch, he closed his eyes, allowing more tears to slide down. He cocooned me in his arms, trying to get as close as possible.

"I'm so sorr ..." I placed a finger across his lips to quiet him. I couldn't re-hash the mess our lives had become. I just needed to be here with him.

"Hey," I whispered. He opened his eyes, the tears wetting his long black eyelashes. "It's going to be okay." I said. His eyes searched mine for something.

"Is it? Do you really believe that?" He took a step away from me and put both of his hands on his head. His voice weak and pleading, he said, "Because I don't see this getting any better."

"What do you mean?"

He dropped his arms to his side dramatically, his face full of pain and confusion. "Do you not understand why I 'm here? Do you really not know how I feel about you?"

Ryan, I mean, I guess I ..."

His temper flared so quickly I jumped. "You guessed what, Jenna? You guess that since I walked out of this room last time my feelings for you have changed?"

"What are you talking about? You have Dana. You were pretty clear ... what was it you said; I needed to 'move on' because you clearly had."

"And you follow Cale around like a love sick teenager. He strings you along and you fall for it every time. Let's see, does this sound familiar; he rejects you, you throw a fit, he buys you something expensive, and you're right back to square one. What's the matter with you? You're better than that, Jenna. Even if he can't see it – I know it."

He turned his back to me and reached for the window. I grabbed for him, pulling on the back of his t-shirt. "Wait one second. Don't think you can just drop all of this and then leave. Why the hell did you even come here?"

He turned quickly, grabbing my face between his hands. "You're supposed to be mine."

He leaned in and touched his lips softly to mine. I melted into him, both physically and emotionally. He was right; I was supposed to be his.

I should've pulled away, but didn't. I wanted to feel needed, loved and all the other things he had promised me. He pulled away from me, searching my eyes for something.

"Ryan,"

"No, please don't say it; I came here thinking maybe, just maybe. But after seeing you when you got back ..."

His lips were back on mine, soft and caring, nothing like Cale's.

"I can be what you need tonight, please. Let me take care of you ... In every way," He whispered into my ear. His soft lips traced down my neck as he pressed his hand flat against my back, holding me close to him. "Let me show you with my body how I feel about you in my heart."

Tears fell from my eyes. I didn't care what the consequences of our actions would be. I needed relief from this emotional nightmare I'd gotten myself into. This was right – I wanted him as much as he needed me.

I ran my hand under his shirt and against his bare chest, feeling every muscle tighten as my fingertips ran over them. He lifted his arms, allowing me to lift his shirt over his head.

Looking up at him through hooded eyes, I laid my hand over where his heart was and felt the steady beat. He covered my hand with his.

"I need you to know something," he whispered.

I kissed his chest lightly. He closed his eyes as I ran my hands up his chest. When I got to his shoulders, I ran my fingertips up the back of his neck and pulled him down to me. Our lips were so close I could feel his breath.

"This will change me, Jenna."

"What do you mean?"

"There will be no one else after you. Even if this is our only night together, for the rest of my life, it will be your face I see." He pulled me into his chest and held me. "I will give everything up for you."

My whole body stiffened — it was all crystal clear to me. Being with me meant he would be giving up his place in The Brotherhood. Going against Cale like this, meant everything he's been waiting for, all of his dreams, would be gone.

That's the moment I knew I would never be good enough for him either. I pushed down a sob, a half-second before it escaped. I took several steps back away from him, cringing against the sting in my chest.

"Ryan, I can't do this. I don't feel that way about you." The lie singed my lips and burned my soul. I knew what I was doing to him, but it was better this way. His expression turned desperate as he stepped toward me.

"Just try, Jen. I know I'm not Cale, but I can be everything you need – I promise." He reached for each of my arms and I moved quickly out of his way.

"No," I yelled. "I don't want this. Don't you understand? If I do this with you I can kiss my chance with Cale goodbye." He looked at me with disbelief.

"What does he have that I don't? Is it the money, because I have money."

"No, it's not that."

"Then what? I don't care that you've already had sex with Cale. He's not right for you – I am."

"What? I have not had sex with him."

"Well everyone thinks you have so what's the difference? Just give me a damn reason why you don't want me."

Confusion swirling in my head … Of course he thought I was sleeping with Cale. Why wouldn't he? I acted like I was, and most likely would have tonight if he hadn't stopped it. But now, I was about to do the same thing to Ryan that Cale had done to me, time and time again – reject him.

"Well that's just great. The least you can do is give me a reason. Shit, Jenna, tell me you think I'm stupid, or ugly, but say something – you owe me that."

With a voice laced with hatred I felt for myself, "I don't owe you anything."

The room went deadly silent. He walked past me toward the door but stopped just inches from it. His breaths were raspy and labored. Even with his back to me, I could sense all the tension rolling off of him. His shoulders raised and fell erratically and he ran his hand through his hair.

The emotion in this room was so thick it was suffocating me. I felt the finality in what I said and knew this would be the last time I was alone with Ryan.

Nausea racked my body as my mind flooded with every laugh, every touch, and every kiss we'd shared. Tears fell from my eyes and I brushed them away hard, pissed my heart was such a traitor to the act I was trying to put on. The pain was nearly fatal. I needed to be strong for him; I was not about to let him give up everything for me.

When he spoke, my heart ached a little harder at the sound of his pain.

He whispered, "Jenna ... Jenna please. Please don't hate me."

I wanted to tell him there was no way I could ever hate him. I wanted to beg forgiveness and wrap my arms around his waist and bury myself in everything that was him. But I didn't speak a word; I couldn't bear to hear my own voice even respond to him. I was disgusted with myself. Nothing I could say could make this any better; it would only cause more pain. And there had been enough of that tonight.

"I need something from you." He laid his head lightly against the door and continued when I didn't speak.

"Please, ask me to stay — just for tonight. Tomorrow I'll leave and that will be it. I won't bother you ever again. But tonight, just let me make love to you like it's just you and me. Let me hold you like you're mine, and kiss you like we have every tomorrow ahead of us." With his head hung low, he turned to me.

"Please Jenna, one word, just ask me to stay and all that I am, will be yours tonight. I will love you with everything I have."

The dark room closed in around me as I focused on my voice. I needed him to believe this.

"You were right. I am his, even if he doesn't want me."

Tears streamed from his beautiful blue eyes and he shook his head in disbelief. "Then what are we?" He pointed back and forth between us. The emotions that swarmed inside of me took over and tears spilled everywhere. My body shook.

"What are we?" he demanded.

"We are nothing!" I screamed. My heart shattered at the sound of my own words. The pain coursed through me in waves.

He steadied himself against the door. His hands curled in fists, but the anger was too much for him. "I can't believe you!" he shouted. His hands moved so quickly, I only heard the pounding of his fist on the door. I cringed as he smashed his hand over and over, yelling out in a rage the whole time.

I lifted my chin higher in an attempt to look more convincing. The numbness from before washing over me again, but this time it was from my own personal betrayal of my heart.

He marched past me, slid the window open and climbed onto the fire escape.

I turned to face him, pleading, "Please come back inside, you've been drinking and if you fall you could get hurt."

He stood, bracing himself on the window frame, looking back in at me. "Now you're worried about me? Wow, you're really something." He glanced over his shoulder toward the ground. "It couldn't hurt any more than what just happened in here." Turning his back to me, he started down the fire escape. "I'm done. Cale can have what's left of you."

I crumbled to the floor as soon as he was out of sight. The whole room spun and I welcomed the darkness I had so desperately fought to keep away.

>CHAPTER NINETEEN<

"I'm not sure I can hide the dark circles under your eyes." Katie dabbed her concealer – covered finger under my eyes one last time as she shook her head at me. "Did you sleep at all?" She knew the answer to that question.

I moved over to the full length mirror she had propped up. My blonde hair was pulled tight and high on my head in a perfectly round bun. A simple string of pearls circled my neck and matched the pearl earrings Katie had picked out. I ran my hands down my sides – straightening the pink fitted bodice of the dress that laid perfectly at my hips, where it met a white and pink striped pleated skirt, which stopped just below my knees.

Slipping my feet into the nude-colored heels that Katie offered, I took one last look in the mirror. I looked nothing like myself – it was perfect.

"You did a great job picking this out, thank you."

Katie gave me a sad look. "Have you talked to either one of them?"

I shook my head. I didn't expect to hear from either of them and honestly, I didn't want to. Cale was too confusing and Ryan was pissed. I was on my own today.

"Maybe you should just skip it. I mean seriously, screw both of them."

I gathered every ounce of energy I had, "I can't." My throat was scratchy and my head pounded from the lack of sleep. I had an internal shaking that started after Ryan left and had not stopped since.

"Well, you look beautiful."

I glanced down at my dress, running my hands over it again. It was a beautiful dress.

"Your ride will be here in a few minutes."

She opened the door and turned back toward me. "Are you ready?"

I pulled my shoulders back and walked toward her. She stopped me before I could get out the door.

"I want you to know that this sponsorship does not define you. You are beautiful, smart and an amazing friend. Remember at the end of this day, no matter what happens, you will still be all of those things."

I hugged her tight. She was the only person in my life that had never wanted or needed anything in return. She loved me for me.

The driver waited outside the dorms. He opened the back door of the car when he saw me coming, "Good evening, Miss Clausen," he said tipping his hat to me. I slid into the back seat, trying to ignore the chill of the leather seats on my legs.

He shut the door, closing out all noise and surrounding me in silence – I felt completely isolated. Time seemed to slow down as we drove past the other students on campus. I wondered if they had stories like mine – if they were happy and satisfied – or if we were all just trying to escape some part of our lives; with the hope there was something better.

The dark tinted windows added to the lonely feelings invading my mind. I twisted my hands in my lap. I'd made a full swing from the poor girl with nobody who cared – to riding in fancy cars and wearing designer dresses while on my way to meet a roomful of very powerful men – but yet ... here I was, still alone.

The Brotherhood House was massive. It sat alone in the middle of the block with a deep front yard, commanding attention in a cold and isolated way. A waist high stone wall separated the grounds from the sidewalk, running from one end of the block to the other – allowing no confusion that this property belonged to important people. The front of the house had matching stone blocks and above the front door hung a huge plaque carved from the same stone. It read, "The House of The Brotherhood". Wrought iron fencing ran along each side of the walk leading to the front door.

When the car stopped, so did my heart. I closed my eyes and prayed the driver would just keep going. When I heard the door open, I gingerly turned toward him but stopped. He leaned slightly into the car, "Would you like me to get Mr. Davis to accompany you to the house?"

I quickly shook my head, "No, that won't be necessary." I gathered up every bit of bravery I could muster and stepped outside of the car. It was eerily quiet. I suddenly wished I had paid more attention to the direction we were going. Cale had given me an idea of where the house was, but I was not exactly sure how to get back to my dorm. That shot down my fleeting thought of running for it.

I started up the walk toward the house, my heels announcing my presence with every step.

The door opened before I could knock and a man dressed in black pants and a white waiter's jacket motioned me in with a sweep of his hand.

"Miss Clausen, please wait here. Someone will be out for you shortly."

"Thank you," I whispered to his back as he left the room.

I stood in the middle of a large open foyer. A crystal chandelier hung from the center of the room and under it stood a large round table with the biggest flower arrangement I had ever seen. I walked toward the table, cringing when my heel slid on the polished floor. To my right there was a large study with a fireplace, to my left – closed doors and an open staircase led up to an open balcony that looked down on the foyer.

I jumped when the doors opened and an intimidating figure started toward me. A small gasp escaped. I lightly placed my finger tips on the table to steady myself. It was the same face, only older. I wasn't sure if it was the wisdom of years lived that made him so attractive, or the way he carried himself. Confidence oozed from him. He expected what he wanted–and he deserved it.

His green eyes locked onto mine as he strode toward me, with a predatory air about him. I held my breath, taking a tiny step backwards.

"Hello, Jenna." His voice was smooth but powerful. He extended his hand to mine and I froze. His smile faltered for just a second, but was quickly replaced. He took a step closer to me and leaned in.

"The evaluation has already begun, please remember your training."

Even though he'd used pleasantries, I knew this wasn't a request–it was a warning. What he was really saying was, 'people are already watching you; don't embarrass me or my son.'

My mother's voice bounced around inside of my head, "Don't miss out on the biggest opportunity of your life." Something inside me clicked.

In that moment, I realized I was done letting these men take control of my destiny. My mom was right, this was the opportunity I was waiting for and I had messed everything up by letting my stupid emotions get involved – just like she always did.

No longer – I was going home with this sponsorship, and if, after that, Cale wanted nothing else from me that was more than fine. Today, I would start making my own path. I was done letting my mother's horrible life decisions dictate my reaction or non-reaction to things. The control was about to shift; this is what I had come here for. No more cowering in the closet, no more messed up little girl.

So I leaned into the most powerful man I had ever met, and whispered, "I know my training sir, and I'm more than ready to become the next sponsored girl for The Brotherhood." I stood tall, straightened my dress and inhaled deeply giving Mr. Davis a big smile. "Now, if the panel is ready for me, I would love to get this started."

Cale's father let his eyes rest on my face for long enough that my heart beat wildly, making me want to squirm, but I stood my ground never looking away from him.

Just when I thought I would lose it, he extended his arm to me and smirked. "Right this way, Miss Clausen."

>CHAPTER TWENTY<

Cale insisted I come to the celebration party. I was in no mood to celebrate; even though I just found out I'd gotten the sponsorship. What I really wanted to do was to climb into my bed and sleep for days and days. But Cale was so excited when he called to give me the news, I couldn't say no to him. Thinking back, I was not sure I'd ever said no to him.

He hadn't mentioned anything about what happened in the alley. I guess we were both taking another 'pass' and I was fine with it. Something inside me knew last night was the final time Cale and I would entertain the idea of being anything more than friends. I needed to move on in my own direction, by myself. No Cale … my choice. No Ryan … destiny's choice.

"How are you doing back there?" Katie walked a few feet ahead of me, holding tightly to Marcus's hand. She glanced over her shoulder and flashed me a quick smile.

"Awesome," I answered in an excited, high-pitched voice stopping both Katie and Marcus in their tracks.

"Why don't you go ahead, we'll catch up in a second?" Katie kissed Marcus on the cheek. He turned in my direction.

"Jen, I don't know what's going on with you and my brother, or you and Cale, or you and ... anything really." He was as comfortable in these emotional moments as his brother. "But you have us, we're here for you." He motioned back and forth between himself and Katie and winked at me.

"I know," I grumbled, feeling like the loser friend I was. "Thanks." He leaned into Katie and whispered into her ear. Nodding her head at him, she turned to give me her full attention.

"What's going on with you," she asked as she walked back to where I stood.

"I don't know." I threw my hands in the air like a little kid throwing a fit.

"Is this all about that stupid fight you and Ryan had?"

"That was not a stupid fight; he practically called me a slut." I had only given Katie parts of the story. Not because I wanted to keep anything from her, but if I was being honest, I couldn't even handle all the drama of it myself ... I didn't want to force it onto someone else. I kept the intimate details to myself this time.

"He did not. He said you were allowing people to assume things about you that weren't true."

"Yes, things like I was having sex with Cale."

"Well honestly, Jenna, you weren't doing anything to make people think any differently."

She was taking his side.

"Are you seriously saying you don't think he did anything wrong?"

"No – the shit he pulled at Midnight was messed up. And I don't even know what to think about last night. But what I am saying is, you need to relax. If you want to be with Cale, then be with him, but don't get so pissed when Ryan doesn't want to be around it. You know he has real feelings for you and he's just trying to protect you."

"Protect me from what?" I huffed as I walked past her.

"From yourself." She said under her breath thinking I couldn't hear her. Her heels clicked on the sidewalk as she tried to catch up to me, but I didn't slow down.

"Remember, I won't be home tonight. Marcus leaves tomorrow for that trip the elders are sending him on. We got a hotel room."

I laughed at the way she sang the last part. Those two got hotel rooms all the time, even though she swore they hadn't had sex yet.

"Can't wait to hear all the details." I laughed as I slowed down and grabbed her arm. She smiled at me and I laid my head on her shoulder as we walked toward the party. "I'm sorry I'm such a bitch," I said with a sigh.

"It's okay, I love you anyway." She threw her head back and laughed out loud. Even if my entire world turned upside down, I knew after everything we had been through in the last few months … I would always have Katie.

The fraternity house was enormous. It had to be at least three stories tall with a porch that wrapped around the first story and a deck around the second.

There were people everywhere. As soon as we opened the door we were drowned in the craziness. A heavy fog of smoke lingered in the large house. The smell of it, mixed with alcohol and sweat was almost too much for my already sensitive stomach to handle. I covered my nose with my hand and tried to block it out. The rooms were wall to wall people. Most stood in little groups along the edges trying to yell over the pounding beat of the music while others transformed the center of the room into a makeshift dance floor.

The party was so loud it was impossible to hear what anyone was saying. This was actually a good thing. I wasn't ready to hear anyone else's opinion of me. Now that I'd been chosen for sponsorship, I was sure there was a target on my back.

Cale would be impossible to find in this mess of bodies; I sent a quick text.

"At the front door, come and save me"

Marcus waved his arms at us from across the room and mouthed for us to stay put, but that was impossible. Katie held onto me as we followed along the flow of people coming into the house. Some drunk in front of me turned suddenly, spilling beer all over himself. The whole crowd erupted with laughter and yelled "Beer foul"! The guy laughed and threw his hands in the air, heading toward a wall where a line of tapped beer kegs sat. The crowd shifted with him and everyone was forced to move in the same direction, whether you wanted to or not. Katie held onto my hand as tight as she could while she pushed against the crowd and toward Marcus.

The volume of the music lowered and the crowd began to chant drunk guy's name. A group of guys lifted his legs above his head, suspending him into the air as he drank straight from the tapper. Everyone around him cheered and counted out loud. Apparently, making it the longest came with serious bragging rights.

Marcus grabbed Katie's hand and pulled us both to him, handing each of us a cup. I looked back at the guy who was still upside down.

"It's called a keg slam. When someone calls you out on a beer foul, you have to slam it straight from the keg," Marcus said leaning into me so I could hear him.

"Sounds like a blast." I said sarcastically as I took a drink. It was flat and tasted like fermented apple juice. "Yuck, this stuff is nasty!"

"What do you expect? I got it when I first got here so you wouldn't have to wait in line. Hey, let's go outside or something, it's way too crowded in here." He wrapped one arm around Katie's neck and the other around mine; turning us both toward the direction we'd come from.

"Are you crazy? I'm not going anywhere until that guy is done doing his keg slam. There's no way we would get through there anyway," Katie laughed. Marcus dropped his arms from our shoulders and shot Katie a quick side glance.

Ryan's voice cut through the other noise in the room. "Well, well … if it isn't my soon to be sister-in-law and my 'newly-sponsored, ex'-best friend'."

I rolled my eyes but my heart dropped when I looked at him, even drunk he was incredible. His dark hair was a mess. I knew he'd been running his hands through it like he always did when he was upset – but it looked good on him. What didn't look good on him was Dana, who sat on his lap. No wonder Marcus tried to usher us out of here.

Ryan wouldn't look at me. He just sat on a dining room chair with little Miss Hottie all over him. His hand was on the back of her neck and I watched as he pulled her down whispering something into her ear. She giggled and I wanted to punch her right in the face.

Katie lightly grabbed my arm, "Come on, let's go find Cale."

Ryan glanced up at me and held my stare. "Yes, Jenna, run off to Cale like you always do. I'm sure he has a BMW or something waiting to make up for last night in the alley."

I brought my hand around, putting every ounce of anger behind it. When I connected with his cheek, it caught him off guard. He lost his balance for a second, dumping Dana onto the floor. I smirked down at her before leaning toward him.

"What are you doing? Do you think this hurts me? Do you want to hurt me?"

He sat taller, getting as close to me as he could, "Why would this hurt you?" he asked in a sarcastic voice. "We are nothing to each other, remember?"

Tears threatened to spill over as I stared at him. I could feel the shaking at my core starting and I knew I needed to get as far away from him as possible. I pushed into the crowd. There were so many people, I had no idea where I was heading or where I would end up, but as long as it was away from Ryan, it was the right direction.

Drunk guy finished his keg slam so the entire crowd started shifting back to the dance floor, the exact opposite direction I wanted to go. The music came back with a thump as I tried to push forward.

"Back the hell up!" Someone yelled and the whole group of people shifted direction. I almost lost my balance, but strong arms grabbed me around the waist. I looked back into Cale's face as he used his arm to clear a path and get us both away from the center of the room. Once at the edge of the room, he pulled me into a tight hug.

"Jenna, what happened? I came looking for you after your text and couldn't find you." I grabbed him around the waist and buried my face in his shirt. Ryan cut me so deeply with the truth in his words – my whole world had changed. He was right – we were nothing to each other anymore.

"Hey!" Ryan shouted from somewhere close. His voice sounded pissed and my heart started racing at the sound of it.

Cale slowly moved me behind him, keeping a hold of one of my hands. I pressed my face against the back of his arm, hoping to avoid what was about to happen.

"Jenna, what the hell? You're just going to walk away from me again?"

Cale tightened his grip on my hand. "Brother, I think you might want to go sit back down." Cale's voice was not angry, but it carried an air of superiority that reminded me of his father. I knew it would not sit well with Ryan.

"Oh, King Cale is telling me I can't even talk with my friend now? "

"I don't think she wants to talk right now."

"Really, well why don't we ask her ... Jenna?" His voice was so intense; I jumped when he said my name. I looked up and locked eyes with Ryan – my chest tightened painfully. Even with all the anger in his voice, his eyes looked desperate. After everything I'd done to him, he was giving me one more chance. "Do you want to talk to me?"

"I said she doesn't want to talk to you, Ryan. Now go the hell home and sober up. You and I will talk in the morning. But you stay away from Jenna – do you understand me?" Everyone stopped what they were doing – all eyes were on us.

Ryan's face suddenly changed. He charged at Cale grabbing him around the waist and pushing him back against the wall of people that stood behind us. I was knocked to the side and hit the ground hard. Random hands reached down to help me up, but I scrambled to my feet and pushed my way toward the fight. Cale had flipped Ryan to his back and had him down on the ground. I could see Cale's fists smashing over and over again into Ryan's ribs as people cheered. But, in no way had Ryan given up, he viciously pounded fist after fist into the side of Cale's head and neck. Both were bleeding; Cale from the side of his face and Ryan from a cut somewhere above his ear. Brothers from the house rushed in, grabbing at each of them as they tried to pry them apart. Marcus grabbed Ryan under the arms and pulled him to his feet as the other's pulled Cale away.

The entire room began to spin. My throat started to close up like someone was choking me. I couldn't get a full breath. Everything around me began to blur. Not here ... not now. I couldn't let this happen in front of everyone.

Ryan's eyes were frantically searching the crowd for me. "Jenna! Jenna!" he screamed over and over, fighting against Marcus. His eyes found me and I instinctively moved toward him, pulled by some unknown force that had been there between us since the moment we met. I needed to be near him, to know he was all right. No ... I need to be near him to know *I* was all right. I shoved against the people between us, trying to get to him. "Ryan!" I yelled frantically.

Suddenly Cale was in front of me, winding his arm around my waist. Marcus fought against Ryan; holding him back as he struggled to get to me. "Jenna, please – wait!" he yelled.

Cale turned me toward the door and ushered me out. I clung to him sobbing, fighting the desire to break free and run back to Ryan.

~~~

I lay curled up in the middle of Cale's huge bed. The aftershock of my crying shook my body as I tried to calm my ragged painful breaths. What had I done? Where would I go from here? I could never look Ryan in the eyes again. I had left him for Cale once again.

The bed dipped when Cale sat down behind me. I rolled over to face him. He reached over and pushed the tear soaked hair from my face.

"Here's some water. I thought it might help you feel better."

I pushed myself up and used the headboard to lean on. "Thank you," I said quietly as I took the glass from him. He held an ice pack against his eye – it was already bruised and swollen.

"Cale, I'm so sorry."

"You didn't do anything wrong. I obviously missed something here. I had no idea Ryan had those types of feelings for you."

"He doesn't," I quickly said, my desire to protect Ryan flaring. "He's just confused."

"Drunk, yes. Confused about how he feels about you? I don't think so." He smiled a small smile and put his fingers on the bottom of the water glass I held in my hand, raising it to my mouth. "Drink, things will be better." I took a large gulp of water and sat the glass on the side table.

"You do understand I don't feel that way about Ryan, right?" I had to make Cale believe, if Ryan had any chance of moving past this and staying connected in The Brotherhood. It was the only way I knew how to save him. My voice dripped with a pleading tone I was not used to hearing from myself.

There was an aching in my throat. I took another big drink of water, trying to put out the burn of the lies that were spewing from my mouth. I love Ryan ... no – I am *in love* with Ryan. He is the one I want and there is no happy ending without him.

I thought I'd be able to walk away from him, but after seeing him tonight, I knew I was dead wrong. The pleading in his eyes and the way he screamed my name ... suddenly, the finality of what I'd done came crashing down around me.

I watched as Cale walked over to his closet, unbuttoning the torn and dirty shirt he had worn to the party. He grabbed a t-shirt off of a hanger and pulled it over his head. I had been so stupid all along and now I'd ruined any chance I may have to be happy. I needed to find Ryan; maybe there was a way to fix this.

"Cale, I'm sorry but I have to go," I said as I started to climb to the end of the bed. The room started spinning and I grabbed onto the blanket to steady myself.

"No, Jenna." His voice trailed off and echoed in my ears. I rubbed my forehead as a warm feeling coursed through me. My head felt heavy and I struggled to hold it up. I blinked rapidly as my vision blurred in and out.

"He doesn't want you anymore, Jenna. That's what tonight was about. You are mine, not Ryan's. He knows it now."

>CHAPTER TWENTY-ONE<

My world was dark. It took some time for the confusion to clear and for me to understand ... the sound I heard was my own breath...in and out, in and out. There was a weight on my chest making every breath a struggle. I wasn't sure how much longer I could force myself to breathe.

I wanted to panic but I couldn't sit up, I couldn't talk, I couldn't even open my eyes. A terrible stabbing pain at the base of my skull throbbed every time my heart beat, sending an explosion of light behind my eyelids with every pulse.

At some point, between the throbs of pain and the sound of my breathing, other sounds began to filter in. Someone moved around the room quickly but it was not clear what they were doing. The noises faded in and out, like someone trying to find the right radio station.

I tried to yell out but my voice refused to work. With every bit of strength in me, I attempted to move something, an arm or even a finger to let whoever was there know, I needed help. Nothing moved. I frantically tried to arch my back or roll my head; it only made the pain worse... I was trapped inside my own body.

Was I dead? Did the person in the room want me dead? Maybe it was safer to remain still. I retreated back inside my head and searched my mind for the last memory. Fighting with Ryan, walking up to the party with Katie ... but that was it — nothing to explain why I would be laying here unable to move.

"Jenna, wake up. You need to try really hard to open your eyes."

I recognized the sound of shuffling feet and suddenly the bed dipped down. The light touch of someone's finger tips moved my hair from my face.

"Please wake up, little one."

Ryan! My mind screamed his name. He sounded worried. Was he scared I was dead? Internally I rolled from side to side, fighting against whatever it was holding me hostage in my own mind. A little flutter in my eye lids filled my body with a rush of excitement. I concentrated as hard as I could, opening my eyes just enough to see in front of me. Even the soft light in the room was painful and everything was blurry.

"Hey," he whispered as he leaned over me.

None of this was familiar. Why had he brought me here? I clumsily tried sitting up but Ryan caught both of my arms.

"Just stay where you are," he whispered, "you're in no condition to go anywhere." He leaned down and kissed my forehead lightly. "I'm so happy to see you awake. Just relax and when you're feeling better, I'll explain everything. You're safe now."

My head spun with questions I couldn't get out of my mouth. I'm safe now? Why, wasn't I before...and where am I? What happened to Cale and why did I feel like this? I wanted answers, but knowing I was with Ryan brought me enough peace to relax. My eyes drooped and began closing. A surge of panic rushed through me at the last second, wondering if I would ever wake up again, but the exhaustion was too much for me – it was dark again.

The second time waking up was easier. I hesitantly propped myself up on my elbows, unsure of my surroundings. The room was shadowed in darkness. I knew I wasn't on campus anymore because of the sounds coming from the open window. Street noises echoed around the room. Cars honked, people yelled and the faint sounds of police sirens rang out in the background. I was somewhere in the heart of the city.

My head pounded and no matter how many times I blinked, my vision was still a little blurred, but I was able to slowly sit up. I pushed myself back so I could steady myself against the headboard. I raised my hand to rub the back of my neck where the pain still lingered. It felt foreign, like I had never moved before.

Directly across from the bed was a door I guessed opened into the hallway. It had several dead bolt locks, but they seemed to be for show. I could see a thin crack of light slipping in from around the door where it didn't fit the casing.

"Looks like a nice neighborhood," I thought sarcastically to myself.

To my right, an old refrigerator buzzed loudly next to a rusty stove. To the left was a recliner chair and a small TV positioned in the corner. The only variation in the box-sized room was a door on the wall where the TV sat. I wondered if it was the bathroom but by the size, it could be a closet.

Lights flashed in through the thin curtains covering a window next to the TV. An occasional wind blew them into the room along with an unpleasant smell, a mix of garbage and fried foods.

A flash of pain struck me and I was suddenly nauseous. I closed my eyes, rubbing my hands up and down my face, trying to erase the memory of the smell.

The darkness outside gave no clue to the time, only that it was late. An eerie feeling settled inside of me, I had no idea what time it was or how long I'd slept. I moved to the edge of the bed and lowered my feet to the floor. The dizziness hadn't gone away, but it seemed better when I grounded myself. Even though I knew the window was only a few steps away, it still seemed too far to go.

The room was chilly and a shiver slid down my spine. My clothes were damp and I trembled from the weakness that consumed my body. Cautiously, I stood, still unsure I could bear my own weight. When I didn't end up in a heap on the floor, I moved toward the window.

The noises I'd heard could only come from a busy street full of people. I was afraid to get too close to the window. I didn't want anyone to see me, but I was too curious not to look.

The window actually looked down into an alley separating the building I was in from the next. I did however, have a good view of the street that ran in front of the two buildings and the store across the street.

The light flashing into the window was from a huge sign that blinked the words "Liquor and Cigs". The street was hectic, packed with people and cars. They stood in the streets yelling to each other. A man lay passed out in the alley below my window. I was safer in this one room apartment than I would ever be on these streets — especially since I didn't even know where I was.

Below the flashing sign stood a middle aged woman smoking a cigarette and watching the cars go by. Out of all the people, I wasn't sure why she stood out in the crowd. Maybe because of the way she was dressed or the desperate look on her face she tried so hard to hide. It was obvious what she was doing — although I'd never actually seen a prostitute before. I watched as she walked over to a car, leaned into the window for a second before opening the door, and climbed in. My heart dropped realizing what I'd witnessed. Why would Ryan bring me to such a place?

A vicious dog came running down the alley barking. He chased away a man sitting next to the dumpster and came back to it. The man had clearly been in the dog's territory. The dog lifted his leg, marking what was his. He jogged back down the alley and out of sight. There was nothing safe about where I was.

Terror consumed me, as I realized all of the new dangers I would be facing if I attempted to leave. I backed away slowly, afraid if I took my eyes away from the window, some of the unknown that lived on the street would jump through and invade my private little room.

I jumped when the back of my legs touched the mattress. Maybe if I went back to bed, this would all seem different when I woke up. I crawled in and pulled the blanket to my chin, praying this was a nightmare.

>CHAPTER TWENTY-TWO<

The sun warmed my face as I lay in my bed. This was my favorite time of day. It was quiet and safe. My mind peacefully faded back and forth between dreams and reality...my own personal fairytale. I cringed as strange things started happening. It was dark and people yelled at me, I ran to get away from them. A vision of a window with curtains blowing in. My chest felt heavy and it I couldn't take in a breath. Someone stood over me. I can't move. I need help! I'm so frightened and I don't know what to do – I need to scream!

"Ryan!"

I sat straight up out of my dream searching the room for the threats, desperately trying to throw the restricting sheets off of me. Ryan rushed to the side of the bed. I frantically grabbed at him and threw my arms around his neck. He sat on the edge of the bed, gathering me up into his lap and held me, whispering, "I'm here, everything's ok … I've got you."

I struggled as I tried to keep the panic from getting out of control. I wasn't sure what I was afraid of, but I knew I was somewhat safe as long as I stayed right here, cradled within his embrace. He caressed my hair while continuing to reassure me things were fine. Over his shoulder, I watched as the curtains blew into the room, reminding me things were not fine.

When he sensed my body relaxing, he loosened his hold. "I know you have a lot of questions right now, but why don't you take a shower. It will make you feel better. Then we can talk."

He took hold of my hands and led me to the bathroom. "I won't leave, I promise." He lifted both of my hands to his mouth and kissed them gently. My eyes searched his face, hoping for a clue to why he was so concerned about my safety. If he wanted me to be safe, this was not the place to bring me.

"You should have everything you need in there. I'll be waiting for you out here."

I stepped inside the bathroom and he shut the door behind me. I glanced in the mirror, but the face reflected back was unrecognizable. My eyes were sunken in and had dark circles around them. My skin was almost transparent. I touched my cheek, but it was like touching a stranger.

On the sink sat a new toothbrush and toothpaste. I looked around the small room, noticing items that looked like they belonged to me. My type of deodorant and my brand of hair products sat on top of a clean towel next to a pile of my clothes. Why the hell would he have all of this?

As I let the warm water hit my face, I decided even if he had kidnapped me, he was right about the shower making me feel better. The blood began to flow to my arms and legs again and I felt stronger – physically and emotionally.

I got dressed and brushed my teeth while I made a mental list of all the questions that needed answered. If he wouldn't tell me what I wanted, I was ready to face this neighborhood alone. It was daytime and the store across the street had to have a phone. I made a plan to call Katie to come and get me if anything Ryan said sounded fishy. I grabbed a rubber band and pulled my hair up as I walked out of the bathroom.

The smell of bacon hit me and my stomach ached with hunger. I hadn't even felt hungry until that moment. He had a glass of orange juice and a cup of coffee poured for me. I sat at the small table as he cooked with his back toward me.

"Feel better?" he asked without turning around.

"A little, I guess." I said with hesitation. I took a quick sip of coffee and cleared my throat.

"Listen Ryan, I don't remember anything that happened after I got to the party, so instead of me asking questions, why don't you just start from the beginning and tell me everything? Start with what day it is, because I have no idea how long I've been here."

He turned around with a blank look on his face as he pushed a plate of food in front of me. "It's Wednesday."

Instantly, my mind started computing all the time and days I'd lost. "How can it be Wednesday? Have I slept that long? What about my classes and who knows I'm here? Did you tell Katie where I was? She probably has the FBI looking for me. What about Cale, does he know where I am? You better start spilling the story before I decide you're some sort of freak and call the police myself. Even though I have no idea where I am … why I'm here … or how I got here." My voice trailed off as I realized how much trouble I was in. I pushed the food away and sat back in my chair as I looked down at my hands. I took a deep breath. "Please, Ryan."

He pulled out the chair across from me and sat down. His stare bore into me, making me feel very small. "I'll tell you what I know, but it's limited. There are a lot of pieces that just don't fit and some are missing altogether."

"Just start from the beginning, please."

Ryan started slowly, being very guarded with his words, fueling my anxiety into anger. "You're not going to like some of the things I'm going to tell you." He said

"I'm a big girl. Just tell me so I can start figuring this out."

"Listen, Jenna, it doesn't work that way. I have to tell you all the pieces so you can help me put it all together. We have to work together on this. So just listen to me, and after I'm all done, you can ask as many questions as you want."

"Fine." I sat back in my seat with a frustrated growl, trying to hide the fact I was scared to death to hear what he had to say.

"After you and Katie got to the party, we …" he pointed between him and I, "got into an argument."

I searched my memory, but it wasn't there. I looked at him suspiciously. There was a reason I'd lost my memory and he needed to get to the point.

"Cale got involved and, I'm so sorry Jenna … I'm sorry for everything. I need to fix this but I don't know how."

"Don't. Don't do this now. We need to put everything that's happened between us to the side right now. At least until you tell me why you've kidnapped me and brought me to live in the ghetto." I tried a small smile, but it didn't happen.

"Okay. Well, after you and I had our argument, Cale got involved." My heart rate picked up speed, but still, I had no memories. "He and I got into a fight at the party and then he took you away."

"You mean we left together?"

"No, I mean he forcefully took you out of the party."

I shook my head slowly at him, unsure of what he was saying.

"You were hysterical and trying to push through the crowd to get to me, but he grabbed you around the waist and basically forced you out the door." He twisted his hands together, obviously still bothered by what happened.

"So after everything settled down, I made Katie and Marcus take me to look for you, but we couldn't find you anywhere."

I sat very still, hanging on his every word. My leg shook involuntarily, I didn't know why.

"I went to the house and demanded Cale tell me where you were. He said the two of you had argued, you left, and that was the last he'd seen of you. I looked for you Jenna, all night, all day Sunday. I didn't sleep, I didn't go to class – I never stopped looking."

His chair made a horrible noise as he slid it across the old linoleum floor so he could sit in front of me. He reached out and placed one hand on my trembling leg, the other he wrapped around my hands.

"Finally, Monday night I went back to the house. I hoped there was a clue to where you were and if he didn't want to tell me, well, I was going to destroy the place until he did. I snuck in, hoping to get a look around Cale's bedroom. Nolan was inside talking to him, so I listened outside of the door." He paused, frowning at the memory.

"They were talking about Katie. All I could hear were bits and pieces. Something about what they said really bothered me – they said Quinn was going over that night to 'try again'."

"Try again? Try to do what?" I asked.

"I don't know. But something about the way Nolan said it made my skin crawl, so I kept listening. They started talking about my brother – wondering how much trouble he was going to give them when he got back. The next topic was you. Cale said you were in the basement and the timing was perfect."

"Timing for what?" I asked, knowing he probably didn't have the answer.

"I told you I don't know all the pieces."

I took a deep breath and shook my head. "This doesn't make any sense. I don't remember any of it."

"First Years are not allowed in the basement of the house so I didn't know my way around, but I had to get to you. It's like a maze down there. It took me awhile, but that's where I found you."

"What do you mean ... found me?"

"You were in a room in the basement, a bedroom." He leaned back into his chair, staring at both of his hands that he had placed in his lap. He curled them into fists.

Fear flared inside of me. "Go on," I urged.

"You were naked."

My mouth went dry and my head started spinning. "What?" I asked in a whisper, "Why?"

"I don't know, but I don't think anything had happened to you. I knew if I left you there, you were in danger, so I wrapped you in a blanket and brought you here."

I couldn't speak. I sat dazed as I let his words sink in.

Panic rose quickly within me and I was on my feet, pacing back and forth in the little space. Questions started spilling out, "Who was in the house? Where was Cale and why was I naked? I stopped, looking at him for something ... anything.

"What is going on?" I screamed.

Ryan's stare never left his hands as I went on my emotional rampage. I rushed toward him.

"Ryan!" I yelled. "Answer me!" He lifted his eyes until they met mine. "I don't know any of the answers."

My body fell back into the chair and I slumped down from defeat. I couldn't look at him but I had one more question.

"How do you know nothing happened to me?"

He was careful when he answered, using a soft tone, "I found unused condoms by the bed."

A flash of what he must have seen when he walked into the room slammed into my head like a wrecking ball. The idea of him seeing me so vulnerable and knowing what he saved me from was overwhelming. I lay my face in my hands and started to shake.

Instantly his strong arms were around me again. I turned toward him, using him as a shelter from the reality of what he was telling me. He picked me up and I held on like a child. He gently placed me on the bed and climbed in behind me. I turned toward him to find the security he always provided. I rested my head on his chest, listening to his heartbeat. He covered me with the blanket and let me cry.

He'd kept his word – he'd save me from the monsters.

"What are we going to do?" I asked.

"They're looking for you."

"Who, the police? Maybe we should go talk with them."

He shook his head. "No, The Brothers are looking for you." His eyes were intense, he was nervous – and it scared me.

"Why would they all be looking for me?"

"I have a feeling there were others involved in what was planned for you – more than just Cale and Nolan." He sat up and dropped his feet over the edge of the bed. I shuddered at the word "planned" but knew he was right. Whatever happened to me was definitely planned out.

"Why me?" I asked softly.

Shaking his head he responded "I don't know. That's what we have to find out."

"We need some answers. We have to fill in the blanks before someone else gets hurt."

All of a sudden the panic was back, like a hammer in my chest. I jumped up and yelled "Katie! Ryan, what have they done to Katie?"

All I wanted to do was scream, but I couldn't get the air in. I scrambled around the room, looking for shoes. "Get up! We have to go get her now!"

"Jenna," Ryan said in a very low but solid voice. "We have to be careful. We can't just go running back to your dorm room and expect to go unnoticed."

"But Katie," my voice was shaking, just like every other part of my body. I knew I had to save her – I didn't know from what, but only that I had to.

"Yes, we'll go get her tonight, but we have to have a plan too."

I went back over to the table and turned the chair to face the bed where Ryan was still sitting.

"You're right, but I have some questions for you."

"That's fine, but I also need some answers from you too."

"Me first." I said with no room for argument. "First of all, where are we? Whose apartment is this?"

"It's mine. We are downtown in an area you should never be in alone. I rented it under a false name – not that anyone in this neighborhood gives their real name." He hesitated but then started again. "Remember when I asked you to leave everything and come away with me? This was supposed to be where we stayed for a few weeks until things calmed down. That's why I have all of your stuff in the bathroom. I've been stashing things here for the last two months. No one would've looked for us here. My brother doesn't even know I have it." As he admitted the last part, he dropped his head. I could tell that he felt shame for hiding this from Marcus.

"Where is he?"

"I don't know. He, Katie and I decided he still needed to go on the trip the elders had planned for him. We all knew something wasn't right, but Marcus thought we should try to keep up the act until we found you. That's why Katie didn't come here with us. They decided she should stay in the dorms like she normally would."

"They decided?"

"I didn't care about any of that, Jen; I just wanted to find you. I let them make all the decisions while I searched for you. Now, It's my turn." He hesitated, confliction darkening his face. His question was lost in the silence between us— silence can be so loud at times.

"We need to make a plan." I said as I stood and grabbed a bag from the floor. I ran around the room gathering items I thought we might need. A flash light that sat on the floor by the stove, paper and a pen I'd seen next to the TV.

Ryan stood in the middle of the room with a distant look on his face. I turned and looked at him.

"Ryan, we have to go get Katie," I said quietly.

"I know," He said but didn't move. I put the bag on the floor.

I prepared myself for what I was about to tell him. "Do you remember when you said I was already Cale's?" His jaw tightened.

"From the moment I met you in that crowded hallway, I belonged to you. My friend – my savior – my only love." I placed my hand over his heart, he covered it with his.

"There was never any room for Cale. It's always been you – it will always be you."

>CHAPTER TWENTY-THREE<

The smooth cement blocks felt cold under the palms of my hands as I slid along the wall toward my dorm room. Almost uncontrollably, my eyes roamed the entrances at either end of the hallway.

Back and forth I scanned, expecting to see the shadow of someone crouched and ready to attack. The lights were dimmed because of the late hour, and I prayed everyone was asleep.

From my spot down the hall, I could see the moonlight stretching out from under my room door. I stood, paralyzed with fear. Part of me wanted to rush to Katie and make sure she was not hurt. The other part realized Ryan and I had no idea what we were dealing with. Whatever she had been through would be my fault – I wasn't sure I could handle that. I could just turn and run, go back home, and tell my mom things just didn't work out. I could pretend I'd never met Katie or Ryan and go back to my old life, never allowing myself to think of Cale or this place again.

But Ryan stood behind me; I could feel the warmth of his body. I looked over my shoulder and he motioned to the door, questioning me with his eyes. I knew it was dangerous for us to be standing out in the hallway like this. I had no choice – I kept moving.

I stood terrified, staring at my door. I could feel the heaviness of the truth on the other side. My hands trembled. Ryan took the key from me, slipped it into the lock and cracked the door open.

The room was still and dark. He slowly opened the door, the light broke through the darkness like it was searching for something – and there she was.

She shielded her eyes from the light. I gasped at the sight of her. I'd seen people depressed before, but Katie was almost unrecognizable. Her face was pale and sunken in, because sunshine was not available in the dark place her mind had gone. I moved slowly toward her. All the color had drained out of her once beautiful and dramatic eyes – they were vacant.

She sat on the couch with her back against the arm rest, legs straight out and arms just hanging uselessly at her sides. Her breathing was slow, deep and deliberate – as if it was almost impossible for her body to remember how to perform this act. It looked excruciating – and familiar. I knew exactly how she felt, but Ryan had been there to help me wake up – Katie had been all alone.

I went to her, first sitting on the edge of the couch. When she did not object, I moved closer whispering her name, hoping she would show some type of recognition.

"Katie, it's me," I whispered as I lightly touched her leg. As soon as I did, she jumped to the corner of the couch and pulled her knees to her chest. Tears sprung to my eyes, as she cowered like a beaten animal. She held onto herself tightly. I couldn't tell if it was to protect her from more pain getting in, or if she was trying to make sure her last bit of sanity didn't escape out. With her eyes wide and breathing rapidly through her open mouth, she rocked back and forth attempting to soothe herself.

I looked at Ryan, hoping he had an idea. His face was pale and filled with terror. I thought for a second he might be in shock.

"Katie, I know something terrible has happened to you and I want to help you." She stopped rocking. Hope surged through me – maybe she was ready to listen now.

"Katie, I don't know why this happened to you, but it almost happened to me too. We need you to help us figure this all out. We can't let this happen anymore."

The sound of her voice was a whisper of what it once had been, but it startled me anyway. "

"Training is not fun, training is not fun. No training for you." She started rocking again, only with more frustration.

"Who trained you Katie? What were they training you for? Who did this to you?"

"Quinn, Quinn is the trainer." She winced as she said his name and buried her face in her knees. "Quinn." She whispered again. I didn't have to look at Ryan to know he had picked up a bag and was stuffing clothes of mine into it.

I moved closer to her and extended my hand. "Katie we are going to take you with us. Come on and get some of your things. I won't let Quinn hurt you anymore." She stopped rocking and looked at my extended hand like she was unsure what to do with it. Her eyes met mine and she spoke as her mind had suddenly cleared.

"They *are* going to kill you, Jenna. Why did you have to run? Now they're going to kill you." Ryan stopped what he was doing and stared at Katie. Her eyes faded back to the darkness. She was no longer talking to me; she was talking at me when she said calmly. "He'll be here soon. They'll kill us both if he knows you were here."

A knock on the door echoed through the room. Katie's expression exploded into fear and panic. I grabbed her arm and tried to pull her up. Ryan was already at the window, throwing my bag to the ground.

"Katie! Get up!" I was begging her. "Please come with us! You don't have to stay." She stood and stared in the direction of the door, as the voice on the other side said her name. It was Quinn.

Slowly she turned her head to me and whispered. "Go, or he will kill us all."

I shook my head wildly, "No, I won't leave you." I whispered, tears running down my face. She was like a robot as she walked toward the door. I knew what she was doing – what she was willing to endure to keep me safe. I couldn't leave her – not like this. She had to come with us.

Ryan grabbed my arm and started pulling me toward the window. "Katie, we'll be back for you tomorrow night – be ready." Ryan whispered.

She whispered, "Tell Marcus, I love him."

Ryan pushed me out onto the fire escape. I fought to get back into the room. I wanted to fight for Katie, and fight for myself, but I knew she was right. Quinn was prepared to kill us all. The best thing I could do for her now was stay alive. We would come back and get her tomorrow and the three of us would run together.

Ryan jumped out of the window and joined me on the fire escape. I was still looking to Katie, waiting for that one little hint she'd changed her mind, but she never looked back at me. She just continued to the door.

Tears poured down my face while agony consumed my entire body. I knew what Katie had just sacrificed to keep me safe, and I could not bear the thought of what she was going through. As we got to the bottom of the fire escape, Ryan jumped off, turned and lowered me to the ground. We ran around the building until we were safely under the cover of darkness.

I dropped to my knees, my stomach retching.

"I know you're terrified for her right now, but we can't stay here waiting for them to find us." He grabbed my hand and led me through backyards and allies. We didn't talk as we ran along holding hands. I knew if he wasn't leading me, I would crumble into a ball and let whatever was going to happen to me, happen. But once again – he was saving me.

We ran until I couldn't breathe anymore. I followed him like a tiny child. I had no idea where we were. My surroundings were blurred from fear and anxiety. I couldn't get her face out of my mind.

"Ryan, I can't … I can't run anymore." I said in a breathy whisper. I stopped and bent over, bracing my hands on my knees. He was coming at me by the time I looked up and did not say a word. He grabbed me by the back of my arm, an attempt to support me so I could keep going. I knew by the look on his face, he was as horrified about leaving her as I was.

After two more dark allies, I started to recognize things. It was a relief to know we were almost back to the apartment. Not in my wildest dreams did I ever think this part of town would somehow give me comfort.

The building we stayed in was as dirty on the outside as it was on the inside. We rushed into the entry way and crossed paths with the woman I'd seen out my window last night. Our eyes met for the briefest of seconds before she looked down.

I continued to follow Ryan up several flights of stairs and down the long hallway leading to our door.

I sat on the bed watching him lock the multiple locks. "I wouldn't feel safe even if this entire room was steel," I whispered. Although I knew he heard me, he did not respond.

When he finished, he fell into the kitchen chair and put his head in his hands. We sat in this little room and let our fears and insecurities drown us. The more I tried to calm myself the more I could feel the panic rising.

Ryan's breathing started getting faster and faster, and I knew he was also struggling with these monsters and wondering why in the hell we'd left her there. I went to him, hoping to find the right words to speak. Before I could say anything he turned and buried his face in my stomach, holding me as tight as he could and cried. I caressed his hair and whispered, "It's going to be okay. We'll figure this out."

He squeezed me tighter and I knew I was the only thing he had left to hold on to. Being together was the only thing that made sense right now. I was Ryan's hold on reality in the middle of all this insanity — the one thing he was counting on. Finally, if only in a small way, I was saving him.

>CHAPTER TWENTY-FOUR<

Morning came in with a flood of light – the type of sunshine that made you believe it carried warmth, but it was only an illusion. I pulled the blanket up and moved closer to Ryan. He was not awake yet and it was comforting to be lying with him. His rhythmic breathing was just what I needed to keep me in a calm place where nothing can hurt you except your own mind.

It was only seconds until the memories of the night came flooding back. I opened my mind to the harsh realities of this situation quickly consumed me ... The burden of fear coming back in full force.

I glanced at Ryan. Somehow it calmed my nerves to know he was relaxed and dreaming. I hoped his dreams were good, because the nightmare would begin as soon as he opened his eyes. I carefully slid myself out of the bed without disturbing him. Fueled by a strong desire to keep things as normal as possible, I went into the bathroom and quickly showered, brushed my teeth and made a mental list of things to do. I would: wake Ryan, make something to eat while he was showering, get a hold of my mom and let her know things were okay with me – I paused for a second, wondering what had happened to my phone.

The emotions rushed me all at once. I grabbed the edge of the sink and a shooting pain rushed through my head and chest; my throat constricted and burned.

"Katie," I whispered to myself, covering my mouth with one hand trying to keep the sob inside. I closed my eyes and whispered her name over and over again. I hoped somehow she was able to feel me and knew I was coming. She only needed to hold on for a little longer.

I stared at my reflection in the mirror. My fear suddenly switched to anger. I thought about Quinn and the things he was doing to Katie. I decided in that moment, I would kill Quinn. I didn't know how or when, but I would take his life for what he'd done. My list was now complete – the most important being, get Katie and kill Quinn.

My every intention was to wake Ryan so we could start working on my list. But when I opened the door and my eyes fell on his sleeping face, time stopped. He looked so peaceful, like a sleeping child.

Kneeling beside the bed, I let my eyes roam over his perfect features. I tried to fight the desire to touch him, but couldn't resist. I used the back of my fingers to brush his cheek.

Stretching, he took a deep breath in and his eyes fluttered. He looked rested and smiled at first, but as he focused in on my face, there was something else in his eyes. I understood – it was sadness.

"Are you all right?" I asked as I rubbed his cheek again.

"No, I'm not." His voice was raspy and soft. "I need you to know I would never let anyone hurt you. I would never just leave you like I left Katie last night." Tears filled his eyes. "I didn't want to leave her; I just didn't know what to do. She told us to leave." He covered both eyes with the palms of his hands.

"I know. We need to focus on getting her here tonight." I gently pulled back on his arms and he dropped them.

"Right?"

He nodded and wiped a tear away. "Get up and shower and I will make some breakfast."

He followed my orders and went into the bathroom. I was shaking as I walked toward the kitchen and opened the fridge.

Ryan had already told me he needed to check in at the house today. He had not been there at all yesterday and people would be wondering where he was. Even though he and Cale were not on the best of terms, he said he thought they believed him when he told them he hadn't found me. So he needed to keep up that act.

"Ryan," he looked up from the food he hadn't touched. "We have to get the police involved. We can't do this on our own."

"No. We have to be very careful, Jenna. This is a dangerous situation and we have to be smart." He stood up and grabbed his sweatshirt, pulling it on over his head. "The Brothers aren't looking for you to talk this out, Jen. They know everyone in this town and if you think they don't have a friend or two on the police force, then you are just naive."

"But don't you think they could help us?"

"We need to have the whole picture so the police are forced into action." His voice was stern – there was no way I was going to change his mind.

"I need to get you and Katie away from here, and then I will deal with The Brotherhood."

He walked over to me and pulled me into a tight hug. "Please promise me you won't leave the apartment until I come back to get you."

I was silent.

"Jenna ..."

"I promise."

~~~

His words rolled around in my head over and over as I paced the apartment. It shouldn't have come as a surprise to me, especially after seeing Katie. He was right; I had no idea what I was up against. But still, I felt like he knew a part of the story I didn't.

I needed to find out who had put me in that basement room and why they were doing what they were to Katie. None of this was making any sense to me. Why us? What was the purpose of all of it? What do they have to gain?

That basement held all the answers, I was sure of it. There had to be some clues to all of this. I couldn't figure out how to find the answer without the protection of the police. I just couldn't see this ending well without them.

If Katie and I went to them, told them everything that happened, how could they not go and look around? How could they ignore it?

I made up my mind. Tonight we would go get Katie, and tomorrow after Ryan left, Katie and I would go to the police ourselves. Guilt coursed through my body immediately for thinking about going against Ryan's wishes. He was trying to keep both Katie and me safe, but I had to take some responsibility in it too.

I wasn't going to just sit here and wait for them to find me.

I needed to connect with the outside world. Maybe I could find some horrible soap opera or talk show to dive into and shut off my brain for a bit. Just some background noise to help me drown out these constant thoughts running through my head would be helpful.

A scream rose up from the alley. I glanced out in time to see the alley dog chasing someone. It was a big dog, a German Shepherd, I thought. That guy must be an idiot to provoke it. I stared mindlessly out the window, watching the action.

"Police have the area blocked off," I heard faintly in the background. I watched the dog as he backed the man up against the dumpster. I shook my head, knowing the dumpster was the wrong place to try and hide.

"...in hopes of finding the girl's roommate."

The man held up his hands in front of him, looking all around for help.

I glanced at the screen and looked away again, before it hit me. The picture was a shot of the front of my dorm building. All other noise left the world and I dropped to my knees.

"Once again, University officials are not commenting on the apparent death of this student, or the name of her missing roommate. Local police are telling us the roommate has not been named a suspect but they would like to talk to this person, to find out if she has any information that could help solve this brutal crime."

I grabbed my head as the word "No" spilled over and over from my lips. She was dead – he'd killed her. I fell to the floor in a ball as shockwaves hit my body. My lungs deflated and refused oxygen. The world dissolved and I lost control of my actions. Somehow though, I made it to my feet. I threw open the door and stumbled down the hallway, weaving between the stair railing and the wall.

The pain in my chest was crippling and I didn't know what to do with it. I clawed at my face and neck, trying to let everything out.

I ran down the steps and out of the building, letting the sunshine hit me in the face. I stood there silently screaming, waiting for someone to rescue me; no one came.

The pain of losing her pounded in my head. My heart screamed her name. Mindlessly I wandered around – I was destroyed. I wanted to die with her, I begged for it.

I turned the corner and started down the alley, running my hand along the bricks of the building to keep my balance. No real thoughts formed in my head, only scattered words: "apparent death", "brutal crime", "suspect".

My legs shook and I knew they weren't going to carry me much further. The shaking made its way up my torso, attacking me violently, taking over every inch of my body until I had nothing left. I leaned one hand against the building and emptied my stomach over and over.

The world spun uncontrollably as I crashed to the ground next to the garbage dumpster. The cement was cold, wet and unforgiving. The burn of scraped skin on my forehead registered for a split second, followed by the warmth of blood. It wasn't enough to make me move.

I decided this is where I would give up, so I closed my eyes and dreamed of death.

>CHAPTER TWENTY-FIVE<

"Hey...hey, are you okay?"

Everything was blurry; I blinked as the outline of a woman came into view. Her face seemed familiar. I squinted against the pain in my head. She stood the alley's width away, obviously uncomfortable talking to me.

"I said, are you okay?"

Using every bit of energy I could, I pushed myself to a sitting position, but the spinning started again. I tried to steady it by closing my eyes and putting my face in my hands.

"Whoever did this to you must've been pretty pissed." I slowly looked up at her again, my vision blotted with white spots.

Her eyes darted to something over my shoulder. "He hasn't left your side."

I glanced over my shoulder to see the alley dog sitting there. It was the same dog that had chased a man down this alley earlier. He looked even bigger up close than he did from my window.

"I've seen that dog in this alley, but didn't realize he belonged to someone." My head hurt so badly, I couldn't even tell her he wasn't mine, I just stared at her. She was nervous but continued. "I was going to try to shake you awake, but your friend made it very clear I was to get no closer to you than this. He is very protective – probably smart to have in a neighborhood like this."

I tried to swallow, but choked on the dryness in my throat. I coughed a few times and my chest felt like it would explode.

"How long have I been out here?"

"Well, I first noticed you when I looked out my window an hour ago. I thought you were dead." I cringed at her relaxed view of death. She talked about it as if it was as simple as asking me what I wanted for dinner.

"About fifteen minutes ago I heard Cujo going crazy. I looked out and some scumbag was trying to get close to you. Of course, your security guard here was not about to let that happen so after he scared the guy off , I decided I would come down here and try to wake you up. The longer you lay here, the better chance someone sees you and calls the cops. When the cops come, they make all sorts of trouble. The last thing I need is a bunch of cops hanging around asking questions."

I must've looked confused because finally she said, "Bad for business, you know?" She attempted a smile, but the action seemed unfamiliar to her. "Anyway, let's get you up and see if you can walk."

She took a step toward me and the dog lunged. I could see the hair standing up on his back and heard the low warning growl. I don't know why, but I reached out and put one hand on his back. He steadied his stance, so I leaned on him as I got myself to my feet. I gave him a quick scratch behind his ears.

As soon as I stood up, I could feel the strength coming back to my legs, but I wasn't ready to walk yet. I stood for a second, looking around. The alley was framed in by tall buildings on either side. I looked up and found my window. The one I was looking out this morning ... when I heard the news about Katie.

"I can help you back to your room." She said from a few feet behind me. I knew she didn't want to get any closer to me because of the dog. "I just live down the hall from you."

I turned to look at her. "You do? I've never seen you before. I mean, I've seen you standing on the corner but ..." I almost felt ashamed that I didn't know she lived in the same building — but it's not like I was out looking for friends.

"It's okay, but a word of advice … when you live in a neighborhood like this, it's very important to know exactly who your neighbors are. Then go about your business like you have no idea who your neighbors are." I nodded my head at her — I knew what she meant. From the window I had guessed her to be middle-aged, but now that I was closer to her, she looked much younger.

"And don't trust anyone … ever," she added.

"Not even you?"

"Not even me," she said flatly.

We walked down the alley and turned the corner to go into our building. There was no foyer or happy manager to greet you. The mixed smell of garbage and mold hit me and was strangely comforting. It was like when you open the front door to your own home and the aroma of your life hits you. This had quickly become the essence of my life — and how fitting it was.

The stairway stood open in the middle of the building, any floor could look down and see straight to the bottom. We headed up the steps to the third floor. My companion never left my side, staying right in step with me.

"What's your dog's name?" she asked.

"Actually, it's not my dog," I said as I reached down and touched his back.

"Well he is now. You should call him Killer."

We continued up the steps in silence.

"His name is Angel," I whispered. Katie's face flashed in my mind. The way she looked when I first met her. Her beautiful smile, her laugh that made you laugh, even if you didn't want to. My heart grew heavy, as I remembered the last time I saw her. I squeezed my eyes shut and shook my head, trying to remove the memory.

We walked down the third floor hallway and as we passed a door she whispered, "This is my room. My name is Becky, by the way."

"Jen ..." She shook her head to silence me.

Leaning toward me she whispered. "It's best if people don't know you're in the hallways, it's safer that way ... always whisper."

I wanted to thank her for helping me. To tell her she didn't have to stand on that damn corner every night. There was more to life than that. But what did I know, my best friend was dead, I was on the run, and I had no idea what I was going to do. I started rubbing my forehead, trying to remove all of the hopeless thoughts. I sucked in air quickly when my hand ran over dried blood.

Then I heard Angel. The growl was deep, low, and quiet, not meant to scare something away, but to gain our attention. He stood at my door, his back end dropped a bit, ready to spring at whatever was going to come out.

Becky grabbed my arm, "We gotta go." I pulled my arm away and took a step toward my door. "If you're that stupid fine, but I'm not waiting to see what that has dog all fired up." She put her key quietly in the lock. She was right, I needed to hide; someone was in my apartment.

"Hurry, please hurry." I whispered right into her ear "They're here to kill me." Just as those words passed my lips, the key turned and the door was open.

"Angel!" I spit out, quickly he returned to my side.

I pressed both hands up against the door, straining my eyes to see through the peep hole. Becky paced back and forth behind me. She mumbled to herself. "I knew I shouldn't have gone down there. What was I thinking? I know better than this."

"SHHH," I said as I waved my hand behind me.

"Someone wants to kill you? And I'm with you, which makes me as good as dead."

I couldn't take my eyes away from the hallway. I needed to see who was looking for me. The hair on the back of my neck stood up when I realized; it wasn't who was looking for me, it was who had found me.

"Do you have any weapons?" I asked, still with my face pressed against the door.

"What?"

I turned toward her, irritated. I didn't have time for these stupid games. "Listen Becky, I know what you do for a living. Do you have anything we can defend ourselves with or not?"

She scurried over by the bed and pulled out a baseball bat. I frowned as she handed it to me – then she pulled a knife out of her purse.

"This is it? You really need to get some serious protection." She shrugged her shoulders at me.

"I'm not ready to die, are you?" She stared at me with shocked eyes, as she slowly shook her head.

"Okay, I'll let Angel out first; whoever is in there won't be expecting a dog. I'll crack him over the head with the bat; you come in with the knife only if we need it, okay?" She nodded.

I turned back to the door where Angel was still standing. I knelt down to him and rubbed behind his ear. I was putting a lot of trust in an animal who had only been "mine" for about thirty minutes. When I stood up, he put his nose right at the door; like he understood the plan. I cracked open Becky's door, and had the perfect view of my door from here.

My heart beat drowned out all other noises. I concentrated on the coolness of the bat in my hand. One hit was all I needed. I knew if I pictured it too much in my head, I wouldn't be able to go through with it. Already, my conscious told me that I couldn't do this; I wasn't a killer. But it was him or me. There was no choice – and when I told Becky that I wasn't going to die today, I meant it. Whoever came out that door would be Quinn – in my mind. A strange calmness came over me. I could do this.

As my door cracked open, I felt Angel stiffen next to me – I tightened my grip on the bat. Whoever was coming out of that door was going to die.

The door opened wider and I could see the back of him. He wore a black hoodie pulled up over his head and a gray denim jacket pulled tight across his broad shoulders. He slowly backed out of the door like he was waiting for someone to invite him back in.

I pictured Quinn's face. He was the one who had killed my friend – the one who had done unimaginable things to her. I wanted to see his face, wanted to see who had found me and for some reason, wanted my face to be the last thing he saw – for Katie.

Picturing her face one more time, I swung the door open. Angel bolted toward Katie's killer.

He didn't have time to fully turn around before Angel had a hold of the back of his upper arm. I lifted my bat, waiting for the perfect shot.

Katie was the only thing on my mind – how she looked the last time I saw her, and what she had to endure to keep me safe. I could feel the rage of her death rising in me. I was ready to make someone pay for all the fear and pain I had felt in the last few days.

The stranger yelled in agony as Angel pulled on his arm in an attempt to bring him to the ground. But something in that yell made me stop. Something made me lessen my grip and scream Angel's name.

"Angel! Come here!" Angel let go of the stranger, but paced between us, not wanting me to get any closer.

The stranger dropped to his knees and then onto his side, grabbing at his arm. I could already see the dark stain of blood coming through his coat as he moaned in pain.

I took a few steps toward him. My bat still raised and Angel between us.

"Who are you?" I yelled, but he didn't respond. I moved a little closer and lowered my voice. "Tell me who you are or I swear I will turn you into a dog toy."

Angel growled and the floor made a terrible creaking sound as I walked a few steps closer.

He slowly rolled over into a sitting position and the hood fell from his face. Tears streamed down his cheeks and I felt my head start to spin as he looked at me.

"They killed her, Jenna. They killed my Katie."

"Marcus?"

>CHAPTER TWENTY-SIX<

"We have to get inside." I grabbed him by his other arm and helped him to his feet. He trembled against me. I used my foot to push the door open further and shuffled him into the apartment, steadying him on the wall. He gasped over and over for air, trying to calm himself.

"They killed her, Jenna."

"Come on." I grabbed the chair and moved it over by the sink, helping him lower himself onto it. He grabbed at me, desperate for something.

"I know." I kept my eyes down. I couldn't let him see her the way she was when I had seen her last. I was afraid that if I looked at him, he would somehow be able to see my memory of her. He was already broken – if he saw what I saw, he would crumble.

"Stay here. I'll be right back."

The hallway was empty. I inched along the wall but kept my eyes toward the stairwell. I tapped Becky's door with the end of the bat and waited. Nothing. I tried the door but it was locked. I couldn't blame her for not wanting anything to do with me; I had known her for fifteen minutes and asked her to stab someone.

Slowly I backed into my apartment and closed the door.

Marcus sat in the chair, his head hanging down. I swallowed to fight off the sob that had a tight grip on my throat. I could feel his terror and disbelief – I knew it well.

"I'm going to get your arm cleaned up. We need to make sure you don't need stitches." The only thing I could do right now was avoid. He'd want to know all the details, and I'd have to tell him. But right now I had to do something other than think about Katie.

The old pipes moaned when I turned on the water to fill the sink. "Marcus," I said as I crouched down and touched his leg, "I'm going to clean up your arm."

He turned his head, looked down at me and put his hand over mine. The moment our eyes met, the weight of his heartbreak hit me and I fell forward onto my knees. His eyes begged me to tell him it wasn't true

– his hand tightened around mine, because he knew it was. He hung his head when he saw the tears falling down my cheeks. We cried together for the one person who held both our hearts.

~~~

I helped him take off his jacket and hoodie. He sat motionless while I cleaned the bite wounds. They were deep and oozing; he never made a sound. There was no physical pain that could overpower what his heart was feeling right now.

I tied a ripped towel around the deepest wounds and began to wash the blood out of the rest of them.

"How did you find this place?" I worried if Marcus knew where this place was, maybe some of the other Brothers knew as well.

"I followed Ryan here one day. I'd noticed he would disappear for hours at a time, and I wanted to make sure he wasn't doing anything that would get him into trouble." Angel, who had been sleeping at Marcus's feet, lifted his head as Marcus slowly stood. "Whose dog is that, Jenna?" Angel stood up, stretched and trotted over to the bed, jumping onto it and making himself comfortable.

"Mine, I guess." Marcus just shook his head. He walked over to the window and looked out through the curtains into the dusk of the night. "How did you get in here?"

"The door was open. I was scared of what I'd find in here – not exactly a neighborhood where doors are left open." In the midst of my panic attack, after hearing about Katie, I'd run out without even shutting the door. I rolled my eyes at my stupidity.

The quietness of the room seemed heavy. I searched for the answers to the questions that he hadn't even asked yet, but I was sure were coming.

"Why are you here, Jenna?" He asked, as he turned to face into the room. I sat on the bed and began petting Angel. My mind had so many thoughts running through it, making it impossible for me to speak. "What happened to Katie?"

I understood I was going to have to tell him everything that happened. What I couldn't figure out, was how to handle the aftermath of telling him the truth. The things I need to tell him would be like a sledgehammer slamming into his chest. I didn't know how to soften it. So I decided to start at the beginning. "Marcus, this is what I know..."

But before I could get anything out, it was happening again; the deep, low, growl I would trust my life with Angel had lifted his head, staring at the door. My stomach twisted as my heart instantly started to race. I motioned to Marcus to be quiet and he quickly positioned himself with his back against the same wall as the door, giving him the advantage of being behind the door when it opened. I moved off the bed, grabbed the bat I'd propped against the door earlier and slid next to Marcus.

Angel effortlessly moved off the bed and stood a few feet back from the door. The hair on the back of his neck was standing straight up and he had dropped his hind quarters a few inches in preparation to leap at whatever was coming through the door.

Marcus looked down at me and whispered, "Let Angel start and I'll grab him – you run." I shook my head; there was no way I was leaving him here. In my mind I was back in my dorm room, begging Katie to go with us.

"No. No, I won't leave you." I couldn't allow one more person I cared for to die fighting for me. If anyone would die tonight, it would be me, fighting to keep Marcus alive.

"Jenna, listen to me," he was moving his eyes back and forth wildly from the door to me. "It will do no good for both of us to die in here. The only chance we have is for you to run across the street and call for help. No matter what you hear, just keep running until you get to that store. Do you understand me?" Angel growled again, bringing our attention back to the door. "That's the only way we both live."

I handed him the bat.

The door knob turned slowly first, and someone tried to lean on the door. It creaked as the locked deadbolt held its place. I tried to swallow but my throat had gone completely dry. I was staring at the knob and trying to listen to every small movement made on the other side of the door, but all I could hear was the pounding of my own heartbeat in my head. Every muscle tensed, but I tried to remain as level-headed as possible.

There was a clinking on the other side of the door. Something was trying to slide into the lock.

"He's picking the lock." I panicked. "He's going to get in." Marcus put his finger to his lips, his eyes pleading with me to be quiet.

I moved directly in front of the door. "Who's there?" The door cracked open and I sucked in my breath.

"Jenna?"

I swung the door open and threw myself at Ryan, he examined my face as I tried to hug him.

"What happened to your face?" I walked backwards into the room, refusing to let go of him. "Jenna, tell me, what happened?"

I wanted to tell him about Katie, and what happened with Becky and Marcus, but I couldn't speak. A thousand emotions swirled in my head but I couldn't form a single word. Tears flooded from my eyes. I grabbed at him, like he was my last breath, holding him as close as I could. His strong arms held me up, while I buried my face in his chest, needing his presence. I knew it didn't make any of this go away, but still, it was all I wanted – to be close to him. He would fix this somehow.

Ryan spun around quickly, as the door slammed behind us; Marcus spoke, "I left her with you, and you said you would protect her. Now, who the hell is going to tell me what happened to Katie?"

CHAPTER TWENTEY-SEVEN

"I asked you a question, brother." Marcus said calmly, but the edge of anger in his voice made it clear he was not asking. Something had changed in him since Ryan had stepped into the apartment. There was a coldness that wasn't there before. He wasn't looking for answers – he wanted to place blame.

Ryan slowly stretched one hand out toward his brother. I wasn't sure if it was a gesture of peace or his attempt to keep some distance between them. "Marcus, please ... calm down and we can talk about it."

Ryan's words set off a firestorm inside of Marcus that played out on his face. He grimaced as if the words had caused him physical pain. The electricity between the two brothers shot out and twisted in the room, making my heart jump into overdrive.

Marcus's red-rimmed eyes bore into his brother, demanding the answers he really didn't want to hear – but needed to know.

Ryan's outstretched hand shook slightly as he carefully stepped in front of me. I slid behind him, leaning into his back and hiding my face from Marcus. Reaching down, I expected to find Angel at my side, but he wasn't there. I made a quick scan of the room, turning frantically to look in all the corners, but he was gone … probably ran out when the door was opened. My heart tore open with anxiety at the thought of being without him. I closed my eyes and tried to calm myself.

"Don't you tell me to calm down. My fucking girlfriend is dead – murdered – and you're going to tell me to calm down?"

Marcus slammed the bat against the kitchen chair, sending it sliding it across the floor toward us. Ryan caught it, slowly setting it up-right next to him, never taking his eyes off of his brother.

"Don't tell me to calm down!" he screamed again. "Tell me exactly what you know."

"That's what we're trying to…"

"Stop … just stop. I don't want the bullshit answer." Marcus ran his free hand quickly through his hair. "I want to know exactly what you know about all of it, and I'm only going to give you one chance to tell me the truth, Ryan."

There was a pause in the conversation as their eyes locked. Something passed between them, some sort of silent communication that confused me.

"I tried to take her, I really did, but she wouldn't let me," Ryan pleaded.

Marcus tilted his head, looking at him with suspicious eyes. "What do you mean she wouldn't let you? Did you ask her?"

Something twisted in my gut as the scene played out in my mind. I couldn't remember – did he try to get her to come with us? The whole scene was clouded with fear; all I remembered him saying was that we would be back. Why wouldn't he have made her go?

I took a step away from him, staring at his back while trying to replay that horrible night. My mind raced, trying to remember the details, while at the same time trying to block the image of Katie's bruised and battered face. It was too much; I just couldn't see it again.

Ryan glanced over his shoulder quickly as he felt the distance between us – our eyes met. My shoulders shook and I covered my mouth with my hand.

"Of course, I tried. All she was worried about was that I get Jenna out of there. So that's what I did." I started to slowly shake my head, knowing he never tried to get her to go.

He turned back to his brother, his voice was low. "I didn't know they were going to hurt her."

Marcus started to pace, never taking his eyes from Ryan. A sarcastic laugh filled the room. Suddenly he threw his arm in the air, pointing a finger right at Ryan.

"But what *do* you know Ryan? That's the real question isn't it?"

My heart had been paralyzed by what was happening in front of me, but my mind knew instinctively that this was not going to end well. I needed to leave … Now!

I moved slowly, trying to avoid attention, until the back of my legs hit the bed. Bile began to rise in my throat as I realized I was trapped. There was one door and both Ryan and Marcus were between me and my only hope of escape. My heart beat hard in my neck and pounded in my ears. A shaking started at my core and quickly spread throughout my whole body – I couldn't contain it. Oh God, not now. I had to keep myself together.

My eyes darted back and forth from Ryan to Marcus, oversensitive to every little move either of them made. Every breath, every twisted expression, every flex and release of fists, felt like fingernails on a chalkboard to my nerves. The tension between them was so overwhelming it consumed me.

Ryan watched his brother out of the corner of his eye, not looking directly at him, but never letting him out of his sight.

Marcus suddenly stopped. His face changed from anger to pure hatred – it made me cringe. I held my breath waiting for him to make his move.

When he spoke again, the words dripped from his mouth like he couldn't stand the taste of them. "I stopped by the house today, Ryan."

Ryan didn't move. Not even a flinch. Marcus continued, taunting Ryan with his words.

"I went to the basement."

An excruciating silence swirled around the three of us. I mentally begged one of them to talk, to break this unbearable weight in the room. Finally Ryan spoke; his tone was low and controlled, "Why?"

Marcus spat out a sound of disgust like he couldn't believe Ryan had the nerve to ask him that. His eyes fell to the floor for only a second while he ran his hand over his face. Ryan motioned for me and I instinctively stepped away from the bed.

The bat in Marcus's hands rose quickly in Ryan's direction.

"Don't move, Jenna," he growled. Anxiety surged through my veins, leaving my face burning, but the rest of me ice cold. An unfamiliar emotion crossed Marcus's face. He nodded his head slightly at me and I realized he wasn't threatening me, he thought he was protecting me. He was trying to keep me away from Ryan.

Once he was sure I wasn't going to move, he resumed his pacing. This time it was a more leisurely pace, almost arrogant. His lips slowly turned up in a small smirk. Oh my God, what did he know?

I covered my eyes with my hands willing myself to calm down. I wouldn't pass out ... I won't pass out. His expression, I couldn't take it. He knew something, but he was waiting for something from Ryan to put it all together.

"Why did you go to the house, Marcus?" Ryan asked again.

"When you're looking for clues about who murdered the only person you've ever loved, and you have a pretty good idea who that someone is – you start in the dark places. The places you aren't allowed to go. Seemed like the obvious choice."

"No, no, no," I whispered shaking my head back and forth. I closed my eyes tightly and covered my ears, trying to drown out everything going on in this room. But I couldn't hide; there was nowhere to go, no way to be invisible in all of this. I felt like I was standing in the middle of an ice-covered lake with cracks all around, unable to move because of the damage – so you just wait until it's your turn to fall in and drown.

"What did you find?" I yelled, dropping my hands from my face, staring at Marcus. Ryan's eyes darted to mine and then back to his brother's.

Ignoring my outburst, Ryan continued, "Marcus, you really have no idea what you've gotten yourself into."

"No brother, it seems you don't know what you've gotten *yourself* into, or maybe you do."

"What are the two of you talking about?" I demanded. Ryan held up his hand, wanting me to stop talking. But this game they were playing was dangerous. It needed to end now before someone did something that couldn't be taken back.

Marcus backed over to the table and reached into his pocket, pulling out several pieces of paper and holding them in the air like he was trying to make a point.

"I'm talking about this, Jenna. I found them in a locked cabinet in the basement of the house." He laid them on the table.

Ryan started growling as he shook his head back and forth. His chest rose quickly with each breath, anger radiating off of him in waves. I was terrified by the way his jaw flexed as he ground his teeth. His eyes darted back and forth between Marcus and me.

Finally he broke, "Jesus, Marcus, I know. I know you were there okay? They all know you were there. You don't need to do this. Just let me explain." His voice was softer than before, almost pleading.

Marcus didn't take his eyes from Ryan, but motioned for me to come over to the table, "Jenna, I found these in a file with your name on it."

"Stop!" Ryan's harsh voice was back and it bounced off the walls as he rushed toward his brother. "They know you have that – you just signed your death certificate. They will kill all of us, don't you understand?"

Marcus rushed his brother, and they stood eye to eye ... toe to toe. Marcus spoke a strained whisper through his clenched teeth, "I died when you let them kill Katie. I will never stop." He looked in my direction, "Jenna, you need to ..."

Before I could move, Ryan grabbed the chair sitting beside him and brought it around, connecting with the side of Marcus's head. I screamed as I watched Marcus fall to the floor. He lay motionless. I rushed to him, lifting his head onto my knees and feeling for a pulse. It was faint.

"Are you crazy?" I screamed.

Ryan mumbled quickly under his breath like a maniac, running his hands through his hair over and over. He paced back and forth until he finally walked over to the television and pulled the cord from it. He stormed toward me and I scrambled backwards on the floor to get away from him. "Don't you move," he growled at me.

He roughly lifted Marcus, putting him on the bed and tying him to the frame. I saw an opportunity, so I jumped up and grabbed the pieces of paper from the table.

His voice was low and threatening, "Don't read that, Jenna." But I continued. A small gasp escaped from my mouth as I fought the reality trying to slam down on me.

His eyes were dark and his face showed no emotion as he stood next to the bed. I looked back down at the papers in my hands, scanning them as quickly as I could.

"What is this?" I couldn't look at him – scared of the pain it would cause me to see him in a different way. He was all I had left, my second chance, my escape. But suddenly I realized, nothing could be farther from the truth. He'd never planned to be my escape; he planned to be my ending.

The papers I held in my hand proved that.

Over and over I read the name that was about to change everything I perceived to be good and safe. I struggled to contain the fear buried deep inside of me since childhood; but it poured out into this small, dungeon – like room – drowning me, closing in all around me, weighing heavily on my chest.

"Don't be afraid," he whispered moving close enough to me that I could feel the heat radiating off his body. He leaned into me slowly, like a lover wanting to gain access. When his chest touched my shoulder, I closed my eyes and leaned into him. Welcoming his closeness, praying he had an answer that would make this entire mess ok somehow. My heart had not yet realized – he was my biggest threat.

"What. Is. This?" I asked once more. His two word answer shattered my already broken world.

"The list."

Shaking my head in disbelief I asked slowly, "Of what?"

"The people who are assigned to you." He let out a long breath, while checking that his brother was still not moving.

I didn't want to hear anymore – he continued anyway. "My brother didn't know any of this until now. He's a true First year in the house, so he knew nothing of the business. I, on the other hand, have had a year of 'special training'." He smiled at me, causing my skin to crawl.

"I am your Keeper Jenna. I've been assigned to keep you safe since you were chosen."

"Chosen?"

"Yes, you were identified as a candidate before you even started school. Cale is your Sponsor, I am your Keeper, and Quinn ..." his eyes fell briefly to the floor but he quickly recovered, meeting my eyes once more, although he couldn't hide the crack in his voice, "Quinn is your trainer."

The visions of Katie slammed back into me and I grabbed at my temples like someone was stabbing me. My vision tilted and I stumbled.

"What have you done? Oh, my God Ryan, what have you done?"

The rational side of me eyed the door, trying to figure out how to get past him. The emotional side was still determined to trust him. The internal struggle kept me from reacting. He leaned down and turned my face up to his, holding my chin softly. His eyes filled with tears as they darted back and forth between mine.

But I knew I couldn't show weakness. If I was going to make it out alive, I was going to have to fight.

"Don't be afraid, it'll be harder on both of us."

He was no longer my Ryan, and the reality that he never really was quickly set in causing a tornado of emotions inside my chest.

I watched as his eyes moved over to Marcus on the bed. A terrifying calmness came over him as his arms fell to his sides. I knew with every cell in my body that he was going to hurt me. Tears began to run down my face.

"You stay away from me," I whispered as I backed away from him.

"You can scream all you want to, no one in this neighborhood is going to help you."

"No, no … you're one of them? Why? Why would you do this?" His stare burned into me.

"I need you to …"

"To what? Let you kill me without causing you too much trouble? You tricked me and used me. You told me you loved me and promised to protect me. I am not going down like this. I will not let you be the one who does this to me. I hate you!" The words were spilling out of me.

I grabbed for the bat lying on the floor. With one quick movement he came at me while kicking the bat across the room. We both froze, staring into each other's eyes.

I could see the door behind him and knew it was my only hope. He was going to have to kill me to contain me. He lunged and grabbed me around the shoulders. I twisted and fought against his hold.

"Stop fighting me and let me explain."

"Explain what? How you killed Katie? How you're probably going to kill your own brother and how I'm next?"

I fought with every ounce of energy I had — swinging, hitting and screaming. I reached up and dug my fingernails into his cheek as hard as I could. He grabbed my hands, holding them to my sides as blood trickled down his face.

"I know you can't understand this now, but I promise this is for your own good."

He twisted me around; pulling my back against his chest as he tightly gripped me around the neck with his thick forearm. His mouth hovered above my ear as his grip tightened, restricting my air flow. He whispered, "All you had to do was shut up and listen, but you never listen to me. I'm sorry, Jenna but I have to do this. I don't want to, but you gave me no choice." And his grip tightened once again.

"Please," I gasped "Don't".

"It's too late for begging, we're out of time." He growled.

I sputtered and gasped, trying to get any small amount of oxygen I could. He leaned closer to my ear and kissed it gently as he whispered, "I do love you, never forget that." Then he tightened his hold around my neck … Katie's face was the last thing I saw.

>CHAPTER TWENTY-EIGHT<

Waking up from something like that is a slow process. My head pounded as every beat of my heart pulsed behind my eyelids. My body felt weightless but I ached everywhere. I choked trying to clear my throat. It burned and felt like I was swallowing razor blades. I gagged again, my tongue so dry it stuck to the roof of my mouth. I turned my head to the side and something ran down the side of my cheek. I reached up slowly to wipe my mouth.

I was restrained – I pulled again, nothing. I tried to move my leg, but it too was restrained.

Panic surged and tears began streaming down the sides of my face. I blinked rapidly, trying to recognize something, anything to tell me where I was. I pulled and pulled against whatever was tied around my hands and feet. But with every movement came searing pain, where the bonds cut deeper into my skin, the fresh wounds oozing and sliding under the straps.

My heart pounded against my chest as muffled voices drifted into the room. I tried to roll to the side, lifting my shoulders as much as I could. My hands throbbed as I pulled on them, frantically scanning the room. This was a bedroom and I was tied to the bed. I laid my head back down, letting the memories creep back in. Ryan was the reason I was here. I knew what was going to happen to me, and so did he.

Cale's voice carried above all the others and it paralyzed me as he summoned Quinn. "She's awake, go calm her down."

My blood turned to ice. Not Quinn...please not him. Ryan spoke next, "I could've killed her, but I didn't know if you wanted her alive. Do you want me to go in and finish her off?"

I threw my head back against the mattress over and over, fighting the splintering of my heart, as tears blurred my vision. I wanted to be furious, I wanted to hate ... but I couldn't. How could he be talking about killing me with the same voice he had promised to protect me with? The same voice he'd said he loved me with. I was going to die today ... there was no doubt about that. But I was going to choose how I died. I wouldn't plead or cry; they would never get that from me again.

Cale's voice was strained and to the point, "No. You had your chance – Quinn will take care of it."

I closed my eyes and begged death upon me. I willed my heart to stop, my breathing to cease. I was terrified of the pain I knew they had planned for me, but more than that, I didn't want to give them the satisfaction of taking one more thing that belonged to me. If this was really the end of my life, I wanted to be the one who was in charge of it. I wanted them to feel disappointment that they were not the ones to cause my final breath.

The door cracked open; I looked over, hoping whoever was coming in next, was here to help me. I really didn't know who I expected my savior to be – there was no one left to come for me. I was completely alone. Katie is dead, Marcus probably is too, and Ryan … well, he's as good as dead to me now. Although, I held out hope for one second – I had to, because I knew without a doubt, that if the door closed behind Quinn, it would be the same as signing my horrific and painful death certificate.

Cale came in first. Something triggered inside of me and I started fighting against the bonds again. He flashed a large smile and chuckled, "Still fighting, Jenna? Just like the first time we met, fighting then and fighting even now."

I tried to scream but my throat closed with the strain and I fell back against the bed, gagging and coughing.

"You really are stupid aren't you? Fight all you want – you aren't getting out of those," he leaned toward me and whispered, "I'm a bit of an expert when it comes to restraints." He walked to the end of the bed and stood there shaking his head at me. "Truthfully, I expected nothing less from you, fighting until the very end. If I had to be honest, it's somewhat admirable – and irritating as fuck at the same time."

The door opened once more and Quinn stood in the doorway. I stilled as all the blood drained from me. His eyes roamed over me and flashed with lust. He was going to hurt me so badly, and he was looking forward to it.

Ryan stood motionless in the hallway behind Quinn. His eyes met mine, but his face showed no emotion. I wanted to call out to him. I wanted to believe that he was going to save me, until the memory of what he'd done came rushing back to me. I realized all over again why I was here – he was the reason. He brought me here, and handed me over to these monsters to dole out whatever twisted justice they felt I deserved. I turned away from him, closed my eyes tightly and tears ran down each side of my face. He wouldn't save me. No one would come for me. No one ever saved me. My body trembled as I realized these were my last few moments alive. Katie's smiling face, my mom, and memories of Ryan holding me flashed through my mind.

A sob surfaced and my chest involuntarily rose off the mattress as I tried to fight it. I rolled my head back and forth on the mattress, trying to erase any good memories I had of him. All along he'd used me to improve his position in the house. All this time I was nothing more than a pawn in his well thought out plan. If he kept me hidden while everyone else looked for me, he could deliver me at the right time, when it benefited him the most.

Quinn stood quietly over by the door, while Cale came to the side of the bed and bent down so he was eye level with me. He took a long, deep breath and then let it out.

"You're such a disappointment, Jenna. I thought you were smarter than this – I really did." He stood and started pacing next to the bed. "I knew you would figure this all out eventually, but I really believed you would see the positive side of it."

He stopped and stared down at me. When he spoke again, his voice was strained, "I could've given you more than you ever dreamed of. Look at you and your pathetic, little life." His voice was getting louder and louder, "I would've given you money, education, travel. With your looks, you would've held the company of the most powerful men all over the world."

I felt the sobs begin again, but I pressed my lips together tightly. I would not give him the satisfaction of even one more tear.

"But you had to ruin, didn't you?" he growled.

I lifted my chin in defiance and smirked.

Pain suddenly shot through my head; I could feel the blood dripping from the corner of my eye before I even knew he'd hit me. He leaned over me, his face right above mine. Spit flew from between his teeth as he hissed, "You almost ruined everything for me. You think some little tramp like you could bring me down?"

I stared right back at him. There were things I wanted to know, things I had a right to know and this was my last chance.

"Katie," I whispered.

He smiled down at me, his eyes slowly moving down my face to my mouth. He ran a finger down the side of my cheek and then stood abruptly.

"Okay … you want to know about your friend, I understand that. It really is a shame someone with Marcus's bloodline and potential would fall in love with trash like Katie." He paused and then waved his hand in the air, "Anyway … after Ryan and I got into that fight at the party, Marcus was sent off by the elders to tell their father how badly Ryan was screwing up. It was the right thing to do, and when Ryan came to see me that night while you were sleeping in my bedroom, I set him straight. You see, for a second, Ryan had fallen under your spell. I understood that, so I gave him the benefit of the doubt when he came back begging my forgiveness. It was a rookie mistake; we've all had it happen. It's the pitfall of having to work with beautiful, captivating women."

"By the time Ryan got his head on straight, you were already gone and he had a job to do."

"We had patrols out looking for you. Quinn stopped by your room and found Katie. As you can imagine, she was very upset and demanding. She freaked out on him and started making accusations against me and The Brotherhood. Some were a little too close to the truth, so Quinn did what he had to do."

Cale glanced over at Quinn and he nodded in agreement. "Quinn tells me she really wasn't Brotherhood quality anyway. I'm sure he could've taught her what she needed to learn, but we prefer the naturals, you see, it's always better to have employees you needn't spend a lot of time training. They can begin earning income right away. But she was never going to be the same, so we killed her — because we couldn't find you. It was a message really, to make sure you understood how serious we were about getting you back."

My gut twisted and I tried to curl into a ball. But the restraints prevented it. So I lifted my head off the bed as far as I could, and rolled as far up onto my side as possible. I squirmed with the pain of knowing what he was saying was true; it was my fault that Katie was dead.

He continued to walk back and forth at the bottom of the bed. "Now you on the other hand, you had a spark. I knew you weren't going to be bought. All the bloodlines could see that when they met you at your interview. But it was okay. It made you more of a challenge; made things look good for me once I got you to agree to be sponsored." He checked his watch and took in an exaggerated breath.

"That is why I sent Ryan after you. He has, well … special training and I was hoping you could be convinced. But then Katie happened and you just refused to be caught – such a shame."

His laugh was cold and made me shiver.

"The only good thing about this is you can be completely erased." He checked his watch again and then looked at me with a strange smile. "Your mom should already be dead by now."

A rush of emotion hit me like a tidal wave, washing over my body and filling me with a desire to fight. I twisted my body, ignoring the stabbing pain shooting up my arms.

"No," I wanted to cry out in disbelief, but it came out in a choking sound. His fist connected with my jaw and I faded out for just a second, but nothing could dull the kind of pain I was feeling inside of me. Blood ran from the corner of my mouth and I did nothing to try and stop it.

"Right about now, the chief of police of your shitty, little home town, is getting a complete confession from you by e-mail." My eyes widened as my mind spun to understand what he was saying.

"School was just too much for you, Jenna," his voice was laced with a sarcastically sympathetic tone.

"The fact that you hadn't gotten along with Katie and constantly felt inferior to her only intensified your feelings of inadequacy. You have such low self-esteem." He smiled at me and shook his head like he felt sorry for me. "And then, when she started her romance with a boy from the prestigious Brotherhood house, the jealousy was just too much for you. You realized no matter how much schooling you got, or how far away you moved, you would always be that invisible, small-town, little piece of white-trash whore you always were."

I shook my head no as the image of what he was saying started to play out in my head. "After you killed Katie, you went to confess to your mom. You were hoping she could somehow redeem herself for all the shitty parenting, but when you saw her, all those years of abuse that she had allowed to happen to you, well ... you snapped. And when she told you that you needed to turn yourself in, you killed her too. They'll find a gun with your prints all over it, along with your cell phone that has pictures of both crime scenes."

My whole body shook, my heart filled with so much pain. I arched my back off the bed to try and fight it – silently screaming. I pictured my mom, so trusting, and excited for my "opportunity". All those years she had only wanted love. She had believed every promise ever told to her, and all she had wanted was for our lives to be better. Everyone had left her too. It wasn't only me that no one had ever come for – it was her as well. I pictured the last minutes of her life and knew no one was coming for her this time either.

Something split open inside of me. That was it — I was officially dead. Not physically, but now it didn't matter what they had planned. I deserved every bit of suffering that was coming my way. He grabbed my chin and I whined as the pain shot up my jaw.

"That's right, just one more person whose death is your responsibility. But who will care about a loser like her and her worthless daughter? No one! And once they find your body, they will close the case. I will, of course, be heartbroken for the girl who I tried to save, but didn't reach soon enough. It really couldn't be more perfect."

He started pacing again and then quickly turned on his heels and walked directly at me. I didn't know that if you get hit hard enough, it doesn't actually hurt. It's more of a noise echoing in your head until the aftershock — when your body tries to hold onto life — that's when the pain starts. The room started to spin, darkness taking over. I inhaled deeply, welcoming it.

"Wake up!" he shook me by the shoulders. "You aren't getting off that easy. I want you to hear this before you die." His face was right next to mine and I struggled as my vision faded in and out.

"I won; there is no one that can take me down. The only thing women are good for is to make The Brotherhood money, or have my sons so I can train them to make more money. I want you to know that was all you were worth, and you couldn't even get that right – and because of that, everyone that ever loved you is dead."

He stood up straight and turned toward the door, speaking to Quinn as he passed him. "Get rid of her. I don't want to see or hear of her again." He grabbed for the handle of the door then stopped. "And Quinn, I don't care what you do to her before she's dead; just make sure it's worth all this chasing."

>CHAPTER TWENTY-NINE<

"Jenna, Jenna, Jenna," Quinn said slowly as he reached down and locked the door.

Shaking his head, he walked toward the bed. "I was really looking forward to training you."

He motioned between the two of us, and in a teasing voice, he said, "This could have been so much more pleasant, but now..." he laughed and stretched his arms out in front of him, bowing slightly to me like he was delivering a gift, "... it won't be pleasant at all.

He grabbed my face, squeezing so hard I could feel the inside of my cheek start to bleed. I grimaced, trying to shake out of his hold, but he held on tighter.

"I don't know what's so special about you. We've had much better looking, much better built girls then you." He trailed the fingers of his free hand down my torso slowly, making me shudder when he reached the top of my jeans, he grabbed the waistband and pulled – I gasped.

"I was surprised when Cale sponsored you, but he said he saw something – and the Fathers agreed." His face was so close to me I could feel his breath, I struggled to move away from him, but he held my face still as he hissed, "What do I know, I'm only the trainer."

He leaned into me and pressed his mouth against mine, like some type of ritualistic tasting of the prey. When he pulled away, my blood was smeared on his lips. He smiled and licked them clean.

All I could do was stare at him. His would be the last face I would ever see, the last voice I would ever hear. There was still a small part of me that wanted to scream and fight him, but I realized I didn't have the desire to get away. Where would I go if I did? There was nowhere ... and no one. So I closed my eyes and prepared to die.

A heavy-handed knock broke through the darkness of the room. I tried to turn my head, but he kept my chin squeezed tightly in his powerful hand; although he was looking and seemed concerned.

He didn't make a move toward the door, only stared in that direction. I watched him as suspicion crossed his face.

Another knock; this one was shorter but just as heavy. Whoever was on the other side was getting impatient.

My heart started racing. I watched him as he slowly stood. I could almost sense fear around him, and it made me even more terrified. At the last second, he looked down at me and growled, "Don't make a sound." I nodded quickly at him, my already messed up emotions seemed to believe he would protect me from the person on the other side of that door. If he was scared – I was scared. Maybe he would protect me.

He crossed the room silently. When he reached the door, he placed both hands on it, leaned in and pressed his ear against it. There was no noise coming from the other side.

He slowly reached for the handle with one hand, his fingertips hovering over the lock. Bile rose and I started gagging on the blood that ran down the back of my throat – I closed my eyes as tightly as I could. I knew I was making noises; Quinn wouldn't like that. So I fought to keep the stomach fluids from coming up. Even with my eyes closed, the room spun. My nerve cells were on fire, my body hypersensitive to every place it touched the sheets. A shiver ran down my back and it felt like millions of needles piercing my skin.

I jumped at the sound of the lock clicking. The room was suddenly filled with the noises of a struggle;

grunting, heavy breathing, skin slapping against skin —
fists meeting bone over and over.

"She's mine," Quinn struggled to get out.
Whoever was trying to get to me was fighting hard for
the privilege to be the one to end my life. They
wrestled around on the floor next to my bed; I
could've just opened my eyes and looked, but I wasn't
brave enough. Watching Quinn beat someone to death
was not something I wanted to do. I kept my eyes
closed — it felt better this way.

My head began to float and my body relaxed; I
took a deep breath. My face fell slack, the pain was
gone. I quietly cheered for Quinn — it sounded like he
had the upper hand. It didn't matter who won this
battle, because I was dead for sure. The award for the
winner was getting to kill me. But I'd already made
peace with it being Quinn — I wanted it to be him, it
should be him.

I heard gasping and gurgling noises as someone
kicked the bed. Someone struggled for breath. It was
over as quickly as it had started. The only sound left
was one person trying to catch his breath.

I didn't know who it was and I was too afraid to
open my eyes. I decided it would be best not to look
my killer in the face. I turned my head away from the
door and squeezed my eyes shut even tighter. I waited
for a blow to my body or the type of invasion Quinn
had planned for me. I wasn't tense … I felt relaxed and
accepting of my fate.

My arms fell onto the bed as the bonds were cut … and next, the ties on my feet were gone. I braced myself as someone helped me to sit up. I wanted to grab onto this person but was so weak I couldn't move. I thought about opening my eyes as the small part of me that was still fighting vied for control inside of me, but the struggle was almost too much as my eyelids fluttered. I always thought physical defeat would be the worst … I was wrong. Physically I was okay, but my mind had been prepared for death, and I couldn't fight that.

"Jenna, it's me, Marcus, open your eyes." I felt the coolness of water slip over my lips and onto my legs. I grabbed at the bottle, desperately trying to drink it all. I coughed and choked as water spilled out over the corners of my mouth when my throat refused it.

"Slowly, drink it slowly." He whispered. "I'll explain everything, but let me get you out of here first – hold on to me."

The possibility of making it out of this room alive gave me the energy to reach up and hold onto him around the neck as he slipped his arms under my knees.

Marcus moved swiftly, his route obviously planned out. I did my job by holding onto him and keeping my eyes closed. I pressed my face against his chest and tried to remain calm. I trusted him, because I had no one else.

I think physically I could run, but if he had put me down, emotionally I would've crumbled. Without a doubt, I would've stood in one place, unable to move, cried and screamed – begging myself to wake up from this horrible nightmare that had become my life. Instead, I held on.

We weaved in and out of rooms, ducking into dark places and waiting until we could move again. His heartbeat pounded loudly in my ear as he held me. Finally stopping, he spoke softly between his rapid breaths.

"Jenna, do you think you can stand?"

I nodded my head and he lowered me onto my feet. I let go of him and, surprising both of us, held my own weight. He handed me a bottle of water. I took a small drink – it went down this time and seemed to help the burning.

We were in the kitchen. I laid my wrists onto the granite counter, welcoming the cooling effect it had on my wounds. I slowly spread my fingers out, fighting the tingling feeling as the blood flow returned.

Marcus took my face softly, a hand on each cheek, careful not to hurt me. Our eyes connected and his desperation passed to me. The sensation made me reach up and hold onto each of his wrists to steady myself. We stood there for several quiet seconds as his anxiety swirled around both of us. He was not convinced we would make it out alive … neither was I.

I knew this may be the last time I ever felt kindness in a touch so I leaned into him, resting my forehead on his. I wanted him to know how thankful I was that someone had finally come for me.

He inhaled deeply and spoke to me in a whisper, "Okay, Jenna listen to me – I only have time to tell you this once. Do you think you can run?" He pointed to a service door in the darkened corner of the kitchen.

I couldn't answer him, but suddenly all my energy was transferred to that door. Freedom was on the other side and I couldn't understand what we were doing just standing here. I started pushing against him, the excitement of freedom flooding through me.

"Wait," he said, pulling me to him, trying to get me to focus back on him. I looked up at him, shaking my head and pushing against his chest. Tears streamed down my face as I fought to get to the door.

"There's an alarm. Once we go out that door, everyone will know you've escaped."

I stopped, motionless as his words sunk in. I wasn't as close to freedom as I thought, it was complicated. Everything was always complicated. Nothing is ever as it seems. I leaned back into him.

"I have a car parked a few blocks away, but I can't carry you and get to the car before someone finds us. Do you understand?"

I nodded again, swallowing and wincing against the burning.

"When we go through this door, I need you to run as fast as you can to the library – don't go anywhere else. My car is parked in the opposite direction. I'm hoping to confuse them by splitting up. I will pick you up; hide next to the building, on the side closest to the dorms, if you get there before me."

"Then what?" I whispered, grabbing my throat as the words came out.

He stilled, staring down at me as his eyes roamed over my broken face. He pushed a piece of hair out of my face and tucked it behind my ear. He knew what I was asking. Once we got out of here, where would we go? The police? According to Ryan, most of them were on The Brotherhood payroll and the others would already have me pegged as a killer. The school? They had to be working with The Brotherhood; how else would they have been able to get all my financial and personal information? My mom was dead and his dad was part of The Brotherhood – we had nowhere safe to go.

He leaned down and kissed my forehead quickly, then pulled me to his chest. I gripped him around the waist and held tightly, realizing we had no 'then what'. Only this moment – nothing was promised after this.

He released me and led me to the door. "Are you ready?"

I nodded, tears filling my eyes again.

"One more thing, if I don't come in 30 minutes, go back to the apartment. I left some things there for you that you will need. Don't look for me." And just like that, he pushed open the heavy door.

It was nighttime and there was a steady drizzle of cold rain falling down. I turned my face to the sky and welcomed the cleansing; I wanted everything that had happened in the last week to be washed away.

"Run!" he whispered and pushed away from me.

I stood, paralyzed, trying to get my bearings. I looked quickly to my right, there was a row of dumpsters, and past them the alley ran straight into a main street. I could see headlights from the heavy traffic. I blinked away the rain, trying to make a decision.

Adrenalin flooded my system. My heart started pumping at a crazy pace in anticipation of being chased. I looked from one end of the dirty alley to the other. I knew it was the quickest way to the library, but I couldn't just run along the main street, so I hurried in the opposite direction, surprised at how alive I felt. I guess my desire to live outweighed any physical pain I was feeling. I stopped by the corner of the house, not wanting to rush out from behind any false sense of security it was giving me.

Marcus was gone; I couldn't see him anywhere. I said a quick prayer that no matter what happened to me, he would be spared.

I heard all sorts of commotion coming from inside the house. The alarm must be going off and I was standing here just waiting to be caught again.

I took off into the darkness, finding a line of bushes at the edge of The Brotherhood property and laid down under their cover. I realized I would have to run across the road. I was so weak; I was gasping for air and trying to get my head to stop spinning when I heard him.

Cale walked along the sidewalk on the other side of the bush. He talked into his phone as his head went from side to side, scanning the area for me. I pushed my hand over my mouth, trying to hold in the terrified whimpers that were trying to escape.

His voice was low but the anger was undeniable. If he found me now, I think he would kill me right here where I lay.

"I don't know what happened, I'm sorry. I'll find her and the rest of them." A car raced up and came to a screeching stop in front of him. The door opened, Cale jumped in yelling something to the driver and they were gone ... chasing after me once again.

My heart started to pound as I realized, for the first time since this began, I was on my own.

>CHAPTER THIRTY<

It wasn't easy getting to the library. I spent most of the time ducking behind cars and crawling behind bushes. My hands were cut and bleeding and my bare feet throbbed. Something inside of me kept me moving.

Once at the library, I was relieved to find a spot on the designated side of the building that gave shelter from the rain. The trees that stood next to the building were casting just enough shadow from the headlights of the traffic to make it a good hiding place. I was pretty confident no one would see me from the road, and I had a clear view of the traffic so I would be able to see when Marcus pulled up.

I leaned against the building; my cheek pressed up against the bricks, wishing I could just blend into this wall and be invisible ... like I wanted to be that first day I came here. I hadn't expected anything unusual to happen to me. Why would I? Nothing unusual ever happens to me. I was the girl who could walk down a street and never actually meet the stare of another person. I hated it back then – hated the feeling of being so unimportant, no one even noticed you. Now I longed for it, but instead, the whole world was looking for me.

The rain continued to come down in sheets of drizzle, confident it left nothing dry. I shivered for the first time since I'd escaped and realized I must be cold.

I closed my eyes to rest; even though I knew it was careless to be unprepared … I was just so tired. The second my eyes shut, Ryan's face appeared and my heart broke all over again. In my memory, he was smiling like the first day we met. He was so handsome and kind that day. Memories began flashing like a movie in my head, the two of us in class, the times in my dorm room with Katie and Marcus and Ryan … sitting in the dark, waiting for me to come home, on the night that changed everything.

My mind flashed memories of his face; the face I longed for, the face I loved … the face that lied and tricked me, then handed me over to the people who were determined to kill me. I couldn't take this anymore; I had to rid my system of him. I rolled my forehead back and forth along the bricks, trying to erase everything about him. He wanted me dead. He'd even offered to come into the room and finish me off … but my heart still wanted to love him.

I heard a rustling sound and opened my eyes just in time to see a hand come from behind me and slip over my mouth. I bucked back against my captor, getting my legs up against the wall and pushing as hard as I could. This was not going to happen; I would either escape or die right here and now.

His other arm wrapped around my waist, pushing me toward the building, pinning me between the bricks and his body. I screamed into his hand. His face pressed hard against my cheek, whispering something in my ear, but I wasn't going to calm down long enough to hear what this madman was trying to say. I knew what he wanted; he didn't need to give me the play by play.

I wildly threw my elbows and kicked behind me to escape his hold. I closed my eyes and arched my back as hard as I could, while attempting to rip my arms from him. When I felt two *thuds* on my side, I instinctively opened my eyes to see what had happened. It was Angel – he stood on his back legs with both paws on me.

Startled enough to stop struggling, the person behind me took his opportunity and whispered in my ear, "It's me, Marcus … don't scream!"

He dropped his hands and I lunged toward Angel, throwing my arms around his neck and burying my face in his fur. Still holding onto Angel for the much needed comfort, I turned and looked up to where Marcus was standing. Angel nuzzled in closer and leaned his weight into me.

"Are you crazy? Why would you do that to me? I thought you were Ryan. I thought you were going to kill me." He leaned down, taking his shoes and socks off. He threw the socks at me and I pulled them over my bare feet while he put his shoes back on.

"We have to go." He reached down and grabbed my hand, helping me to my feet. "I drove by a carload of the Brothers over by the clock tower and got nervous that they recognized me. So I left the car and ran over here as fast as I could. Jenna, we have to find somewhere to go, there are too many people looking for you. We're not safe out here."

"Back to the apartment?"

He nodded his approval and I turned toward the street.

"Wait," he said as he grabbed my arm.

I turned toward him, willing him to hurry with my eyes.

"There's something I need to tell you about Ryan."

Warning alarms sounded in my head and my entire body stiffened at the sound of his name.

I yanked my arm from his grip and Angel growled a warning at him. "Don't talk to me about

Ryan! I don't want to hear his name – do you understand me? We stood staring at each other, rain covering both of us. Silence filled our standoff as he contemplated his next words. My heart raced with anger and betrayal. How could he bring him up? His brother had just tried to kill me and what was I doing? Standing here, trusting him. How stupid could I be?

"There' something you need to know." He said.

I interrupted him, not wanting to hear anything he had to say about Ryan, "No, there is something you need to know. I survived your brother and I will survive you. If you have any ideas of hurting me, also know this, I will kill you without hesitation."

I walked past him to the back of the building and stole a glance around the corner to make sure no one was there. When I turned, his eyes were on me.

"I would never hurt you."

I huffed out a sarcastic laugh and tried walking past him but he grabbed my arm. "Please Jenna, I need you to believe me."

I looked up into his blue eyes, the familiarity of them made my heart skip a beat, and pissed me off at the same time.

"You aren't the first Kitson brother to make that promise to me ... forgive me if I am not one hundred percent trusting." His eyes flashed understanding; he nodded once and dropped his hand.

"Back at the house, you said you'd left something at the apartment I would need. What was it?"

"I left the papers I found in your file. I tucked them between the mattress and the box springs."

I needed those papers. If there was any chance that I could get the police involved, or anyone to listen to me, I need some sort of proof of what was going on inside that house. Something solid, more than my word, because as Cale had so kindly pointed out, I was easily erased. I nodded my approval at him.

"One more thing; there's also a bag of money, new ID's for us and a couple of guns."

My heart stopped and the world spun. I put my hand against the bricks to steady myself. It had never occurred to me there might be another option. I could run.

>CHAPTER THIRTY-ONE<

The run back to the apartment was easier than I'd thought it would be. Less than an hour ago, I thought I was going to die, so I guess anything is easier than having someone beat the life out of you.

Angel took the lead, scouting ahead and checking around all the buildings. I was confident no one would surprise me by jumping out; Angel would have them by the throat before they could touch me.

So our biggest concern was the people on foot and in the cars. Since all the sane people had found somewhere to hide from the drizzle, which now resembled a light sleet, all we had to do was hide from the traffic.

My feet were past the point of throbbing and had simply lost all feeling, but they somehow kept me upright and moving forward. My chest felt like a cement block had taken up residency on it, but I continued to suck in the frigid air, each breath harder than the last.

We came out of a half-empty parking lot to the backside of the building I'd been calling home for the last week. I knew the only way to get to the apartment was through the alley where Angel and Becky had found me. My throat tightened at the thought of being out in the open with only an occasional dumpster to hide behind. Marcus and I stood with our backs to the building. We both desperately needed a rest.

How'd you get all that stuff?" I took a deep breath and looked around the corner. It was dark and there were people sleeping next to the dumpster. The street was relatively quiet tonight, but the other end of the alley was brightly lit up from the stores across the street. Angel had already started trotting down the alley.

"What? He asked in a breathy whisper.

"The money, the guns, the ID's – how did you get all of it?"

"You can do a lot of things when you have the right amount of money."

I nodded at him.

"But when, when did you do it?"

Angel had circled back and the light tapping of his toenails grabbed my attention as he came back around the corner, obviously irritated we didn't follow him the first time.

"Let's just get inside and I'll tell you everything." He nudged me with his arm, encouraging me into the open alley.

We slid along the wall of the building quickly, trying to be as quiet as possible. I kept watch in front of us while Marcus kept his eyes behind us. We stepped over the people that slept by the dumpster and made our way to the edge of the alley. Knowing we were about to step into the light of the streets, I gave Marcus a pointed look – he nodded once and followed me out into the artificial light. We kept our eyes on the ground and ducked once again into the darkness of the building entrance. I stood bent over, my hands on my knees, trying to fight off the hyperventilation that threatened to take over. Marcus stood at the door, looking back and forth making sure no one was rushing into the building. His breathing echoed off the filthy walls. When he was sure no one was following us, he came over and rubbed my back softly until I could breathe again.

I looked up the open staircases and wondered how I'd ever make it up that far. The warmth of the building made my frost-bitten feet burn.

Marcus gave me a small smile, "Almost there."

We started up the stairs, staying close to the banister – once again with me leading and Marcus watching to make sure no one came in the front doors.

Once we reached my floor, we moved so our backs were against the wall, still watching over the banister for anyone approaching.

The hallway was empty except for the trash that lay along the wall between each apartment door. The darkness of the hall seemed almost inescapable and the grime and dust hung in the air like a blanket.

"What if someone is in there?" My panic rising before I could control it. I turned toward Marcus and rocked back and forth – the room started to fade out. "I can't do this."

"You stay with me. Pull it together!" He shook both of my shoulders. I met his eyes and he whispered, "Please don't leave me now – I need you."

I closed my eyes and took in a ragged breath. I saw Katie's face – I could do this for her. I would live through this and bring her killers to justice. When I opened my eyes, I felt more in control. He looked at me with hopeful eyes and I nodded to him letting him know that I was okay. I turned toward my door and started down the hallway. We crept along, trying to avoid making any noise. As I stepped in front of Becky's door, it opened. Her facial expression dropped and panic crossed her face. She started to slam her door but I stopped it with both hands.

"Becky, wait!" She pushed against the door as I tried to keep it open. Suddenly, she stopped and the door flew open. Marcus's fearful eyes darted back and forth between her and me, not knowing what to expect.

"Please leave – I don't want your kind of trouble."

"I'm not trying to get you in any trouble; I just wanted to know if you've seen anyone coming from my apartment?"

She took in a deep breath and crossed her arms in front of herself as she glared at me. "No."

I nodded my head at her and stepped out of the doorway as she started to close the door.

Before it was shut completely, she looked out and whispered, "Do you remember the advice I gave you that day?"

I nodded my head and she shut the door.

I stood staring at her closed door. Marcus leaned in and asked, "What advice did she give you?" Goosebumps rose all over my body as I her words sunk in.

"She said, 'when you live in a neighborhood like this, it's very important to know exactly who your neighbors are, and then go about your business acting like you have no idea who your neighbors are.' We can't trust her, we have to get our stuff and leave now!"

I rushed to the apartment door and Marcus stepped in front of me, unlocking the door and pushing it wide open. Angel rushed in and jumped on the bed.

"You get the bag, it's in the shower - and I'll get the paperwork."

I ran into the bathroom and pushed the shower curtain to the side – I gasped. It was there, just as he said it would be. There was several hand guns in the bag with what appeared to be a couple boxes of ammo. The guns lay on a bed of more money than I'd ever seen in my life.

Sweat beaded on my forehead as I took the whole thing in. There it was the rest of my life in a black duffel bag. I adjusted the top gun so I could zip the bag, but noticed an envelope with my name on it. I recognized the handwriting right away … it was from Ryan. I tentatively reached for it, unsure if I wanted to know what was inside. I took a deep breath as I pulled out the hand written letter.

Dear Jenna,

If you are reading this letter, it means you are still alive and I've done my job. I now pass that responsibility to Marcus. He will keep you safe, I have to believe that. I know he'll explain all of this to you, but I wanted you to hear it from me first.

Jenna, I do love you. I know right now there isn't a part of you that could ever believe it, but please try to understand … you are the most important thing in this world to me.

When I was trained, I was told I would be a body guard. I believed my job would be to keep people safe. I never imagined what that actually meant.

I became suspicious when Cale told me to spend as much time as possible with you. He said I should make sure you trusted me, but I could never tell you what my assignment really was. I decided to dig deeper into what the business side of The Brotherhood actually is.

I put it all together the night I found you in the basement. A part of me always wondered if The Brotherhood's business was illegal; but prostitution and high-end escorts? It makes my stomach turn to know what generations of my family have been involved in.

I'm so sorry I didn't tell you then, Jenna – I should have. I just wanted to protect you, and I thought if I could get enough information and go to the DCI myself, you would never have to be scared again. I wanted you to know I could and would protect you no matter what. I wanted you to believe I would always be the person that would come to save you.

I went to Cale and pledged my loyalty to him. I promised him I would bring you in. I'm sorry; it was the only thing I could think of to keep off his radar.

After we left Katie, I knew I was in over my head, so I spent the next day gathering everything in this bag. My plan was to go back for her that night and the four of us were going to disappear.

I messed up Jen. I messed up badly and it got Katie killed. I had no idea they would do something like that. I should've never left her; I should've made her come with us.

Marcus lost his mind when he found out about Katie, and I can't blame him. I would've been the same way if something like that happened to you. The Brotherhood knew Marcus had been in the house and the kind of information he had. According to them, he had to die. They were crazy about trying to find him.

Cale told me if I didn't deliver you that night, they would not only kill my brother, but they would kill your mom. I was never a big fan of your mom, but I knew you wouldn't want her harmed in any way.

I'd planned on telling you everything that night, but when I got there and saw Marcus, I knew he wanted to kill me – and would if I didn't do something – and that meant you both would be dead for sure.

I panicked; I had to calm you both down. After I made you pass out, I waited until Marcus woke up and I explained everything; then we came up with a plan. We needed more information and more time.

I would take you to Cale — I hated this part, Jenna ... please believe me ... this was not an easy option, it nearly killed me.

I would sneak Marcus in and he would get you out of the house. Once the alarm goes off, everyone would rush to find you and I would grab all the information I could get from the files that Marcus had discovered.

I plan to fax all the info to the main office of the DCI and hope someone important sees it. Then I will do whatever it takes to get close enough to Cale and kill him. He will pay for his part in Katie's death. I will do this for you and for my brother. I don't know how else to make it right.

Marcus is to leave with you to help you start a new life. He knows what he needs to do. I understand that you'll never want to see me again, and I can accept that — as long as I know you're alive. I love you and you being alive and safe are the most important thing to me.

Thank you for walking into my life that day. I'm forever changed because of you. Please understand my heart is broken and will never heal ... it will never stop wanting you. No matter how long my life is, your face will always be the one I see every night, your love will be my craving, our memories always precious to me.

This isn't easy ... saying goodbye. Every part of me wants nothing but to be near you, to hold you, to love you — and to feel your love back. I'm sorry I failed *you. I'm sorry I couldn't be the one to come when you needed me the most.*

All of my heart,

Ryan

Marcus's arms were suddenly around me. I turned in toward him, grabbing onto his shirt.

"We have to go get him," I pleaded.

He shook his head, "No. He doesn't want that, Jenna."

I started struggling and he tightened his arms around me. "They will kill him," I yelled as I pounded against his chest. "There's no way he'll get close enough to Cale to kill him. As soon as they figure out you're the one who took me, they will know he helped you. They will torture and kill him."

He was silent, avoiding my eyes. "You know that don't you? He knew that! What did he do Marcus? What did you both do?"

He grabbed my face in his hands and made me look at him. "Yes, he knew that, we both knew it. The only way to get close enough to possibly kill Cale was to get caught. He knew they would start looking for him as soon as they knew it was me that came for you."

My legs buckled and Marcus caught me.

"He's dead isn't he?"

Marcus laid his head on top of mine. "Maybe the DCI got there first or maybe he was able to get Cale alone or ..." his voice cracked and faded out.

"Marcus?"

He just shook his head against mine and I knew – Ryan was dead.

There are times in your life when reality is just too painful and even your own heart can't allow you to feel it. I held Marcus as he cried – I felt nothing. I was completely broken. I closed my eyes – a thought crossed my mind. I reached around Marcus and grabbed a gun. I watched the light reflect off the cold, gray metal as I lifted it to my head and pressed it against my temple.

"What the hell, Jenna," Marcus screamed as he pushed me against the sink and pulled the gun from my hand. I looked at him with no emotion ... I wanted to die.

"You don't get to do that!"

My body started to shake.

"My brother died so he could save your life. You don't get to do that!" he said again. Tears suddenly started and ran in steady steams down each side of my face. I pushed him away from me and he fell against the opposite wall, just as defeated as I was.

I walked out of the bathroom and into the hallway, stopping in front of Becky's door. I banged as hard as I could until she opened it with the chain attached. Her eyes were crazy with panic.

"Come with us," I said.

"What? No, go away!" She started to close the door and I pushed against it.

"We have money and guns. Come with us – we can save you from this life."

She paused, staring at me through the slit in the door. "Why?"

I dropped my eyes to the floor. My chest heaving with the heaviness of what I knew I was going to say next. "Because, someone saved me from this kind of life and I want to save you too."

Marcus was suddenly behind me. "We have to go now."

I looked at Becky again. "This is your one chance. Please, come with us."

Tears filled her eyes as she looked at me one last time … and closed her door.

I closed my eyes and shook my head; I had failed her too.

Marcus reached out and touched my arm with urgency. "Now … we have to go now."

We ran down the hall but, slid to a stop when we saw Angel. Something wasn't right. He stood at the top of the stairs, staring down and growling ferociously. Every fiber in my body knew what was about to happen. That's when we saw him, slowly climbing the steps toward us. Our eyes locked and he smiled like he had seen his best friend "Hello, Jenna," Cale said calmly.

I fell back onto Marcus like I'd been shot in the chest and he grabbed me, trying to keep me on my feet while he drug me backwards.

"No! "I screamed. My feet shuffled along the floor, trying to regain my balance, but the terror that flooded through me wouldn't allow it.

Angel stood his ground, barking a feverish warning for Cale not to come any closer. He shifted his weight on his haunches, ready to attack. I wanted to scream and call him back, but I had no voice – no rational thought formed. Marcus continued to scurry back to the room, holding onto me.

"Jenna," Cale sang out my name like he was so happy to have finally found me. "There's no use hiding. There's nowhere you can go where I can't find you."

My whole body vibrated with fear. The top of his blonde hair was barely visible above the stairway... he climbed once step at a time, getting closer and closer to me. I watched as Angel ran, in what seemed like slow motion, and lunged toward him.

In one swift move, Cale reached inside of his jacket and pulled out a gun.

"No!" I screamed as the deafening sound of a gunshot echoed off the walls of the open staircase Angel let out a yelp as his body twisted abnormally and then slumped over, falling forward. I heard every step his body hit on the way down.

My knees gave out. Marcus pulled me the last few feet into the apartment and slammed the door, locking every lock. He reached into the bag and pulled out two guns, shoving one into my hand. I grabbed it and held on tight. He switched the safety off and suddenly, it registered what he was saying to me. "Just aim and pull the ..."

Marcus spun toward the door lifting his gun at the same time as the wood door splintered. Cale busted in and fired at Marcus without hesitation. The impact of the gunshot threw Marcus backward and onto me, causing us both to fall onto the bed.

"Marcus!" I screamed, trying to get out from underneath him to see where he had been shot.

Cale marched over to us, pulling Marcus off of me and throwing his lifeless body to the floor. He stood over him, shooting several more times, making sure he got the job done.

Quickly, all of his attention was on me. I made a move for the door but he grabbed me by the hair, throwing me back on the bed. Climbing on top of me, he straddled my body, using his weight to make sure I couldn't move.

"Beautiful Jenna …"he seethed while pushing his gun against my forehead. Rage overtook him and spit spewed from his mouth as he spoke just inches from my face.

"I'm going to kill you slowly and painfully. It won't be quick like those low-life Kitson Brothers or that mutt."

He reached into his pocket and pulled out a long-bladed knife. I bucked against his body weight, desperate to escape my fate. My eyes searched frantically for any type of weapon I could use against him

He grabbed my chin, holding it in place and forcing me to look at him. I whimpered, "Please…"

"Oh, we are so past that." He smiled as he pressed the tip of the knife to the skin just under my eye. I let out a blood curdling scream as he slowly moved it down my cheek, slicing open the skin until he reached my jaw line. I felt the warmth of the blood gush from my open wound.

He stood up, keeping the gun to my head with one hand, and flipping the knife around with the other. "You almost did it – you almost brought me down. Hell, you almost brought the whole house down. But you see this?" He held the blood covered knife up in front of my face, making sure I could see it, and then whispered through clenched teeth. "This is my proof to you that I win."

He raised the knife up and brought it down with such brutal force, that at first, I didn't feel it slice into my thigh muscle. But then he twisted it, and the pain shot through my entire body like an electrical jolt. I let out a guttural, gurgling sound and tried to grab his hand that held the knife, to keep it still.

"You may have gotten away if it weren't for my girl Becky. She's what I like to call my side job. Through the house I make big money, but with girls like Becky … they keep the money flowing every day. When I put the word out I was looking for you, she said you'd been here, but hadn't seen you in a while. She promised she would call if she saw you again – and she did." He grabbed the knife and twisted it as he pulled it out slowly. I groaned loudly, reaching down as I tried to put pressure on the gash, blood oozing out from between my fingers. I rolled to my side. A strangled scream stuck in my throat as I prayed I would pass out.

Looking down at me, he sneered, "You make me sick. As much as I want to draw this out and make you suffer, I honestly can't stand to look at you anymore." He shook his head in disgust.

"Really is a shame." He raised the knife above his head and I closed my eyes, picturing Ryan's face.

A shot rang out – my eyes sprung open, and for a split second, surprise crossed Cale's face. Then a circle of blood began to form on his chest, slowly getting bigger. His eyes rolled into the back of his head as he fell to the ground. Becky ran over to me and using both her hands, put pressure on my leg wound. I touched her hand.

She hesitantly looked at me, fear and panic in her eyes, I smiled as much as I could. Tears began to run down her face. "You said I needed more protection." She let out a small laugh, "You were right."

"Why did you save me?" I whispered.

She shrugged her shoulders.

I welcomed the darkness as it came. I could hear Becky yelling my name, but she sounded so far away. A part of me wanted to stay with her, but I just couldn't. Everyone I loved was dead, and I wanted to be too.

CHAPTER THIRTY-TWO

I moved my fingers; it was hard to do and I didn't know why. I moved them again and felt something furry. I heard a faint beeping noise and then the weight of the sheets over me registered. I was in a bed – and by the sounds and smells, it was a hospital bed.

There was movement under my hand and suddenly a wet cold sensation. It was licking, something was licking my hand. I moved my fingers again. There was a rustling noise and the bed dipped next to me. Something nuzzled my chin – Angel!

I tried as hard as I could to open my eyes, blinking against the bright lights. Someone stood next to the bed on the other side of me. I blinked again, trying to figure out who was brushing the hair from my face.

"She's waking up, go get the nurse." Ryan! That was Ryan. My heart rate shot up as I tried to speak his name.

"Shhh, it's me. You're okay, just relax. I slumped back onto the bed, trying to remember everything that had happened. I opened my eyes just as all of the memories flooded back. I reached for him and he leaned down, embracing me.

"Marcus?" I whispered. He stilled and slowly shook his head. My stomach twisted. "My mom?"

"She was hurt pretty badly, but she's going to be okay. She's still in the hospital, but I've talked with her almost every day. She can't wait to see you." I smiled and nodded my head but couldn't hold it in any longer. I cried into his shoulder as he held me, telling me everything was okay now.

I pushed him back suddenly and whispered, "Cale, is he ... is he dead?"

"Yes, he's dead." Relief flooded through me and I ran my hand through Angel's fur. He lifted his head and I noticed the shaved areas of hair and the staples holding together his surgical sites. I winced as I tenderly ran my fingers over them.

Ryan let out a small laugh, "I brought him here for a short visit because the doctor said it would be good for both of your healing. I got him up on the bed, thinking he would stay for a couple hours, but he made it pretty clear he wasn't leaving you. He only gets off the bed when he needs to go outside or when the nurses are bathing you. Stupid dog even makes me feed him on the bed." I laughed, but then looked at him.

"How are you alive?" I asked reaching for his hand.

"After I faxed the information to DCI, I waited for Cale and his guys to come back. I figured it would only be a matter of time before they figured out I was involved. But they never came back, so I left to go and look for him. The guys that were with him, told the DCI agents he had just figured out that I was involved when Becky called him. He never had a chance to come after me."

I smiled. Ryan leaned down and whispered, "Jen ... I am so sorry. I should've never ..."

I reached up and put a finger across his lips. His eyes were full of tears when they met mine. "You were going to die to keep me safe." He dropped his head and I held him and we whispered, "I love you," over and over again to each other.

Becky came running back into the room pulling a pissed off looking nurse right behind her. She came to a stop when she saw my eyes were open. She looked over at Ryan as he wiped tears off of his cheek. I smiled at her and reached a hand out in her direction. She hesitantly took my hand, moving over to the side of my bed.

"Thank you for saving me," I said.

She cleared her throat, trying to keep her emotions in check. "Do you remember in the apartment, right after I shot Cale ... you asked me why?"

I nodded my head at her.

She shifted her weight back and forth between her feet. "Well, no one had ever tried to save me before you did that night. I did it, because I was hoping maybe we could save each other."

I thought for a second – had I ever saved anyone? I'd spent my whole childhood hiding from the monsters and my teenage years trying to be invisible ... But had I ever really stopped and looked at the people around me? There were people that needed to be saved; kids that were living in similar situations to what I had grown up in, women who, like Becky and my mom, were stuck in a life they didn't know how to get out of.

It was time for me to stop being invisible – stop waiting for someone to come and save me. It was time to be seen and do the saving.

"You want to save each other huh?" I asked as I smiled at her, squeezing her hand. Her eyes got big as I pulled her into an embrace. I held her for a minute and then whispered in her ear, "I think we're on our way to doing just that."

Thank you so much for reading, Chasing Jenna. Although this is a fictional story, I want to take this opportunity to bring to light the real life horrors of the sex-trade industry. One of the most common things people have pointed out to me after reading this book is how frightening it is because it could so easily happen.

The reality is, not that it could happen, but that it *is* happening!

Every day, all over the word, men, woman and children are sold into the sex-trade industry for the sick profit of others. Please, if this story moved you at all, think about giving to a charity that helps prevent the sale of human beings and assists with the rehabilitation of those who have been rescued.

Thank you.

About The Author

If they'd known about ADHD when I was little, my Ritalin dosage would've been OFF THE CHARTS!

It goes without saying; I spent A LOT of time by myself after the teacher moved my desk out into the hallway. ** Silver lining** with all that alone time on my hands, I used my imagination to make the world interesting.

When I was little, people said I had an "active imagination". In elementary school, teachers called me a "daydreamer". My high school counselor said I needed to "learn how to focus" and my college professors warned me to "buckle down". Before I knew it, it was time to "grow up".

So that's what I did, I grew up, got married and had five kids. I work as a full time nurse, I'm active in my church, part of the most amazing book-club, blog about books with my best friend and cart small humans to school, football, theater, dance ect. Oh yeah ... and write when I can and now people say I'm "talented".

Moral of my story: Hug your kids, embrace their differences...love them for who they are. Someday, the traits you think are struggles now...Might be what makes them the happiest!

Micki lives in small town Iowa with her husband, kids and a fat Cocker Spaniel named Joey. She is the author of Winds of Darkness, released in February of 2012 and Chasing Jenna, released November of 2014.

You can find her at the following social media sites:

Goodreads:

Facebook:

Twitter:

Pinterest:

Blog: Mickisue@blogspot.com

Acknowledgements:

Thank you to my Lord and Savior, Jesus Christ, who I give all glory to. I thank him for the blessings in my life.

Thank you to my family for the sacrifices that are made to allow me to follow my dream. Without the support of my husband and children, these characters would never get a voice.

To Author K.J Bell. THANK YOU for making me cry. I needed it so badly. It was in that moment, I had to decide if I really wanted to pursue this dream, or if that is all it would ever be...a dream. Without those tears, I don't think I would've ever realized how much I was willing to work toward my goal.

To the many ladies in my life that I endlessly bother with chapters, paragraphs, sentences or sometimes just ideas... knowing that you are always there to push me along is sometimes the only thing that keeps me going.

To my invaluable BETA readers, who loved this story from the beginning and never let me give up on Jenna, Thank you!

Made in the USA
Middletown, DE
23 February 2015